THE
SPIRIT OF MILLIE MAE

THE
SPIRIT OF MILLIE MAE

Sheila Newberry

ROBERT HALE · LONDON

© Sheila Newberry 2003
First published in Great Britain 2003

ISBN 0 7090 7329 1

Robert Hale Limited
Clerkenwell House
Clerkenwell Green
London EC1R 0HT

The right of Sheila Newberry to be identified as
author of this work has been asserted by her
in accordance with the Copyright, Design and
Patents Act 1988.

2 4 6 8 10 9 7 5 3 1

Typeset in 11/13½ pt Baskerville by
Derek Doyle & Associates, Liverpool.
Printed in Great Britain by
St Edmundsbury Press, Bury St Edmunds, Suffolk.
Bound by Woolnough Bookbinding Limited

For the young Betty, Joan, Pam and John,
who showed plenty of wartime spirit
themselves as they, too, left home for Scotland.
With my love,
Sheila

Author's Acknowledgement

My grateful thanks in particular to:

My husband John and his sisters (wartime and post-war memories of Scotland, Surrey and London which reinforced my own recall); Joan and Michael Laker (for memories of pre-war/wartime Romney Marsh and other parts of Kent, many of which we shared, including the interest in planes of the era); Arthur G. Clarke (sometime merchant seaman); the late Barbara Waters and 'Moses'; Jonathan, number one son, for sharing his discovery and delight in a cache of old newspapers nose-wrinklingly smelling of soot . . . . Also affectionately remembering two indomitable district nurses of those years, Clarkie and Muriel.

Bibliography

Compiled by Lukins, A. H. Edited by Russell, D. A., M. I. Mech:E *The Book of Westland Aircraft* (The Harborough Publishing Co Ltd, 1943)

Mondey, David *The International Encyclopaedia of Aviation* (Hamlyn, 1988)

McDougal, Philip *Kent Airfields in the Battle of Britain*, 4th edn (Meresborough Books, 1992)

Major, Alan *Hidden Kent* (Countryside Books, 1994)

Romney Marsh and Rye, 4000 Years of History (Addax Publishing, 1992)

PROLOGUE

1934

Swirling smugglers mist, as Millie Mae described it, almost obscured the tin roofs of the Last Stop Garage on the edge of the Romney Marsh. Not dire like the freak blizzards in Chicago, but worrying for those in transit. So, the illuminated messenger with winged heels over the pumps was spotted with heartfelt relief by the pilot of the sputtering light plane circling the area.

The glass windmill connecting hose to pump whirled as Tess Rainbow fed petrol into the tank of the motor cycle combination. 'Just enough to get me home, Tess. . . .' The needle quivered, then steadied, on the half-gallon mark.

On this dismal Saturday afternoon, three days before Christmas, it would be dark by four, she thought, then they might as well turn the sign to CLOSED. Pop would demur, for any business in these difficult times was welcome. The garage funded his passion for restoring small aircraft; he had gained his expertise in the Royal Flying Corps towards the end of the Great War.

Pop was closeted in the old barn right now, with a two-seater plane which was once flown to Australia, Pop pointed out to justify his extravagance.

Even at twelve, Tess was aware why her father often shut himself away from his family: Pop was still fighting to come to terms with their dreadful loss. The children had been forced to grow up quickly, not to display their own grief for their mother, the wonderful Millie Mae.

'Don't be afraid to cry if you can't help it,' she'd said once to Tess, 'but keep smiling through, eh?' The spirit of Millie Mae, the memory of her generous personality kept them all going on.

Not having cash to buy the plane from a fellow enthusiast long unemployed, Pop had offered his car in part exchange, plus free petrol for three months, which had not gone down well with his elder daughter, Roma, whom he had recently reluctantly taught to drive, and even though it was the sedate tourer, not the rakish Morgan sports car in which Millie Mae, that irresistible saleswoman had sallied forth with her haberdashery samples.

Still sulking, when the horn summoned them, Roma flung her precious black fake leather motoring coat at Tess. 'Here - *you* go, and wrap a scarf round your mouth.' Tess suffered from bouts of bronchitis each winter. Her robust sister was not always sympathetic when Tess was laid low, for Roma was at an age to be out and about enjoying herself after typing in a local solicitors' office all week, not administering cough medicine and inhalations.

Tess was only half aware that the trees on the other side of the deserted road appeared disembodied, with branches peeping eerily above the gauzy white, for the noise of the unseen small plane was disturbing, like a wasp buzzing round and round a jam jar trap she imagined.

Returning the petrol nozzle to its rest, she waited while the motor cycle was kick-started, then she gazed upwards, shading her eyes. Was the plane trying to make a landing? Why here and not the airfield at Lydd, not many miles away? She shivered, despite the long coat. This month there had been two air crashes in Kent, mercifully not fatal, in thick fog. Then the engine abruptly cut out and Tess knew the plane must be gliding downwards.

Her father's hand touched her shoulder, making her start. 'Run short of fuel; homing-in on the garage, I reckon,' he said.

A sharp whistling, then a definite *crump*. The plane had crash-landed in the meadow, where they kept a small flock of Marsh sheep. Their springer spaniel, Fly, began a frenzied barking from the house.

Tess and Pop ran at full-tilt across the road, brushed through a gap in the hedge, which Roma had fortuitously fashioned when learning to reverse the car, and pounded across the rough grass to the ditched plane.

12

'Silly fool,' Pop panted, being heavily built, 'didn't keep the nose up, tipped it over. Lucky the ewes are in the fold - look, there's the propeller—'

'Here he is, Pop!' Tess shouted. The pilot had rolled clear of the machine, and lay with hands shielding his head, as if expecting an explosion and flames.

'Just as well you ran out of petrol,' Pop pronounced. They could make out the name of the little monoplane, resting tipsily on one wing after cartwheeling to a stop: SPIRIT OF MILLIE MAE. It gave them both quite a jolt.

'Written her off, I reckon. You're no Lindberg that's obvious, and she's no *Spirit of St Louis* . . . Made the headlines today, you did - "missing, from parents' Scottish retreat: never flown solo before, son of Leo Tann, wealthy aircraft manufacturer". I met your father in the Corps, we were actually in business here together after the war - the last time I saw you, you were two years old.' He sounded strident.

Tess gave him a warning nudge: 'Not now, Pop. I wonder why he didn't say he knew the family, this morning?'

'Guilty, as charged,' the pilot said huskily, struggling up. One arm hung limply. 'Hurts like hell; landed on my shoulder. Have you any idea what you look like in that coat? A little Hollywood gangster . . .' Laughter bubbled from his throat. Tess caught hold of his good arm; Pop steadied him the other side.

'Where were you going?' Tess ventured shyly, as they progressed slowly toward the house. Roma was loquacious, but Millie Mae had been the biggest chatterbox of all time. She said Tess was the serious one: she wouldn't be surprised if she became a writer one day. Well, you only had to watch her scribbling away to know she would - and wasn't it *inspiring* living where they did? Think of *Puck of Pook's Hill*, Kipling, of course, and the *Ingoldsby Legends*. Tess took after Mae, her grandmother, who wrote romantic poetry. Her family only discovered her secret after she died young.

Moray Tann looked at the sign, Last Stop Garage, with Roma's fiercely chalked addition, when she was mad at Pop: '*To - nowhere*,' he said slowly. 'But - maybe I was heading this way all the time.'

'Then you're here,' Tess told him simply.

'She's right: Nothing much between us and the sea,' Pop added. 'But

13

you've landed on your feet, as they say: light planes are my business, though I come by mine legally.'

'Coming in? It's cold with the door wide open,' Roma called plaintively from the house. 'Hope you haven't mucked up my best coat, Tess.'

Six-year-old Barney held the toasting fork to the glowing coals, while Tess took the scorched slices from the prongs, covering the uncooked side with cheese and placing them on a tin plate in the ash pan under the grate. Her usually pale, freckled face was flushed in the heat. Her braided hair was almost as red as the coals, her eyes greeny hazel. The baggy dungarees disguised her spindly limbs. Sitting back on her heels she looked younger than her age. There were so many questions she wanted to ask their unexpected visitor, but no chance with Roma around. Before Pop lit the fire with the paper tomorrow, she'd cut out the piece on the *Spirit of Millie Mae*, and pasted it in her scrapbook after the romantic wedding pictures of the Duke and Duchess of Kent. She lifted a warning finger to Fly, inching near the plate of sliced cheddar.

Moray rested in Pop's armchair. His attention was on Roma, as she attempted to put his arm in a sling. He nursed a small glass of whisky and water in his good hand, which Pop said to drink up quick for the shock.

'You may have to brush off cinders, but there'll be a *heavenly* smell soon. Millie Mae, our mother, said nothing tasted as good when you're cold and hungry, even if the cheese sticks to your teeth,' Roma observed brightly, her good humour restored. She didn't meet many attractive young men after all.

With his soft flapped helmet removed, Moray Tann was revealed as just a young feller like Pop said, about Roma's age. She was almost seventeen. Aware of the effect she was having, she leaned closer so her silky bobbed blonde hair brushed his chin. She pinned the cloth in place. '*Done!* Not bad as nursing's not my vocation.' She smiled at him as she straightened up. His eyes were blue like hers; he was as dark as she was fair, with high cheekbones. His quirky mouth gave the impression he was smiling, but it was obvious he was in pain. He did not comment on the mention of Millie Mae.

'We lost my wife two years ago. Car crash.' Pop stated baldly. 'It's cheese on toast most nights since she went, the kids are learning, but—'

'Are you going to call the police?' the young man asked abruptly.

14

'Not tonight. The accident may have been reported already; if so, the local bobby will come knocking on our door anyway. You really ought to speak to your father first, or I will, if you wish, even though we parted on heated terms, you might say. My guess is *you* did, too? You should see a doctor though—'

'Please, no. I'll be all right.'

Tess solemnly presented him with the first supper plate.

'We usually stay in the kitchen in the evenings this time of the year, as it's the warmest room. You'll have to sleep in here tonight, I'm afraid.' Pop said.

Barney spoke at last. He had similar colouring to Tess. They took after Pop for the auburn hair. Pop still had a brush of it with a fierce moustache. 'He c-can have my bed, Pop.' He'd begun stammering after Millie Mae died. Tess was protective of him, because of it. She was closer to him than to Roma. She and Barney idolized their father; Pop and Roma often clashed, yet they accepted her as Pop's golden girl, because she reminded him so much of Millie Mae. He'd married her when she was Roma's age, not much older himself. Wartime prompted hasty marriages, but theirs was set to endure.

'Thank you,' Moray said. He had hardly touched his supper. 'I'm sorry, but is it possible I could go to bed now – last night, in a field somewhere, freezing cold . . .' His hands were shaking from the delayed shock.

'I'll change the sheets,' Tess jumped to her feet.

'No, please, no fuss,' he managed. She fielded the plate as it slid from his lap, the toast landing face down on the lino. The dog scooted under the table with his prize. He wasn't named Fly for nothing.

'I'll take you, young feller,' Pop said firmly, before Roma could offer. 'Fill a couple of hot water bottles, Tess, Barney can deliver them, eh? Roma, ring old Dr Broad, and tell him it's not time to put on his slippers yet.'

Monday morning, Christmas Eve, Tess and Moray, insisting, despite his broken collar-bone, he was in need of exercise and air, walked along country lanes until they came to the tarred fishermen's huts and converted railway carriages. They passed boards proclaiming FRESH COD, oily-chained boats, picking their way over long ridges of shingle along the deserted beach at Dungeness, wary of stumbling into the dips. It was a chill day, with gruel-coloured sky, lumpy with cloud, and a rolling sea. There was a solitary fishing smack on the horizon. Fly sniffed at rotting seaweed, and barked at the gulls.

Roma was working until lunchtime, and Pop was manning the pumps; Barney was watching out for their Christmas dinner, a plump capon from a friend in lieu of a garage bill, and a box of groceries, ditto. Moray's parents were collecting their son later. The *Spirit of Millie Mae* had now joined the other plane in the barn. Pop would work on it when he had time. He'd said little to Moray's father on the phone, but agreed to that.

'We came here Boxing Day afternoons,' Tess observed now. 'Millie Mae said we should walk off the excesses of Christmas. Once, we were frosted with snow, and Barney moaned about icicles hanging from his nose, it was so perishing cold. Another time we scuttled home like drowned rats – that's when the ritual of cindery cheese began – Millie Mae always turned disasters into fun.' Except for the last time . . . She turned, called to Fly, because she didn't know Moray well enough to let him see the tears welling up in her eyes.

'My father loved her, too,' he said quietly. 'That's why he and Pop Rainbow parted company.'

'Did your father tell you that?' she asked, startled.

'No. It was Ma, after Dad named the plane. She said it wasn't fair, bringing up old memories – it had taken her long enough to get over it all. She thought we – my young sister Sally and I – should know he had once considered being unfaithful to her, to us, only your Millie Mae wouldn't have allowed it.'

'I'm glad – not about your mother, of course, because it must have been awful for her.' Tess said simply. This was grown-up talk but she got the gist of it, as Moray had, when he was younger.

'We were in Scotland then, we beat the retreat as my mother put it, back to where she came from, the Moray Firth. Dad was building up his business, and eventually we moved down south. There have been other women since in Dad's life . . . I guess your parents followed his progress.'

'They never said. We didn't know you existed.'

They turned to walk back. Tess whistled for Fly to follow.

'It must be beautiful here in the summer,' he said. 'I was curious, when I knew I was born here. I learned how the marsh was reclaimed; about smuggling and shipwrecks, the dykes, The Royal Military Canal, the Mermaid Inn at Rye and medieval churches built on great mounds because of the threat from the sea. Maybe that's why I flew here.'

To see Millie Mae for yourself, she thought, only you found Roma instead. She'll probably forget you, when the next good-looking boy comes round, but I won't. 'You came at the wrong time of year, then,' she said aloud.

'You're right, it's almost as cold as it is in Scotland!'

As Roma arrived on her bicycle, a large car swept round in an arc and stopped by the house. Moray's parents! Roma rushed indoors to alert her family, who were just sitting down to lunch.

'Tess, show them into the sitting-room – did you light the fire, Pop?'

'I did,' he assured her. 'Put our plates in the oven to keep warm. Barney.'

'I'm not going until I've scraped my plate,' Moray said solemnly.

The knocker thudded. Tess hurried to answer it, followed by her father.

'Nothing's changed, I see,' Leo Tann observed, gruffly, standing with his back to the fire. His wife was seated. She wore a Cossack cap and cravat in curly black astrakhan complementing her silver-grey wool coat. Her ankles were neatly crossed, giving a glimpse of pure silk stockings, and shiny black court shoes. Millie Mae would have approved, Tess thought. She always looked smart. Mrs Tann gave her an amused glance, guessing what she was thinking.

'You're wrong there,' Pop said bitterly. 'You won't have heard, *we* don't make news, that we lost Millie Mae a while back . . .'

'I'm so sorry,' Jean Tann said, after a long pause. 'The trouble between us was . . . long ago. We are grateful to you for helping Moray, aren't we, Leo?'

Leo was shorter than Pop, who was over six foot, his slighter build disguised by the heavy tweed overcoat. He'd removed his hat, but not his leather gloves, for the hastily lit fire had not warmed the room sufficiently yet. 'Yes, thank you. No point in polite conversation, is there? Is Moray ready?'

'I'll find out, shall I?' Tess departed in some relief.

Tess waved, hanging on to Fly's collar. She hugged to herself Moray's promise. 'I'll write to you, Tess. Dad wants me to go to university, then

17

join the company – that's what we quarrelled about – but I want to join the air force, like Dad did, because all these little wars we keep hearing about will turn into one big war in Europe again – *he* told me that, after all.'

To Roma he said merely; 'I hope we'll meet again, one of these days.'

'I'll advise you when the plane is ready for collection,' Pop said to Leo. They actually shook hands, before Leo got into the driving seat. 'Don't be too hard on the boy,' Pop added. 'You and I were young and impulsive once.'

Leo gestured at the run-down buildings. 'You know, I feel somewhat responsible . . . ironically, it was a good day for me when you kicked me out. Contact me, if things get worse, if you need a job. I owe you a favour now.'

The car moved off smoothly. It would be 1940, wartime, before the young people met again, far from the insular Romney Marsh.

It had been an eventful two years since the *Spirit of Millie Mae* briefly revived the uneasy link between the two families. A king had died, his successor had never been crowned, but 12 May 1937 saw the coronation of his brother, George VI. A month later and the Last Stop Garage closed down.

Pop swallowed his pride, wrote to Leo; then had to prove his worth as an engineer within the Tann Corporation. Other decisions, equally stressful, were made. Pop would be moving around, involved with confidential projects concerning the imminent threat of war: at this time he could not provide a proper home for his children. Roma, now nineteen, seized her independence, with a job with a London travel agency and a bed-sit in Earl's Court. Tess and Barney went to live with Pop's aunts, Peg and Ida, in the flat over their corner shop in Bromley. Pop promised to send for them as soon as he could.

Tess desperately missed the marsh. The transfer to the high school was bewildering at first, but she made up her mind to work hard and do well. The aunts were kind, but unused to children or dogs. Aunt Peg ran the shop, a role she enjoyed; Aunt Ida was responsible for domestic duties and the business accounts. They had been comfortable with this sharing of responsibility for many years; now they, too, had to adapt to a new way of life.

There was no more cindery toasted cheese. They sat with the aunts each evening in the stuffy parlour overlooking the street, with buses going past and the street lamp outside. When homework was done, she was permitted to listen to the wireless until bedtime at 9 p.m; Tess was now fifteen years old.

Their only release was when she and Barney walked Fly in the recreation ground after school, but the dog was reluctant to leave the flat in colder weather. He had canker in his ears due to fire worshipping and Aunt Ida wrinkled her nose at the smell and requested he be removed while she sprayed the room with Mitcham lavender. Tess applied special powder to Fly's sore ears when they were in the rec. It didn't matter how much Fly shook his head there. Barney looked on wistfully as other boys called him to join in a kick-around with a ball. What would the aunts say if he scuffed the shoes Aunt Ida polished so determinedly every morning, or ripped his grey flannel shorts? Maybe the old dungarees which they'd worn in their Romney Marsh days would have looked comical to their peers here, but Tess, equally stuffy in gabardine mac and velour hat, wished she could turn back the clock.

Sometimes, in bed, she would lie awake and wonder what the future held for them both. She would comfort herself by re-reading all the cheery messages from Roma: *I wish Millie Mae could see me now − sending forth travellers all over the world!* and the later cards from Europe when Roma travelled abroad herself. Millie Mae would indeed have been proud of Roma, Tess thought; and her lively ambition: rewarded when she became a courier for her company. Roma was a free spirit, unlike Tess and Barney.

Tucked in her scrapbook were three letters from Moray, written before he reached a compromise with his father and went to university. She hoped he had achieved his dream of joining the air force.

Life changed dramatically again: there were sandbags and shelters; school was disrupted; evacuation discussed. Gas masks; and planes droned overhead. The despair, then the euphoria of Dunkirk. Roma joined the WAAF. Pop was drafted to Scotland to an aerodrome there, and word came at last: *Pack your cases − arriving weekend − taking you back with me!*

OPERATION EAGLE was about to commence, Hitler's bombers were poised to blaze the way for the Panzer troops. Roma, at Biggin Hill, along with many other young women, was about to play a vital role in tracking enemy aircraft in the Battle of Britain, when in August 1940, Pop, Tess, Barney and Fly embarked on the long journey to a fishing village in the Moray Firth.

PART ONE

THE MORAY FIRTH

CHAPTER ONE

On a scorching afternoon, the train was already packed with uniformed men and women, and King's Cross station was a maelstrom of noise and bustle. Pop had managed to book a sleeper: he guided Tess and Barney through the crush, steering round embracing couples, depositing them there, with their luggage.

'We'll need more than the jam sandwiches the dear aunts made to fortify us. I'll take Fly to stretch his legs, see what refreshments are available; you get comfortable; it might look cramped, but we must think ourselves fortunate.'

Tess took off her panama hat and her blazer, which she rolled up, and tossed on to a top bunk. She shook her head in relief: her hair had been cut to shoulder length after heartfelt pleas to the aunts. 'What will your father say?' Peg worried, but she wielded the scissors, and the end result was passable.

'Thank goodness,' she remarked, 'I don't have to wear that hat again – I said I'd jump on it when I left school, but I find I can't!'

'I-I've got to go to a new school,' Barney sighed. 'You're lucky, Tess.'

'I'll be keeping house for you and Pop,' Tess reminded him. 'Not so lucky,' but she grinned so he'd know she was joking. I'll be eighteen soon, she thought, I've been treated as a child until now. Roma was working at sixteen. I'm old enough to join up, too, but Pop says I'm not strong enough; anyway Barney needs me, and I suppose it's a small step towards independence.

There was a sudden hush, then panic among those still milling on the platform as they became aware of the blood-chilling rise and fall of the siren.

'*Pop!*' Tess cried, as station staff rushed to slam and lock all the doors on the train, which was gathering steam. She opened the window. '*Pop,*' she shrieked again, as she spotted him running towards their carriage, pulling the panting dog behind him. 'I can't open the door – *they've locked it* – oh Pop!'

Pop heaved Fly through the window to her. 'Calm down, you two! Take these bags, Barney, stand back, I'm climbing in!' Sweating from his exertions he tumbled at their feet, as the flag was waved, the whistle blew and the journey began, just as the last notes of the warning died down, and the All Clear began. 'False alarm; everyone's getting very edgy. Never mind the holes in my knees,' Pop winced, then winked, as he saw their concern. He shoved the window shut. 'Look – jam again, but home-cooked pastries I charmed from the WVS, and milk. We'll keep the flasks of tea for later.'

What jam! tinned apricot, with sticky fruit oozing sweetness, encased in soft pastry triangles. They sat on a lower bunk, jam spurting and trickling down their chins with each blissful bite. They steamed steadily away from London, air raids and bombs, and Tess thought, we'll be breathing sea air again. I'll always remember these delicious pastries, Barney tearing open the paper bags and licking the jammy smears; tepid milk about to turn, and the smouldering heat and promise of today. She wiped her hands on her hankie and took her pencil and notebook from her bag. No aunts to ask: 'What are you writing?'

Pop quoted Millie Mae, softly: 'Let the muse be undisturbed . . .'

A new page, a new chapter in my life, Tess thought, eager to begin.

Pop woke them early, as the train crossed the Forth bridge. Tess, with Pop's arm round her shoulders, stood by the window looking down through the massive girders at the dark water flowing far below, reflecting the flushed sky.

'It's beautiful, Pop,' she breathed. 'It's – *awesome.*'

'I'm hungry,' Barney yawned.

'Jam sandwiches?' Pop suggested slyly. Fly flipped one ear.

Barney hauled himself up onto the top bunk, pulled the covers over his head. 'Wake me up at the next stop, Pop! I'd r-rather starve.'

They boarded a local train from Aberdeen, where Fly drank a large bowl of water and they were showered when he shook his dewlaps, while they partook of baps and hot coffee. The carriage was claustro-phobic in the midday heat, but they followed the coastline and glimpsed to their delight, the glistening sea and sweeps of sand below towering cliffs. Once, they chuffed past a gathering of raspberry pick-ers, who watched the train go by. They gazed longingly at the brimming chip wood baskets and imagined the luscious taste of the soft fruit.

The smell of fish soup pervaded the steep street of grey stone and slate cottages which regarded the harbour, where they left the bus. No time for exploring today – they climbed, cases in hand, until Pop said, 'We're here.'

The cottage was the end one of a terrace, and their landlady greeted them, with the teapot keeping hot on the range and fillets of fish coated with seasoned flour ready to toss in the iron frying-pan half-full of bubbling dripping.

Mrs Munro, brown hair in a bun, pinny covering her plain dark dress, smiled shyly, showing Tess what was what. 'I'm round the corner, next street, three doors along, should you need me, lassie – my son Gregor and I have moved in with my brother while you're here.'

They were together, as Pop promised, but it didn't feel like home, not yet.

That night, Tess changed into a flannel nighty, a parting gift from Peg and Ida, who feared the nights would be cold by the North Sea. She selected a book from the shelf. This must be Gregor's room, she supposed, from the choice of reading. There was a full set of Joseph Conrad, that sailor writer, a well-thumbed book on ornithology, fat exercise books into which she would not pry, and a pile of *Boys Own Papers* which she could pass on to Barney.

She settled down on the narrow, hard bed, huddling under coarse, grey blankets to dip again into an old favourite, *Treasure Island*. Barney tapped his coded goodnight on the party wall. He was sharing with Pop.

Tess felt a sudden misgiving. This was, after all, an alien place. Pop had warned them that they would be mostly on their own, that she might be lonely when Barney went to school. Even the local accent was hard to comprehend. 'The women round here all work,' Mrs Munro had said. What would she find to do all day? Then she realized that she would have time to write.

*

The late afternoon sunlight was caught in flash of silver as the fishermen deftly sorted their catch. Plump cod and herring slithered into piles, the undersized specimens free to all comers. The local lads, leaping on and off the harbour wall on to the jetty, yet alert for the first sign of the returning boats, now scrambled for this bounty. They chattered shrilly in Gaelic.

Tess and Barney stood at a distance. 'Get to know people,' Pop had urged. This was easier said than done, she thought ruefully. The group of older women, black clad, gossiped. They knitted with one hand only, securing the alternate needle in a loop on their belts.

The test, she discerned, was to see which boy could achieve the longest string as the tiny fish were threaded expertly through the gills. In triumph, the most nimble-fingered presented his granny with a necklace of quicksilver.

Barney unexpectedly darted forward and managed to grab a miserable four fish, despite being roughly elbowed aside by bigger boys, and bore them proudly to his sister. 'Look, supper!'

She grimaced. 'Poor little things, why didn't they throw them back? I'm not sure I fancy preparing them – I've never dealt with heads and tails before.'

'I'll d-do it! I know how,' Barney offered eagerly. Earlier, they had watched the younger women of the village gutting fish with lightning strokes of their sharp knives, their aprons silvered with scales. They had almost choked on the pungent odour as the doors of the smoking sheds opened and closed.

Barney observed then, 'They only bite the middle out of their sandwiches', as the fishwives paused briefly for refreshment.

'The edges are fishy from their fingers, that's why the gulls get the crusts.' The sound of the screaming seabirds brought back memories of Dungeness. Tess's eyes smarted. She was still homesick after all this time.

'Would you like this?' A tall young man with curly sandy hair, proffered a fine cod in red, damp hands. His eyes were very blue, like Moray's. Maybe *he* had stood on this very quay in the holidays, at Barney's age, she thought. The young pilot who had literally dropped out of the sky was still her hero.

'Thank you. It's very kind of you,' she said, echoing the aunts' polite rejoinders. 'I'm sure we shall enjoy it.' Yet, she did not take the fish. Barney, who was becoming less inhibited each day now they were released from their strict regime, had no qualms, pretending to stagger under the weight.

The young man smiled at Tess as she brushed back the strand of fiery hair which fanned her flushed face. 'You are the Rainbow children?' he asked.

She nodded. He must think her younger. Barney was nearly as tall. Millie Mae was right, she took after her grandmother in more ways than one.

'And you are Gregor, aren't you?' Barney asked in return.

'That is so. You are staying in our house.'

Surely he must resent that, Tess thought; we are usurpers, no denying it. Mrs Munro was a widow, no doubt glad of the rent for the cottage, with a son to support. But Gregor was a grown man, not the youth she supposed. He had obviously been out with the boats today.

'We must go,' she said abruptly to Barney. 'Goodbye.'

She was unaware Gregor was watching them as they went up the hill. He would be teased by his companions which was nothing new, for he, too, was a fish out of water, but there, he'd got in first with the lassie which was not like him at all.

Tess hovered anxiously over Pop as he ate. He'd returned later than usual and the baked cod had unfortunately dried out. Pop kept his thoughts to himself as he tackled the fish and mashed potato. He couldn't tell them how exhausted he was, now he was working on the great bombers. It appeared he had taken his family away from the proximity of blazing London, just in time. And what of his beloved Roma? *She* was living and working with danger, no doubt of that. He lay awake at night, fearing for her safety. The Luftwaffe could cross the Channel in six minutes. If it wasn't for the miracle of radar, which alerted the South Coast aerodromes of impending attack, and the courageous young pilots of the Spitfires and Hurricanes . . . But now the London docks were burning. Bombing by day intensified, the flames a beacon for the raiders who followed at night. Retaliation meant ordinary folk were suffering in Berlin, too.

'So, you encountered young Gregor at last,' he said, pushing aside his plate with some relief. 'It was good of him to give you the fish.'

'I gutted it!' Barney put in proudly. He exchanged glances with Tess. She smiled. What a mess he had made, but she didn't tell tales.

CHAPTER TWO

R oma was snatching a long-overdue break in the afternoon of a
day packed with drama. She lay on her bed, fully dressed, apart
from her shoes. She was tense, alert for the next emergency, finding it
difficult to 'switch off'.

She put up her hand and unpinned the elaborate front coil of blonde
hair which most of the girls favoured to counter the severity of the
regulation collar-length style. The blue of her uniform suited her, the
fitted jacket emphasized her full bust, trim waist and curvaceous hips.
Roma was fully aware that several of the young pilots found her very
attractive and that rumour had it she was top of the 'if-only' seduction
list, which, she suspected wryly, didn't even exist. This was hardly the
time for romantic entanglements, they all knew that, although some,
like the abruptly departed fourth occupant of this room, patently could
not help themselves. For this girl it had all ended in tears.

The others had gone to the canteen: Roma was hungry, but too tired
to make the effort. She was past catching up on her sleep. Her head was
pounding from sustained concentration of bending over the maps
spread out on the big table; silently, swiftly, pinpointing the danger
areas, all too aware of the unseen, daring and deadly conflict in the
skies overhead. Outnumbered, but bloody minded, those young men
who risked their lives for their country and compatriots, too often paid
the price. Like Janie's fiancé: the transitory friend they would probably
never see again, despite their assurances.

She thought wistfully of her family, reunited in Scotland. It seemed
a world away. She was on her own, as she'd been since the Last Stop
Garage. She'd put a brave face on it, of course, but missed them dreadfully at first. The colourful cards she dashed off meant she didn't have

to write too much, betray that she was unhappy in that cramped bedsit in London. Then that cheerful optimism, passed on by Millie Mae, resurfaced; she rose to the challenges that came along. Poor Tess: restricted now as none of them had been when their mother was alive, just when she should have been spreading her wings, too.

The tapping on the door startled her. 'Come in!' she called, sitting up and tucking the frivolous loop of hair behind her ear.

'Phew!' exclaimed the unexpected visitor, putting down her laden kitbag thankfully. 'Room for another one in here, they said; sorry to disturb you.' She removed her cap aiming it at the bed in the corner.

'You hit the right spot,' Roma told her wryly, swinging her legs to the ground. The newcomer was a tall, slim girl, with short black hair slicked back with brilliantine, and a dimpled face. 'I'm Roma Rainbow, and you are——?'

'Sally Tann – not *the* Roma Rainbow – Millie Mae's daughter?'

They looked at each other incredulously. Moray's sister, Roma thought. 'None other,' Roma acknowledged. 'You're a long way from home——'

'Surrey? Hardly.'

'Oh, I just thought you must have come from Scotland – my family are there now. Pop works for your dad, but they don't socialize, so we don't know what you're all up to! Had anything to eat? New to all this?'

'Yes, to the first question, and as to the second, well, I've just finished my training: I'm replacing the girl who reluctantly let on to being pregnant.'

Roma said impulsively, 'I hope we can be friends, despite the differences between our parents.'

'Oh, I've always wanted to meet your family; you especially. Moray really fell for you, you know – don't look so surprised! – he didn't imagine his feelings would be reciprocated, being a callow youth at the time. He knew Dad wouldn't approve, so he wrote to your sister, hoping for news of you – she even sent him a snap of you, all glamorous, in a black leather coat.'

'It wasn't *real* leather. . . . I had a whole sheet of those polyphotos, taken at Jerome's,' Roma recalled. 'I didn't know Tess had pinched one.'

'Ma caught sight of it once, and said you were Millie Mae all over again.'

'I hope she didn't mind too much.'

'No, because you see, she and Millie Mae were friends before my dad made that silly confession, and spoilt it all.'

'I never knew that, either. You look like your mother, by the way.'

'Oh, I'm not nearly as glamorous as Ma!' Sally said frankly. 'She didn't fit in at the back of beyond, like your mother did. Ma came from a remote place, but she was brought up in a rather grand house, and went away to school in Edinburgh. I imagine Millie Mae made her time on the Marsh more bearable.'

'And what is Moray doing now?' Roma tidied her hair.

'Oh, he's a pilot; we always knew he would be. I'm not too sure where he is now and anyway, perhaps I shouldn't say – but when he's next on leave, we three should get together, don't you think?'

The warning blared before Roma could answer.

'Let's spend the day exploring, take a packed lunch. You'll be incarcerated tomorrow, after all,' Tess reminded Barney.

'I wish you wouldn't use words I d-don't know,' Barney reproved her.

'I'm trying to increase your vocabulary: imprisoned, in school, I mean. But I'm only joking,' she added quickly, 'You'll soon make friends. Coming?'

'Coming,' Barney said. 'And so are you,' he told Fly sternly.

As they walked along the soft sands at Silver Strand, the sandstone cliffs rose above them, cormorants zoomed low over their heads; in the clefts of the rocks, jackdaws, pigeons and herring gulls chattered and swore. Fly became animated, investigating this and that, as in the Dungeness days.

In the rock pools where Barney crouched, having darted ahead, there were hermit crabs, wearing protective whelk shells, scuttling about, and limpets and mussels to turn over amid the glossy trails of seaweed. 'Tess, come and see this!' Barney called constantly. '*Leave!*' he added, to the curious dog.

She rested against the rocks, pencil flying across the pages of her notebook, unaware, as she made little thumbnail sketches in the margin – instant illustrations, she thought – that she made an appealing picture herself, even in her old school dress, run up, with economy of material, by Peg. The dress was too short, but she enjoyed the warmth of the late summer sun on her bare legs.

Gregor didn't mean to startle her. 'Good morning! Would you object if I joined you for a wee while?' He wore baggy shorts, frayed at the hems, had rolled up his sleeves. Tess was suddenly aware that she was staring at his bronzed limbs, covered with golden fuzz.

She swallowed; then, 'You're not fishing today?' She turned her book over. Her writing was to her, intensely private.

He opened his knapsack. 'No, I'm done with that. I should return to college at the weekend. I am training to be a teacher. Unless I decide otherwise.' He produced a bottle of lemonade. 'Would you care for a wee drop? It's thirsty weather.' Then Barney came running up, his pockets bulging with treasures.

They shared the tepid drink, then Gregor and Barney scaled the cliff to a deserted cottage at the top. He called down to Tess so that she did not feel left out, because she'd said she had no head for heights and would stay put.

'My great-grandfather lived here, Tess. They took the roof off, to avoid the tax, you know. It is left to me; maybe I shall live here one day.'

Tess shaded her eyes, looking up. As they disappeared within the gaping doorway, a white bird rose up, beating its wings in a great flurry of annoyance, and she caught her breath in delight, for the bird was haloed in the sunlight. Could she capture the essence of the moment she wondered, in words?

They shared the flask of tea. 'Sorry, no sugar, I have to battle with the rations, Pop and Barney both having a sweet tooth,' she said, as Gregor drained the stained bakelite cup in one thirsty gulp. There were enough soft baps with a smear of butter and sliver of cheese; apples for the three of them, and dog biscuits and a billycan of water for Fly.

'Shall we walk further? That is, if you should feel like it, Tess?'

'I'm not an invalid,' she said firmly, knowing that Pop must have told his mother about her heart murmur. 'I like walking, it's good for me.' Millie Mae never made anything of it, she thought, it was the aunts worrying – and look how I *ran* that time when Moray Tann landed in our field.

'I am sure you are not. I only meant, you might think it is time to go back.'

She knew then, they could be real friends. Imperceptibly, he short-ened his long stride to match hers, while Barney dashed in and out of the breakers.

They paused within a huge, crumbling sandstone arch, the interior encrusted with bird droppings. 'One fierce storm,' Gregor said, 'and it could fall down.'

Tess shivered. Their voices seemed to bounce off the stone walls. Nothing was predictable, she thought: how long would they be living here; how long would the war go on; when would they see Roma again?

Gregor showed Barney the piles of rotting seaweed. 'Lift a bit, Barney – see what happens.' Tiny, shrimp like creatures flew into the air. Barney was fascinated. 'Sandhoppers,' Gregor grinned.

Tess aired her knowledge. She hadn't been able to resist the natural history books on his bedroom shelf. 'Fodder for the turnstones!' she informed her brother loftily.

Gregor's whisper tickled her ear. 'I recall that expression. . . .'

'I was born by the sea, too, you know,' she returned.

He coaxed her a short way up the cliff, and she was very aware of his firm clasp around her waist, as he showed her how to wedge herself behind a jutting rock. 'The tide will be in shortly, this is the best place to see it.'

'See what, Gregor?' Barney asked. But he wasn't telling. They looked down at the spuming sea, dashing furiously against some huge rocks. One was hollowed out, enabling them to see right through it. The spray smacked at their faces, salting their parted lips, then the sea burst spectacularly through the blowhole, with a thunderous roar. Tess, exhilarated, became aware that she was clutching at Gregor's arm. Pink flooded her cheeks like the tide. She released her grasp immediately, turning her face away.

'Shall I join you on the morrow?' he asked, as they parted at the door.

Tess hesitated. 'Barney will be at school.'

'After lessons, perhaps? A stroll before tea? It seems a pity to waste the good weather; all too soon the evenings will draw in. Winter here will no doubt be more severe than you have experienced in the south.'

She nodded, and he walked on to his uncle's house.

Barney couldn't resist telling Pop that evening, 'Guess what! Tess has a boyfriend – Gregor! He's really nice.'

'*Beast!*' Tess expostulated.

Pop weighed his words carefully. 'I'm pleased you've found a companion, you two, he's a clever chap by all accounts. But, remember, he will be away very soon.' Tess was a grown woman now, like Roma.

That night, Tess slowly leafed through Gregor's notebooks – now she knew he wouldn't mind. When she finally succumbed to sleep, the open pages were pressed between her cheek and the pillow.

She dreamed near dawn that she was running across the strand to meet Gregor, but when at last she came up to him, she found that it was Moray, no older than when they had last met, smiling at her.

CHAPTER THREE

They crossed over the road and turned into a parallel street, where the church stood above the school, both guarded by black railings and clanging gates.

'D-don't come any further,' Barney pleaded. 'Pop told them I was coming.'

'But I should—' Tess worried.

The vehemence of his reply startled, wounded her. '*No*, Tess! Millie Mae wouldn't fuss over me, like you do. If we'd s-stayed in Bromley, I'd have been g-going to secondary s-school, and – you c-couldn't come in with me, there.'

She stepped back. 'Go on then.'

'You won't be waiting at the gates at four, will you?'

'I certainly won't!' She swallowed her hurt. 'Have a good day. Come straight home and get changed; remember we're meeting Greg at the harbour.

There was an asphalted playground, a vegetable garden with a patchwork of plots, some more well tended than others, and beyond that, scrubby grassland stretching down to the shore, curtailed by a brick wall. Barney immediately saw it as an escape route, but he knew he wouldn't dare bunk off school.

Boys were already sparring in the playground, while big girls mothered apprehensive five-year-olds, pulling up socks, and retying hair ribbons.

'Where's the fire?' shouted one large lad, pointing at Barney's newly cropped hair. He flushed miserably, but was saved by the clanging bell, and the opening of the school doors.

This was a school for infants through to leavers: most fourteen-year-old boys joined their kin on the fishing boats, the girls gutted fish, or went into service, or stayed at home to help bring up the younger children. There was always casual work to be had, in particular raspberry picking in late summer. A few seized their chance when they took up a scholarship to a higher school, in a town like Inverness; Gregor had been one of these.

It would have been some consolation, in that stark lofty room with the rows of double desks facing the austere, gowned headmaster behind his table, occasionally to be able to glance out of the windows that Barney sat alongside. If only he could glimpse the sea, he thought; but the early Victorian architect, knowing that children were easily distracted, had placed the windows too high.

Barney was set gruelling tests in all subjects: navigation and Morse code were a mystery to him; even the history questions, normally a favourite subject, naturally had a different bias. The maths were more advanced than he was accustomed to. His doleful expression as he stared at blank paper prompted smothered sniggers from his classmates. He knew if he tried to explain to the frowning master, his stuttering would intensify. He had already been told, 'Speak up, boy, I can't hear you!' A leather thonged strap, the tawse, lay beside the register. It did not take much guessing as to its purpose.

He spent a lonely lunch hour lurking by the bicycle sheds. Unexpectedly, a lanky boy came up just before the bell tolled. 'Nearly time to go in,' he said laconically. 'It's not so bad here, but it takes ages, before they accept you. I should know, we moved here a couple of years ago; my father's the minister.'

'But you're Scottish,' Barney pointed out, 'that makes a difference.'

'Not really,' the boy grinned, pointing to a prominent chipped front tooth. 'Watch out, and don't let 'em stir you up into any fights – that's my advice. I'm Douglas Glenn, by the way. I've got three brothers – two are in the forces.'

'I've two sisters, one in the WAAF, Barney said proudly, 'one here.'

When he ventured back into school, he was told he was demoted to a class with children a year or two younger than he was. They were not exactly friendly, but it was better to be ignored, he thought, than the object of ridicule.

Barney sneaked away, trailing after a couple of boys who were beachcombing, while Tess sat patiently on the wall, absorbed in the rhythm of the fishwives. One looked over, and smiled. Tess thought, she knows I'm waiting for him.

Gregor apologized. 'I had to pack, Mother insisted. Where's Barney?'

'Oh, I'm not sure – he must have followed those boys.'

He was reassuring. 'Give him a little rope, Tess. Safety in numbers.'

They walked, as she had years ago with Moray, along a very different stretch of shore. No crunch of shingle, but soft sand which sneaked into their shoes. They didn't talk of Millie Mae of course, or the Last Stop Garage, but paused to look at a purple starfish and the sad remains of a dead seal.

The other lads ran back along the top of the cliffs, calling mockingly in passing. Gregor shook a friendly fist in reply. They were almost at the blowhole, and Barney was still not in sight. Fearfully, Tess stared out to sea: suppose he had been swept off his feet by the fierce sucking of the receding tide? Gregor had warned her to keep her distance from the rolling sea.

'Sit down,' he said, 'I believe I know where he will be.' He'd seen the bright glistening of her eyes. He went swiftly over to the blowhole, climbed inside and re-emerged with Barney, damp, bloody-nosed and raging.

'Barney!' Tess was shocked. 'You've been *fighting*!'

'They got me first!' he shouted. 'They said I hadn't any r-right to have it, 'cause I don't b-belong here. Three of them jumped on me, but I h-held on – *look*!' He had a green ball, like a large glass grapefruit, shrouded in torn net.

'A fishing float – quite a prize.' Gregor ignored the blood that Barney was smearing on his sleeve. 'Sit beside Tess, Barney, I want you both to listen.'

'Even if you tell me not to fight, well, I will, if they g-go for me again.' Barney's temper hadn't cooled. He ignored Tess's proffered hanky.

'You must fight your own battles, of course, but it's better to find a way to make friends. It takes two, or more, to pick a quarrel – d'you understand?'

'Take it, I don't want it!' Barney growled, thrusting the globe at Gregor. Then he dashed back to the blowhole.

'Leave him, Tess, he'll get over it.'

Ten minutes later, she watched as Gregor showed Barney how to make a little boat from driftwood, a rather dessicated cork, a matchstick and paper from her notebook. He made a notch with his penknife: 'More paper, Tess, please? And your pencil? Scribble a message, Barney, poke it well within the groove, so it'll keep dry, we hope – then launch your wee boat!'

'I don't know what to put.' Barney was still disgruntled. Gregor smiled, wrote something himself, folded and tucked the note in the slit in the little boat. It sailed on the tide, returned, then was buoyed by the waves.

'Time to go home, I think. I'm sorry that this will be our last walk together for a while, when we are just getting to know one another,' Gregor observed.

'You are eager to go?' she asked impulsively.

'I am. Well, I was,' he answered honestly. He smiled down at her upturned, earnest face. 'But I shan't stay at the college long, I have decided to join the merchant navy, I can finish my studies after the war.'

When they reached the harbour, one of the women came towards them, frog-marching one of the other boys. 'Say it then, Geordie,' she demanded.

The unfortunate boy, with a fat lip from Barney's fist, eyed his adversary. 'Sorry,' he muttered, then scuttled off like one of the hermit crabs.

'I'm sorry, too,' his mother told Tess. 'Fancy fighting a new boy like that. I said, they'll have the wrong idea about the rest of us.'

Before supper, Tess pressed her best dress on the wrong side, a little fearfully in case the flat irons were too hot. She slipped on the pink crepe with the sweetheart neckline and cap sleeves, which had been Roma's. It was on the loose side; if only she had a voluptuous figure like her sister.

Gregor had said he would call to say goodbye – surely he meant tonight? Straining on tiptoe, she regarded herself in the little mirror on the bedroom wall, set at the right height for Gregor for shaving.

'I'm not sure this colour goes with red hair,' she said aloud. If only the dress had been green, to emphasize the colour of her eyes.

'You look nice,' Pop told her, after supper. He rustled his newspaper.

'She's waiting for Gregor,' Barney told his father.

'Mind your own business, eh?' Pop reproved mildly, winking at Tess.

The disappointment was great. Gregor called briefly to apologize, 'The lads insist they take me out tonight for a farewell drink; I seem to have earned their approval at last, deciding to join up – I do hope you understand.'

'Goodbye, good luck,' she whispered, knowing the others could hear.

She parted her bedroom curtains later. It was not quite dark. The menfolk were grouping in the street below, talking. Soon they would all walk to the pub, which was a male preserve. The smell of fish soup persisted, mingling with rank tobacco. Then Gregor came along, looked up, just as if she had signalled. Tess was not to know that, silhouetted with the lamplight behind her, she presented an ethereal figure, in that demure nighty, her hair still crackling with static electricity from its vigorous brushing.

He called out. It was a moment before she realized what he was trying to impart. The men turned, looked up too, amused. 'I'll write!'

She hugged those words to her, as she closed the curtains. It was what Moray had said – but she was too young then, which was why he had lost interest, but this time. . . .

Barney tapped goodnight, letting her know he'd heard and seen it all.

'Goodnight!' she tapped back. '*Or else!*'

'Look what I found, Tess,' Barney said, as she stared pensively out to the horizon a few days later. The little craft had been caught up on the rocks. She dug out the paper with her nail file. It read: *Back with the tide!*

'I made a big batch of scones, then realized that with Gregor gone, they would be stale before my brother and I could eat them all.' An unexpededly long speech from reticent Mrs Munro, as she offered Tess a tin plate with six floury scones piled on it, still warm from the oven.

'Thank you,' Tess said. 'Will you come in? Would you like a cup of tea?' She would be glad of the company, for she had been wondering how Barney was faring at school. He was uncommunicative when he returned.

She felt a little awkward, making the tea in Mrs Munro's kitchen, while she sat at the table like a visitor, with hands clasped in her lap.

'Did Gregor get off all right?' she ventured.

'Aye,' Mrs Munro sipped her tea.

'Is it strong enough?' Tess asked. Pop joked that her tea could hardly crawl out of the pot, but it wasn't surprising when rationing was now so strict.

Mrs Munro nodded. 'Aye. Thank you.' She declined a second scone.

'Did – did Gregor tell you Barney is teased at school?'

'He did. They're not a bad lot round here.'

'I'm sorry, I didn't mean—'

'I know you didn't. Leave him to it, that's my advice.' Mrs Munro pushed back her chair. 'I must get home.'

'You'll miss Gregor.'

'I always do. But this time, it is different, you see.'

'You didn't want him to leave college, to go to war?'

'He's a gentle sort, but he will do what he thinks is right. His father was the same. He served in the merchant navy in the Great War. He came through that, but we lost him to the sea, anyway, when Gregor was a wee lad.'

They were at the door. Mrs Munro turned. 'It's not just me who will worry, there is Moira, at college. He must put romance to one side, for now.'

Why is she telling me this? Tess wondered. She opened the door. 'Thank you again for the scones. I hope you'll come again, Mrs Munro.'

'Aye. Did he not tell you about Moira, then?'

'No. We – we've only just met, of course.'

'Ah,' Mrs Munro said enigmatically.

CHAPTER FOUR

Tess tapped uncertainly at the keys of the typewriter Pop had brought home for her. He had secured the little portable to the carrier of the folding bicycle issued to him at work: the promised staff car had not yet materialized.

Roma, Tess thought ruefully, would have laughed at her attempts – hadn't she claimed airily to be able to type sixty words a minute? Roma seemed to succeed in everything. Tess wasn't even sure she'd be able to *think* on the typewriter, but she was determined to persevere.

'Careful with the paper,' Pop said: 'There's a war on you know'

'I do know, Pop. How much did you pay for the typewriter?' she asked, anxiously. They had been hard up for so long it was difficult to take in that now things were easing financially, even though there weren't the goods to buy.

'Never you mind,' he told her, grinning. 'When I mentioned to a colleague, my daughter wants to be a writer, he asked his wife if she wanted to hang on to this, and she said if you could make good use of it, well, take it.'

Now, she was just unlocking the hammers stuck together in mid strike, when she became aware that someone was at the door.

'Blow!' she exclaimed. She draped the cover over the machine and paper.

'Hello, Tess, I said I'd be back on the tide – that's if you read my message,'

'Gregor! Oh,' she floundered. 'You said, you'd write . . .'

'I'm sorry, there wasn't time – may I come in?'

He looked unfamiliar in the dark-blue jacket, worn over a roll-neck sweater, with the silver merchant navy badge glinting on his lapel. She

41

wished she was wearing the pink dress, despite the definite nip in the air, not Roma's old slacks turned up twice at the ankles, and a jumper that had shrunk in the wash.

'Embarkation leave,' he explained, 'I couldn't go without—'

'Seeing your mother again, of course,' she supplied quickly. Her hand trembled as she gave the tea leaves a stir.

'Aye. Just a quick cup, Tess, nothing to eat, thanks. Mother is planning a hefty meal.' He noticed the typewriter. 'I have interrupted your writing?'

'It doesn't matter, really.'

They drank their tea in silence. Then, 'I must go,' he said. 'Think of me.'

'I will.'

The brief visit over, she wondered why he had come. She felt foolish now having looked out of the window the night before he left, for believing he meant it, when he said he'd write. She thought, I suppose he was just being kind when he befriended me – and Barney, too, of course. If only I could stop myself from all this romantic imagining – but then, if I lost that, how would I be able to write?

She uncovered the typewriter, pulled the paper free of the roller, screwed it up, then, remembering Pop's words, smoothed it out again. 'Romance,' she said aloud. 'What do I know about it? I want to be . . . *stirred* like – like the teapot, to be all hot and steaming like the tea.' She grinned sheepishly and carefully reinserted the paper. 'Wonder if I could write a story for *Girl's Crystal*? Exciting – with a heroine much more like Roma than me.'

'Look, girls,' Angela Castle exclaimed: 'See that lady pilot in white leather? That's Jeanne de Cas- um, Casallis?'

'*Mrs Feather*!' Pat interrupted, as the cameras flashed, and the delightfully dithery star of stage and radio, climbed aboard, waving to her fans.

'If she can fly she can't be as feathery as she seems,' Joan concluded.

They were at the Lympne air show, and celebrities were there in force. It seemed they all wanted to learn to fly, like the Castle sisters.

But flying lessons were expensive and their only link with the world of aviation was their father, who was a trusted engineer to the famous . . .

Now, how could she airily despatch her heroine, Angela, a beautiful blonde, in her black leather-look coat, into the sky?

Pop passed her the letter that evening without comment. It had obviously been delivered to him by hand. *Miss Tess Rainbow* – written with a flourish.

'Go away,' she reproved Barney, trying to peek over her shoulder. There was a card within the envelope. She read it twice.

'I'd better put you out of your misery, I suppose,' she told them. 'It's from Mrs Tann, Moray's mother. She's here, she says, because of the bombing. She thinks it would be "rather nice" if we were to meet. She suggests Saturday afternoon. Her chauffeur will collect us – you are both invited, too.'

'Not me,' he said evenly. 'You two go. Time to heal the breach, I reckon.'

'I can't, either,' Barney reminded them. 'I'm spending the day at the Manse – Dougie says his mother makes the best fish and chips with crispy batter – and I can b-borrow a bike – and have races round the box hedges.'

He only faltered once, in that speech, Tess realized, pleased. A friend like Douglas will give him confidence. He's relied on me for too long to protect him.

'I'll make your excuses,' she said. 'Clear the table, Barney, and wash up please, while I RSVP.'

Whatever she wore, she wouldn't impress Mrs Tann, Tess decided. But the postman, courtesy of Roma, saved the day.

Don't get much time to wear civvies nowadays, read the enclosed note. *This should fit you, I hope. Love to all, Roma.*

The lightweight jumper suit was in russet wool. Simple but smart; round-necked and long sleeved; no doubt Roma had livened it up with a silk scarf, or a punched leather belt. What a pity she had to wear rayon stockings and clumpy school shoes with it, she thought, trying the outfit on in her room.

She opened the little attaché case of treasures: her scrapbook,

Moray's letters, Roma's cards, the snapshot of Millie Mae cuddling Tess as a baby; there it was, cocooned in cotton wool – the silver monoplane brooch. Moray had enclosed it in that first eagerly awaited letter. The *Spirit of Millie Mae*? She had kept it secret, never worn it. Now she pinned it to her jumper.

Tess was overawed by the size of the house on the hill, sheltered by Douglas pines; even the cheerfully sparking log fire failed to make the drawing-room cosy on an autumnal afternoon. She sat opposite Jean Tann, as elegant as she remembered her. The armchairs were winged, with deep-cushions: Tess worried about rising decorously, when it was time to partake of tea.

'That colour complements your hair,' Mrs Tann observed, unexpectedly.

'Thank you.' She didn't know why she added, 'The costume was Roma's.'

'Your sister has very good taste,' Mrs Tann said. 'Ah, here he is – I sent him to get changed; I told him he wasn't dressed to receive a young lady.'

'I wasn't dressed at all, Ma, well, only in pyjamas and dressing-gown,' commented an amused voice. Tess, heart pounding, knew immediately who this was, but the wings of the chair obscured her view.

Then Moray stood before her, leaning heavily on crutches but smiling. His hair still flopped endearingly across his forehead. 'Sorry, but I'll probably fall over if I try to shake your hand. It's been a long time since we met, Tess, and some things don't change do they? I'm temporarily grounded after another crash landing; nothing heroic I'm afraid, only a smashed leg this time.'

'Sit down,' his mother ordered. 'He's still suffering from shock, but he won't admit to that, or that the plane was all shot up before he brought it down safely. The RAF sent him as far away as possible, here to me, so—'

'I can't make any more trouble for a bit,' Moray finished, with a wry grin.

'I have to confess,' Jean told Tess, 'I asked you here as a diversion, to stop him fretting, being so far from the action. I'm glad, really, it's just you.'

'You didn't prepare me for another shock – that Tess was all grown up.' With difficulty, he put the crutches aside and subsided slowly into a chair.

'It was a surprise to me, too, but it's years since we met,' Jean reflected. She looked keenly at Tess. 'I certainly didn't take into account that you probably have a young man in tow who might object to you visiting Moray?'

'I—' Tess faltered. 'A friend, that's all. He has gone away,' she added.

'Then I imagine you are free to see who you like,' Jean said. 'I should warn you my son has had a succession of girlfriends since his days at university . . . don't frown, Moray, it's true! Well, I'll leave you to fill in the gaps, as it were, while I see what the housekeeper is planning to serve up for tea.'

'You stopped writing to me,' she said simply, after a long pause. The intense gaze of his blue eyes was disconcerting. He was not smiling now; she guessed that had been for his mother's benefit.

His forehead was beaded with sweat, as it was after that other crash in the *Spirit of Millie Mae*. He must be in pain. She touched the hand gripping the arm of his chair. 'You don't have to make excuses,' she said, when he didn't answer. 'I was only a little girl; you were really interested in Roma.'

'Who obviously never gave me a second thought. It was an adolescent thing. As Ma bluntly remarked, I didn't lack female company thereafter. *You* remembered me; you're wearing that brooch – I admit Ma bought it for me to send you. I didn't write, if I'm honest, being embarrassed by the intensity of your replies. Alarm bells rang, if you like: I detected a hint of puppy love—'

'Now you've embarrassed me!' But she did not withdraw her hand.

'I'm glad you don't look like Roma, like Millie Mae,' he said unexpectedly. 'It's easier for Ma, you see. Well, shall we pick up where we left off, Tess? On that windswept beach when I talked earnestly about the past and quarrelling with Dad – nothing compared to what you'd been through, losing your mother – I was merely a disturbed youth, you were a serious little girl. What d'you say?'

'I think we should begin again, from here,' she said.

'Good. May I ask a new friend to assist me from this chair, slide my crutches into position, and to escort me to the door, which Ma tactfully closed, and to point me in the direction of the downstairs office, as Ma calls it?'

As Tess bent over him, Moray's arms went firmly round her waist, surprising her. His face was very close to hers. 'I'm *glad* you're all grown up, Tess. Let me kiss you – put the seal on our pact of renewed friendship.'

'Please . . .' she protested, but, of course, he took that as assent. Will he know, it's the first time for me? she thought. I hoped Gregor would kiss me, but he didn't, and now— She closed her eyes as their lips met.

When he released her, she belatedly helped him to his feet, hoping he wouldn't realize she was shaking. I'm all stirred up, she thought, bemused. I don't feel grown up at all, just young and foolish, and thoroughly confused.

'I said, joking of course – did you have jam sandwiches?' Pop repeated.

'What? No, smoked salmon, and crusts cut off: I filled up on Madeira cake and fruit scones – there was real butter!'

'You'll be going again?'

'I'm not sure. I suppose – it depends on how long Moray is at home.'

'I gather that, as before, he has been rather brave but foolhardy.' Pop looked at her searchingly. 'Don't let that young feller break your heart, Tess. He's got too much of his old man in him, you know.'

'They don't seem to get on.'

'That's why.'

'Pop, does it still – worry you – you know, about what spoiled the friendship between you and Moray's family?'

'It wasn't that I ever doubted Millie Mae, her love for me, for us,' he answered obliquely, 'it was knowing that Leo invariably succeeded in getting what he wanted. That's what I admired about him when we first met; it was what I eventually feared. Jean has dealt with it in her own way, but it can't have been a happy marriage. Why d'you think she is distancing herself from him right now? Wouldn't Millie Mae have stayed with *me*, kept the family together, whether we were in danger of being bombed out, or not?'

'It seems strange Mrs Tann wants Moray and me to renew our friendship.'

Pop reached out, tweaked her hair affectionately. 'She didn't count on you losing your braids and becoming a beautiful young woman.'

'Oh Pop! Don't be silly,' Tess objected.

'Of course, Moray finds you attractive: as did Gregor. Millie Mae should be here for you to confide in: Roma is too far away. This isn't a carefree time for you, Tess, as it should be. It's asking a lot of you to play mother to your brother, to housekeep for me . . . but don't fall in love with love, as they say.'

'I'll try not to,' she said simply.

CHAPTER FIVE

Tess didn't see Moray again for some time, for shortly after her visit, Jean wrote that he had been rushed to the local hospital, then transferred to Edinburgh for urgent surgery: *It is touch and go; he has developed a serious bone infection. No visitors other than family. I have sent for his father.*

Tess, biting her lip, passed the note to Pop, while Barney looked on.

'Wait a few days before writing to him, I should,' Pop counselled, noting her shocked expression. 'Though I imagine Jean would appreciate a reply.'

Tess received another letter to which she hadn't yet responded: from Gregor, written before he embarked for dangerous waters, where the hidden U-boat menace was ever present and cargo vessels and their escorts ran the gauntlet of torpedoes and grim confrontation. When she met his mother she recognized the marks of strain on her face, because Pop, constantly fearing for Roma's safety, bore these too. Tess felt constrained regarding mention of Gregor, recalling Mrs Munro's enigmatic words just after he left.

Dear Tess
You must be wondering why I came to see you – it was not how I Intended it to be. I wish we'd had more time to get to know each other properly. Parting will be the test, won't it? I think I love you.
   Yours
                Gregor

P.S. Back on the tide – I promise!

If only he hadn't written, 'I think': yet Tess was aware that she would have expressed it like that, herself. Seeing Moray again had been an unsettling experience. The unexpected kiss: maybe it had amused him, but that thought hurt. Would he regard her as a possible link once more between himself and Roma, when – if – he recovered from this serious setback, she wondered.

Multi-coloured combinations, knitted with scraps of wool, hung stiffly on washing lines on freezing November days. The fishing boats were heading for Iceland. The women conserved energy, not chattering; bulked out with layers of clothes, scarves, working automatically with bone-white fingers, selecting slippery fish to pile in the crates. Food vital for the survival of a nation under siege.

The Battle of Britain continued, the anticipated invasion did not take place; but the horrific bombing of London and other great cities and ports intensified. Women flew Hurricanes and Spitfires now, if not yet in combat, delivering replacement fighter planes. Factories worked at full tilt producing armaments.

Although remote from danger as such, Tess and Barney heard the roar of great bombers lifting off in formation at nightfall, then there was the long, tense wait for their return during the early hours. Pop was often away overnight at the base: he kept things to himself, but Tess felt his responsibilities keenly.

She walked along the shore mid-morning, taking a break from writing, when she needed to clarify her thoughts. She did not venture as far as the blowhole, for the searing wind buffeted her along, forced her to keep her head down. Dribbling weather, she described it ruefully to Pop, but she was not laid low with bronchitis. It was Fly who wheezed, loath to budge from the kitchen. 'You're getting ancient, poor old boy,' she told him, 'but keep going until Roma comes home.' It was months since they had seen her.

One Sunday afternoon, she, Pop and Barney climbed steadily uphill from the village, past the fields where great globular turnips, which the locals called neeps, were grown. These had been pulled by hand and were now stored. They followed a track to the forest, bundling dry fallen wood to drag back as they were running low on fuel and snow was in the air. They felt triumphant at their resourcefulness, though Pop pretended to frown on the small neeps which Barney had found in a pocket of long grass, and produced when they reached home.

'They either rolled off the b-barrow, Pop, or they chucked 'em.'

There were hints for using such staples broadcast over the wireless. Tess was becoming a good, plain cook. Today, she mashed the cooked neeps well, added pepper and a spot of butter. She liked to follow in Millie Mae's culinary footsteps. The neeps went down well with lamb chops fried in their own fat.

Pop was actually home in time to eat with them. He complimented her on the first course, then said casually, 'Moray Tann is home I hear, for further convalescence, but it doesn't look as if he will be flying for some time, if ever. The surgeons saved his leg, but mobility will always be a problem.'

'You'll go and see him, Tess, won't you? Can I come this time? They say he's a *hero*, at school,' Barney asked, adding, 'What's for pud?'

'Yes, to the first question. It's roly poly with treacle – if I can scrape the pudding off the cloth, more flour than suet, I'm afraid.' Moray will be devastated, she thought, as he lives for his flying. I must visit him soon.

In the event she went alone. Jean paid her a brief visit while Barney was at school. 'I don't think he is up to answering a young boy's questions on aerial combat yet, but he wants to see you. For some reason he thinks he got off on the wrong foot with you last time. Do come and reassure him, Tess!'

He was resting on his bed. Tess was shocked to see him so thin and haggard. 'Don't worry, you're quite safe,' he said sardonically, after his mother had excused herself. 'You can move faster than I can, after all.'

'I brought you some sweets.' She delved in her bag, to cover her blushes.

'You shouldn't spend your ration on me, but thank you; chewy mints, good. I need something to get my teeth into.'

'You sound bitter,' she said, then instantly regretted it. 'I'm sorry, you have every right to feel like that, Moray.'

'I didn't have any right to tease you, kiss you, last time,' he said, then added in a lighter tone, 'but I couldn't help myself, after all those starchy nurses wary of the boys in blue, when I saw that fabulous hair and those luscious lips.'

She blushed deeply again, to her chagrin. 'Stop mocking me! Roma sent her good wishes to you. Did you know that she and your sister are in the same unit; that they are great pals? It's a small world, isn't it?'

'Sally wrote to me in hospital – you have to be *in extremis* to receive a letter from her. I gather that your sister is popular with the pilots,' he said, wryly. 'And don't bristle again, Tess, it's not as if I said she's a popsy—'

'She's not!' She hated that silly expression.

'See, you *are* bristling! We didn't argue in the marsh days, did we? Can't we be like that again? It's the tonic I need, uncomplicated friendship.' He held out his hand. 'Shake to that?' He added, as she hesitated, 'No spooning – after all, you have a boyfriend, or, sort of, eh? Is that what you want me to say?'

She slipped her hand in his. 'Yes,' she said. I'll write to Gregor, she thought, tell him to, well, wait and see. When Moray meets Roma again, he won't have eyes for anyone else. Because isn't that how it is for *me?*

The week before Christmas, Tess was determined they would celebrate, and decorate their temporary home, for Roma was hoping to be with them. They had a note each today. Tess, having heard extracts from the others, merely said, 'Oh, mine's the same,' refolded and stuck it casually in her pocket.

Roma had been rather indiscreet and Tess didn't want to upset Pop. It wasn't often they had breakfast together. Pop looked quite relaxed for once: pleased at the prospect of seeing Roma. 'Though I reckon she won't think much of the tin tub or the WC, even under a covered way. Millie Mae could put up with a lot, and did, at the garage, but she liked a proper bathroom, too.'

Roma's letter to Tess, said:

Shush! We – Sally and I – might cadge a lift in a plane, as old Swindon's flying north. If you haven't got a spare bed, Sally says I can stay with them at nights as they have plenty of room. Anyway, I hear you're about to get an invitation to Christmas Dinner with the Tanns, but I'm not sure if Pop will accept if Leo decides to put in an appearance.

Tell Moray I am looking forward to seeing him – if the rations will run to it, I might make him some toasted cheese! Just like I did at – the Last Stop to Nowhere.

Roma didn't make that, it was *me*, Tess thought, and who is Swindon?

'Fancy coming up to the forest with me, later?' she asked Barney, now that school had broken up. 'We could pick some of that holly we spotted last time. Maybe Dougie would like to come with us?'

The high ground was already rimed with white; lazy flakes floated in the air, settled on caps and shoulders, then vanished; their feet crunched on the path. The air was colder than it had ever been on the Romney Marsh, but it was just as exhilarating, even though Tess couldn't talk much, or she got out of puff.

The boys raced ahead, alarming Tess as they disappeared from view among the trees. She hurried as best she could. She heard the ominous cracking of the branch before she spotted them: Dougie bending over a sack half-full of holly, but jerking up his head in alarm, as Barney fell from the tree, landing with a jarring thump on his back. In his gloved hand was a sprig of scarlet berries.

'*Barney*!' Tess shrieked, stumbling over a root, nearly going flying herself.

Barney was trying to say something. He moved his hands, to her relief, for surely he couldn't do that if he'd broken his back, indicating he was winded.

'Don't move him until, you're sure,' advised Dougie, the boy scout.

'Can you . . . run for help, Dougie? It gets dark so early, and we don't want to get stuck up here – no one knowing.'

'I told my mum where we were going, but she'll think I'm back at your house – don't move, will you, Tess? I'll be as quick as I can.' Dougie actually picked up the sack, slung it over one shoulder and dashed off through the trees.

Barney was still gasping, blinking his eyes rapidly. Tess knelt beside him, cradling his head. 'Don't worry Barney, you'll be all right.' Oh, please hurry, Dougie, she prayed silently. I don't know what to do!

She cried with relief when Barney managed to sit up. A hand touched her shoulder. She scrambled to her feet, whirled round. Gregor stood there, wearing his dark, oiled wool jersey, and cap. Afterwards she would think, I didn't even feel surprise at that moment.

'It's hard to run uphill in rubber boots,' he said ruefully. 'Mother thought you'd be here, for the holly. Dougie cannoned into me half-way: he's gone to warn her, she did some nursing in the last war.

Now, Barney, what's all this?'

Amazingly, Barney was on his feet. 'I was winded, that's all,' he said, without hesitation. ' Did Dougie take the holly? Half of it's mine.'

'He did, and you needn't think you're going to look for any more today,' Tess said grimly. Then, 'Whatever are *you* doing here, Gregor?'

'Four days' leave – got a lift from the docks – then – well, it doesn't matter, does it? However much Barney protests, he needs to be taken home to get over the shock. Ready?' Barney nodded, shrugging away Tess's hand.

As the boy sloped determinedly ahead, Gregor slipped an arm round Tess's waist. 'Tess, I had to come home – to see you. When you didn't answer my letter, and Mother wrote you were visiting Moray Tann, I thought—'

'You thought I'd cast you off!' she finished, then wished she hadn't.

His grip tightened. 'I know my own mind now, but do you? He's not for you, Tess. Oh, we need his sort right now, especially in the air, but he's irresponsible. Did you know, he took his father's private plane once and flew off – no licence, no permission – crashlanded at the back of beyond.'

'He landed almost at my feet, Gregor, just like Barney did today,' she said. 'I'll tell you about it sometime, but not today – here's Dougie, see?'

CHAPTER SIX

It had been an uneventful journey, albeit noisy, in the belly of the bomber. Both Roma and Sally fell asleep on the last lap. They awoke to a bumpy landing, clutching one another apprehensively.

'You girls OK?' An engaging Canadian accent; she thought fleetingly, before she clapped her hand to her mouth, the voice was more attractive than the man. To her, he was old, compared to the youthful pilots she knew. He was actually thirty-seven, muscular, shortish and balding, the rakish moustache making a statement. He was a sergeant pilot, delivering a replacement plane.

While the navigator took care of the kitbags and Sally, Old Swindon hurried Roma to the scrubby grass fringing the turning apron of the runway. They were in a grey, barren place, under colourless skies, with motionless great planes on the periphery like wary mammoths keeping their distance one from the other.

'Let it all come up, I should, you'll feel better afterwards.' The grip on her shoulders as she took his advice, was reassuring rather than intrusive.

'We haven't been properly introduced,' he told her, as she straightened and made to apologize. 'You coming along at the last minute.'

'You're Old Swindon,' she said weakly. The wind seemed to blow the words out of her mouth, along with saliva. A handkerchief was passed unobtrusively. She mopped her face, still shaking.

'Thanks. I guess I knew they dubbed me that,' he said drily. 'Your cap's askew – hey, let me do it – and, of course, you are the young pilots' dreamboat – Roma Rainbow, wow, what a name!'

They waited by the big plane, sheltering under a wing while the wind chucked icy rain in their faces. The staff car hurtled toward them and screeched to a stop inches away.

'*Pop!*' Roma cried, joyfully, as he clambered out and held out his arms. 'Heard you were coming, unofficially, an hour ago: stayed on, despite it being Christmas Eve, so I can take you home. I've got use of the car over Christmas. We thought you weren't going to make it, after all. How are you, Roma?' He sounded breathless, as if he had run, not driven fast to meet them.

'All the better for seeing you,' she said, hugging him.

They drank tea in the mess with Swindon, who disclosed he'd been seconded to the base. 'Sorry, you'll have to find your own way back,' he told the girls.

'We won't waste time worrying about that yet,' Roma said. 'We've got too much catching up to do.'

'Here's Dad!' Sally exclaimed, jumping up to greet him. Leo didn't embrace her, as Pop had Roma, but his face was transformed by a beaming smile. He nodded to Pop and Roma, then turned to Old Swindon.

'Hello again, Swindon, glad to have you here,' he said.

'You know each other already?' Sally sounded surprised.

'I know your dad's head of the Tann Corporation; I applied for a job there in '38, but joined the RAF instead. I know you're also involved here, sir,' Swindon put in, grinning, 'why else would I give two hitch-hikers a lift?'

Leo declined to join them in a cup of tea. 'I understand you're going to stay with us, after your family reunion, Roma?' he asked.

Seeing Pop's stricken expression, Roma said quickly, 'No – you'll squeeze me in somewhere, won't you, Pop? But Sally and I are certainly hoping we'll all get together sometime over the break.'

Leo looked at Pop. 'You received Jean's invitation? Yes, you must come to us. Give Tess a rest from the stove, eh? Make the most of having Roma home. It's the first Christmas for a while since we've all been together, too.' He turned his attention back to Swindon. 'Thank you for looking after the young ladies. I'll call back for you later, after you've settled in. You must have dinner with us, stay overnight, and tomorrow, of course. Ready, Sally?' He addressed Pop again. 'Second thoughts?'

'We'll come. Thank you,' Pop said evenly. 'Around midday?'

'Fine. We'll see you then.'

They drank their tea. 'You've a first name, surely?' Pop asked Swindon.

'They call me by my surname because I guess what comes before is hard to swallow: Cedric. Do I look like an Anglo-Saxon? I'm named for a great-grandfather – *he* might have been, for all I know. Old Swindon, that's what your daughter let slip earlier. And how about you?'

Pop grinned. He liked him, Roma could tell. 'Always Pop,' he replied. 'Since my own flying youth. Would you admit to Percy?'

'Nope. Certainly wouldn't,' Swindon said cheerfully.

In the car, Pop said to Roma, 'Nice chap, he's obviously taken with you – and before you say it, Roma, he's really not old enough to be your father.'

'I wasn't going to say that! But thanks, Pop.'

'What for?'

'For giving in about Christmas lunch. I know it was hard for you.'

'Not as hard as I imagined. Leo's right – Tess, for one deserves some fun, though a certain young feller'll be disappointed she won't be seeing him.'

Barney was at Dougie's, so Tess was by herself when Gregor called early that afternoon, while Roma was airborne. He carried a step-ladder.

'You might be glad of this, if you want to fix a holly wreath,' he said.

'Come in,' she invited, adding ruefully, 'look, I'm smothered in flour – trying to make four sausages into a dozen sausage rolls – I haven't had time to put up greenery, let alone make a wreath, and I can't find any drawing pins.'

'Here.' He produced a small box from his pocket. 'I'll do my best with the holly while you roll the rolls.'

'I made two little ones with the scraps,' she said later, rubbing her hands under the tap at the sink. 'Let's have a taste, and a cup of tea.'

They sat on the lumpy rexine-covered sofa by the parlour fire, making small talk and sipping tea. Gregor admired the branch of spruce doing duty as a Christmas tree; it was the piece which had snapped from the tree and from which Barney had plummeted the day before and which had been retrieved by Dougie. Tess pulled the curtains to shut out the depressing view of the back yard. It felt cosier, despite being a small, dark room, with the oil lamps lit. They used candles upstairs, mindful of wartime economies. Tess was long used now to doing without electricity.

Gregor moved Fly's head gently from his foot. 'Tess, have you thought about what I said yesterday, when we were walking down the hill?'

She shook her head. He reached for her hand. 'I love you, Tess. Even though we've known each other such a short time.'

'What about your girlfriend?'

'Mother told you about Moira? That's all she is: a friend. Mother approves of her, I know, being a strict Presbyterian like herself; but Tess, she really likes *you*, too. We could win her round.'

'She's been very kind to me. I'm not sure how I feel; please give me time.'

'Time isn't on my side, Tess,' he said simply. 'I'll be on a tanker when I return, ferrying fuel across the Atlantic for British planes.' He cleared his throat. 'May I ask for a couple of books from my – your room, please?'

'Why not fetch them yourself?'

She sat on the bed, plucking idly at a loose thread on the bedspread, watching as he squatted by the bookcase, pulling out a volume here, one there, slotting them back in place. She knew he wanted to take them all.

He plumped down beside her. 'They'll make me think of home, of you, this room.' He moved the books aside, brushing her hair away from her face as their lips met.

It felt good, just how she had imagined it would be, the night she had watched him from the window in this room. I'm stirred, but not disturbed. She smiled at the absurd thought. I mustn't waste time dreaming: when Moray sees Roma again . . . She slid her arms tentatively around Gregor's neck. Why hadn't this happened before he went away, she wondered? His breath was warm, uneven, as he kissed the pulse in her throat. 'Oh, Tess,' he murmured.

They panicked when they heard Roma's voice calling, 'Where are you? Tess – Barney? Aren't you going to welcome the prodigal daughter home?'

'Just as well, perhaps,' Gregor said ruefully. He sat up and so did she.

Pop waited at the foot of the stairs, reminding Tess of how he had regarded Roma in her headstrong youth, when she flounced to her room refusing to say where, and with whom she'd been that evening. That was towards the end of their time in the Romney Marsh, when Tess, woken by screeching tyres, witnessed the row from her doorway. She'd vowed then never to upset Pop like that, herself. But Pop and Roma were long reconciled.

'Just came to collect these.' Gregor indicated the books under his arm. 'Hello, Roma. I mustn't intrude. I'll pop in tomorrow morning, if I may. 'Bye, Tess,' and he was gone, closing the door behind him.

'Boyfriend?' Roma whispered, as they hugged. 'Looks nice.'

'He is!'

'You look as if you've just been kissed.'

'Shush! I have.'

'Good for you, little sister,' Roma said. 'I'll stick up for you, I promise.'

Pop wisely said nothing about Gregor being in her room. What he did say, went down well. 'You won't have to stuff that chicken after all, and worry if the stove'll get hot enough to cook it – you can take that chance on Boxing Day. We're going to Strand House for Christmas lunch. I got my arm twisted, didn't I, Roma? Let me take a proper look at you, I haven't had a chance yet.'

'Let me get changed first, then I'll be more like the Roma you know,' she said blithely, 'You show me my bunk, Tess, and Pop, won't you go and fetch my errant brother home? Anyone would think he didn't want to see me!'

'I can take a hint,' Pop said. 'I've been thinking for some time that Tess needs another woman to talk to,' hoping she would take his meaning.

Woman? Tess thought, bemused. Does that mean that Pop's accepted that I'm an adult now, old enough to think for myself, like Roma?

Tess revealed the presents hidden under her bed. 'Pop gave me some money, said go shopping and be extravagant for once. I've wrapped them all. When Barney's asleep, we'll arrange them round the tree. Barney's pal supplied the decorations! We left ours behind during our move, I suppose.'

'Remember when Millie Mae had us all making silver stars and moons, covering matchboxes with gold paper and putting tiny gifts inside?' Roma reminisced. 'That was the Christmas we were poor as poor, before she went out and got herself a job, but we never realized, due to her ingenuity.'

'I had a grey felt mouse, tucked up in a Swan Vesta bed. I stroked his head, said goodnight and closed the box firmly at bedtime,' Tess said. 'Rather like I do to Barney.' She grinned as he tapped on the wall. 'I can hear you.'

'I had a magic wand, a bauble fixed to a toothpick. I tried to fix a spell on Barney, just a baby then, to stop him taking Millie Mae's attention away from me – shall I have another go?' They interpreted the rapping as 'Don't you dare!'

'And Pop had a lipstick kiss on a note which said 'Pop Goes the Weasel! I Love You.' She said she was sorry she hadn't had time to make anything better, but Pop said, never mind, I'll have the real thing now, thank you.'

'Oh, Roma, if only I was glamorous and confident like you,' Tess sighed softly. 'Here am I, in plain old flannel, and here you are—'

'In saucy cami-knicks, I know. I didn't pack my jimjams, your presents being more important, and my hair's à la Veronica Lake . . . I'm shivering, so lend me your dressing-gown, there's a good girl. Anyway, you can't have looked at yourself properly lately in the mirror, little sister. D'you know what Moray wrote to Sally? "Tess doesn't know it yet, but she's about to break a few hearts!" So are my days as *femme fatale* number one over, young Tess?' Roma joked.

'Now you're teasing – so was he!' Tess retorted.

Pop sat on in the parlour. The fire was almost out, the warmth diminishing, but he had his nightcap, a small glass of whisky from the half-bottle Roma had presented him with. They'd talked, after Tess had excused herself and gone to bed, guessing the two of them needed time on their own. They hadn't spoken of their involvement in this war, of their fears for what the future might hold.

'Time you were married, Roma, you're almost twenty-three,' Pop said gruffly. 'Anyone in mind?'

'Top secret, Pop! Anyway, I reckon Tess'll marry before I do, I can't believe how she's changed.'

'Not on the inside, I believe. You're both Millie Mae's girls, even though you appear quite different. You've both got guts; I'm proud of you.'

'Thanks, Pop. I'm proud of you, too.'

'I gather you think Tess is in love? Gregor's a fine young man, I just hope he doesn't well, jump the gun, if you get my meaning. I can remember all too clearly what it was like to be young and ardent.'

'I'm not sure you've got the right chap, Pop.'

'What d'you mean? Not *Moray*, surely?'

'I mentioned him earlier, and Pop, I could read her face like a book . . .'

Pop put a hand across his eyes. Roma had left home long ago, and it was possible Tess would follow suit sooner than he had imagined. If the war dragged on, then Barney . . . He gave himself a mental shake. I'm nearly forty-four – Millie Mae's been gone eight years, wouldn't she want me to find love and companionship? Not that I've any idea how to go about it.

CHAPTER SEVEN

It was eleven o'clock when Pop reminded Barney to pack away his Gloucester Gladiator biplane model kit, to brush the wood shavings off the table and to put the cap back on the balsa cement. 'Why you have to be in such a hurry to finish it, on Christmas Day? When you've done that, go and get dressed immediately – you're not going to Strand House in your pyjamas surely?'

'Dougie hadn't finished my present yesterday, can we go by there?' Barney was absorbed in peeling the residue of the cement from his fingertips.

'Get a move on, then! I've just remembered I haven't shaved.' He rasped his chin reflectively, then looked keenly at his son. 'I hope you haven't pinched my only razor blade? I *thought* you were concealing something, my lad.'

Barney produced the double-edged blade from his pyjama pocket, which made his father wince. 'Sorry, Dad; I was going to put it b-back – it might need cleaning – but it's got the b-best cutting edge for model-making.'

Luckily, his father turned his attention to Tess, who was drying up the breakfast dishes, so Barney sidled past him double quick. 'What d'you think, Tess, should I wear my suit? Where's Roma? Not having a bath, I hope.'

'No hot water,' Tess said wryly. 'She says she'll cadge one at the Tanns'; I'm here because there isn't room for two in front of the mirror. Yes to the suit, though your shirt needs ironing, and I haven't got time for that.'

'I'll give it a good shake. You're obviously waiting for us to disappear upstairs before Gregor comes.' Pop dodged the balled-up tea towel she aimed as he went out. 'You'll dazzle him in that outfit, Tess,' he called back to her.

She looked down self-consciously at the sequined emerald angora jumper, Roma's gift, together with a pair of black slacks, high-waisted, which was just as well, because the jumper was fashionably brief. 'Just right for dancing; I coveted it, but there was only this one – never mind where I acquired the coupons.' Roma tapped the side of her nose. 'Here.' She tossed a bag casually to Tess. 'Hope they fit. I bet the aunts frowned on brassieres, didn't they?'

'Thanks, Roma! Mmm, they did – well, for me, but not for themselves, with those suits of armour they hung on the airer! Used to make Barney giggle.'

'Not giggling, *goggling*, more like it from bigger boys,' Roma said frankly, as Tess tried both presents for size. 'Surely you don't need that awful vest? Oh, Tess, sleeves and all! It's bound to be much warmer there, than it is here.'

'Don't count on it. Anyway,' she said defensively, 'like on the Marsh, you need warm underwear here.' However, she obediently divested herself and quickly dived back into the snugness of the jumper.

Then Gregor arrived, seizing the opportunity to swing her off her feet and kissing her with surprising abandon. 'Happy Christmas,' he murmured, when they were forced to take a breath. 'Sorry I couldn't get here earlier, but Mother gave me plenty of chores to do, despite me reminding her what day it was. She sends greetings to you all, by the way.'

'Put me down,' she laughed. 'We haven't got long, I'm afraid, we're off to Strand House for lunch. Roma's doing, obviously. She works with Sally Tann.'

His expression clouded. 'I thought we'd walk along the cliff path after lunch, to the old house perhaps, plenty of privacy there. We should talk—'

'You needn't worry about me and Moray, Gregor. Roma's putting on her war paint! This is for you.' She handed him a parcel. 'Not much choice locally, but you'll be writing lots of letters. Watermarked paper, look, and envelopes lined with blue tissue, not scented fortunately, but quite romantic, I thought.' Then she realized he was bound to read more into that than she intended.

His hands caressed her back as he kissed her again. 'Soft wool, all warm, from _you_.' His grip tightened. 'Am I right – you're wearing it next to you?'

'Not quite,' she said demurely. 'Quick, where's my present from you?'

More cosy wool: she wound the long cream scarf round her throat and wondered fleetingly if his mother had knitted it; better that than Moira!

'I thought – keep your chest warm – I mean. . . .' Being fair skinned, he coloured-up easily, as she did. They had a lot in common, both taking their family responsibilities seriously, she thought, both trying to appear more experienced than they were in the game of love.

'I know what you mean! Thank you, Gregor, just right for battling along the beach against the wind,' she told him. Hearing Pop's heavy tread coming downstairs, she added softly, 'I won't _ever_ forget you.'

'That's an odd thing to say.' He looked perplexed.

'Perhaps, but I mean it.' She squeezed his arm. 'We have to go now, and so do you. I'll see you before you leave tomorrow, won't I?'

'You will. Happy Christmas!'

Jean graciously took the credit for the turkey and all the trimmings even though the feast had been prepared by the two women hovering discreetly in the background. They would have their fair share later. They had worked for Miss Jean's family since she was a child, and their loyalty was to her, not to Mr Leo, here when it suited him, acting the master of the house. He might be a highly successful businessman, but the staff here knew that Strand House was hers. She sat at the head of the table, her husband at the end.

Roma chose to sit between Moray and Swindon. Sally was on his left. Pop, Tess and Barney were on the other side of the table with condiments for their own use, no laughter as there was over the way, when Roma and Swindon reached for the mustard simultaneously. Swindon couldn't take his eyes off Roma, which was hard on Sally, Tess noted sympathetically. Her own sparkling outfit had apparently gone unnoticed, despite Roma's prediction, apart from words of approval from Jean. 'You look very bright and pretty today, Tess.' Still, Gregor liked it, she thought, wasn't that all that mattered? Neither she nor Sally could match Roma in her swirling black moire skirt and red satin blouse with bishop's sleeves. Moray, opposite Tess, sat silently. She avoided eye contact with him, remembering her assurances to Gregor, earlier.

'You need to stretch your legs, Barney, after all you put away,' Leo told him. 'There's something I'd like to show you. It's a good walk across the grounds; you come, too, Pop, and Swindon.'

'Sure; sounds good,' he agreed.

'I'll come!' Sally seized her chance. Wrapped up warmly, they departed.

'Be back before dark,' Jean called after them. She turned to Roma. 'Didn't you girls want to go? If you hurried, you could catch them up.'

'Freezing outside, and I can hardly walk a few yards in these heels,' Roma said frankly. 'Actually, it's my chance to ask you if I might have a bath here – hot water's rationed at our place – while they're away.'

'My dear, of course you can!'

'I don't want to desert you, of course.'

'There's Tess: we'll hog the fire together, won't we?'

It promised to be a stimulating afternoon, Tess thought wryly. She would have liked to join the walkers, her shoes were sturdy enough, but she hadn't been invited. At least she wouldn't have to sit with Moray, excusing himself before the pudding was brought in ablaze. It was obvious he was having a bad day. No one offered to help him negotiate the stairs, knowing he would refuse.

'Take your time. Plenty of towels in the linen cupboard,' Jean told Roma. She opened the door next to the bathroom. 'Are you all right, Moray? I'll bring you a cup of tea in a while. If you hear splashing, it's Roma.'

Roma wallowed blissfully. She'd never stepped into a sunken bath before, or turned on gold-plated taps. She emerged from the scented water reluctantly, removed the bath cap and shook her hair free, lifting it off her damp shoulders before enveloping herself in a pink towel. The anguished yell from Moray's room startled her. She didn't stop to think, but padded out and peered anxiously round his door. He was sprawled on the floor, wearing pyjamas,

'Fell off the bed,' he said angrily. 'Knocked the bloody sticks out of reach. Well, aren't you going to do something? Or are you going to laugh?'

'Shut your eyes,' she ordered. 'I'm not decent. Nor are you! I don't find your predicament amusing. Stop feeling sorry for yourself! The plaster'll have protected your leg. Grip my shoulder.' She hauled him up under the armpits. His leg, plastered from thigh to toes, was a dead weight.

'That *hurt*,' he groaned, as she heaved him on to the bed. 'Too late, I'm afraid,' he apologized, opening his eyes just as she struggled to cover herself with the now gaping towel. 'Don't be cross, but how can I ever forget you, like that? Don't flounce off, please . . .' Abruptly, he turned his face to the pillow.

'How can I, when you're crying,' she said helplessly. 'I didn't know men did until I caught Pop unawares after Millie Mae died – but I've seen it often since – young pilots devastated at losing good friends, afraid they'll be next . . . I've comforted them – oh, not how you imagine, Moray, believe me. I've *talked*, I've always been good at that, and I'm getting better at listening.'

'I tried to talk to Tess, she was willing to listen, but—'

'She hasn't been through what we have, thank God,' Roma finished for him. 'Look, I must clear up the mess I made in the bathroom, get dressed, then I'll come back, and you can tell me how all this is really affecting you. Will that help? But, I mustn't stay long—'

'Please, long enough.'

'*Spirit of Millie Mae*,' Leo said, forcing open the great barn doors, and leaving them open so they could see inside. 'I couldn't bring myself to part with her, but she's not been airborne since you repaired her, Pop.'

Together Pop and Leo shifted the rotting tarpaulin which had protected the plane from years of bird droppings and the unwelcome attention of rodents. She still gleamed in the gloom, her name just visible.

'Like to climb in the cockpit, Barney?' Leo asked.

'You b-bet I would!' It was Swindon who hoisted him aloft, via the footholds. Barney's face was ecstatic as he brushed away the cobwebs festooning the cockpit, examined the joystick, the altimeter and the compass.

'I didn't realize she was still here, Dad,' Sally said. 'After all that fuss, when Moray—' She broke off, for Swindon was looking on with lively interest.

'I decided Moray wouldn't fly her again; now he can't, anyway.'

'Just who was Millie Mae? An old sweetheart?' Swindon asked Leo.

'She was my wife,' Pop said evenly.

Swindon looked swiftly from one to the other. 'A free spirit, I guess.'

'A free spirit,' Pop agreed gruffly.

'Will *Millie Mae* ever fly again?' Barney called down to them excitedly.

'Maybe, when you're old enough to pilot her yourself, Barney. She's yours, that's if your father agrees. She can stay here until you're ready for her, in a few year's time. Pop must be the judge of that. How about it?'

'Pop, c-can I have her? *Please?*'

'I reckon that'll make it right.' Pop answered enigmatically. 'You'll have to make do with models, 'til then. Down now, Barney, we'd better get back.'

Sally slipped her arm through Swindon's. 'Don't ask me what that was all about,' she whispered.

'I'm guessing an old wrong's just been righted,' he whispered back.

Barney raced ahead in the growing dusk to tell his sisters his exciting news. Pop and Leo walked side by side, not talking, but maybe finally at ease.

'You don't think Roma's gone to sleep in the bath, do you?' Jean said, finally waking from her doze, to Tess's relief. 'Why don't you go and see, Tess?'

Tess could hear voices from Moray's room. She told herself sternly there was nothing wrong in that; rapped on the door, hoping it wouldn't appear as if she was eavesdropping. Roma ushered her in.

'Leading the search party, Tess? I'm trying to persuade Moray to put on a happy face, to come down for the games Sally has in mind.'

'Yes, do come.' Tess unhooked his dressing-gown from the door. I'm about to commit myself to Gregor, she thought, I can't let him down for someone who would never fall in love with me – not with Roma around.

'You should have brought your boyfriend, Tess,' he said.

'He couldn't desert his mother. Here.' She passed the dressing-gown.

'I'll help you downstairs,' Roma said, draping it round his shoulders. 'Tell them we're on our way. Tess. Someone in the hall—'

'It's only Barney,' Tess reported, looking over the bannisters. 'He seems very excited about something. Oh, and here are the others!'

*

She pretended to be asleep when Roma slid in bed beside her and said, 'Oh good, I can warm my cold feet on you. Tess, are you awake? I believe I've rekindled an old flame. He saw more of me than I intended, but I won't enlarge on that!'

'He's very vulnerable right now, don't lead him on.'

'It wouldn't do,' Roma agreed. 'Oh, I'm good at rallying the troops as they say, but I can't see myself as a nurse; I'm not saintly enough! I yearn to dance the night away, bombs or no bombs; I've got excess energy, like Millie Mae, though she channelled it to our survival at the Last Stop Garage.'

'Moray's the same, I imagine.'

'We're too alike. We need a steadying influence. I have the feeling that Jean would encourage any relationship between you two.'

'Well, Pop wouldn't,' Tess said flatly.

'Anyway, what are we talking about? There's Gregor—'

'Yes, there's Gregor.' But he won't be here, and Moray will, and if he asks to see me, I'll go because I won't be able to help myself, Tess thought.

They were whispering, but the rapping indicated; 'We need our sleep!'

'Time to turn over,' Roma yawned. 'Don't kick me out of bed! 'Night.'

' 'Night.' Tess suspected that sleep would evade her for some time.

CHAPTER EIGHT

'**I**'m not sure Roma remembers how to roast a chicken,' Tess told Gregor as they left the house on Boxing Day morning. 'And Barney ends up with pea-sized potatoes when he does the peeling.'

'Let them get on with it,' he said. 'We must get our walk in before the snow comes down and blots out the path.'

She wore his scarf round her head as well as her neck, at Pop's insistence, and had borrowed a pair of Barney's socks to wear inside her boots. Gregor, too, had warm seamen's socks, turned over the tops of his boots.

They didn't converse much as the track was narrow and slippery; Tess followed in his footsteps. She tried not to look down. The sea far below swelled angrily, leaving clutching fingers of foam on the deserted beach. She was relieved when they reached the cottage. They sat in the old inglenook, with their backs braced against the board which protected the soot-encrusted wall. She was aware that he was breathing fast not from the trek but because of their close proximity. She wasn't nervous, as she would have been if she had visited this forgotten place alone. She moved imperceptibly closer, as if to sap some of his warmth. He did not unsettle her as Moray had.

The hand he clasped firmly was enclosed in a warm mitten, and he seemed to be studying the intricate Fair Isle pattern. The mittens had been given to Tess when the guests' presents were distributed yesterday. *Happy Christmas from the family* the label said.

'I wanted to buy you a ring, but I can't afford it, not yet. I have no right to ask you to marry me anyway, having nothing to offer, except this ruin of a place. I have to admit Mother's right when she says we've known each other no time at all, that we're too young for getting wed.

68

When this war is over I must return to college and finish my course, or I'll never be able to support a wife. I love you, Tess. I'm sure of that. Will you wait for me?'

The slight hesitation betrayed her. 'I—' She must be honest. 'I've hurt you, I'm sorry. I don't want you to go away. I'll worry about you – I *do* love you Gregor, but your mother's right about one thing: I'm afraid I have a little more growing up to do.' She unwound the scarf, looked up at him anxiously, sighed when his arms embraced her.

After a while he said, 'Don't laugh, but I knitted the scarf myself: the seamen's mission provided me with several hanks of wool, which proved a devil to wind and unravel. I learned to knit when I was a wee lad at school. It grew longer and longer as I thought of you.'

'I'm not laughing, Gregor, really. I'm impressed!'

'I was all Mother had, after my father died. She's a strong woman, Tess: she bought our cottage with the insurance money, and worked hard to give me a good education and a secure future. As I said, she is certainly not set against you, but she reminded me that you also have family responsibilities.'

Why me? she thought. Why can't I be like Roma, in control of my own life?

She kissed him impulsively, then disengaged herself from his arms. 'We'd better go, Gregor. Just be sure to come "back on the tide" . . .'

We've both got doubts, she thought. I must see Moray again, before I can begin to get over my infatuation for him.

'I hear from Swindon,' Pop told Roma two days later, 'that you and Sally are being driven back to Kent by Leo first thing tomorrow morning.' The hurt he felt at the lack of communication between them was palpable.

'Oh, Pop, Sally sprang it on me this afternoon. I'd love to stay the week, but I can't miss this chance. Jean is as upset as you are; she had no idea Leo was leaving again so soon, but he had an urgent summons from the works. Moray tried to persuade his dad to take him back too, he wants to be nearer the action, to convince the medical board he can go back to his squadron, even if he can't climb into a plane yet. Of course Leo had to refuse: he said Moray must wait until after his cast is removed. Now, they're not speaking!

'By the way, Sally and I aren't going straight back to base – we've three more days' leave, after all, so I'm staying with her in Surrey. We might go shopping in London, take in a show – if Herr Hitler'll allow it.'

'Take care,' Pop said gruffly.

'We know where all the tube shelters are, Pop! Life goes on there, people dust themselves off, pick their way over the rubble, go to work, where they can; shops, pubs and theatres stay open. "London's burning", they say, but they always add "Britain can take it". The spirit there is really inspiring, amazing.'

She's excited by the element of danger, Pop thought, afraid for her, and there's nothing I can say. Millie Mae rushed at life headlong, too.

Tess, flanked by Pop and Barney in the doorway, waved goodbye until the car was out of sight. It was barely light, the street as yet untrodden by the lugubrious, early workers. Fortunately, the expected snow had held off.

'Wonder where Leo got the petrol,' Pop said heavily, ushering them indoors. Leo's parting words echoed: 'Keep an eye on Jean for me, will you, Pop? She's worried about Moray, the row we had. She blames it on me, of course.'

'That man,' Pop added to Tess, aware that she had heard, 'hasn't really changed. She's not on her own, after all.'

'No, Pop, but I guess she's lonely. Maybe you should look in on her soon.' It would have solved her own dilemma if Moray had left too, but then, that would have thrown him together with Roma, and despite her sister's protestations to the contrary, Tess knew she was strongly attracted to him.

'I wish Roma had eaten something . . . where's the frying pan? I'll cook breakfast, shall I? We need more than porridge this morning, eh?'

'Only two rashers of streaky left, Pop,' she worried.

'Fair shares for all,' he assured her. 'Barney, lay the table, will you?'

Tess knew immediately by the shape of the parcel what it contained. Her first rejection: she'd been hopeful that her eighty-page story would turn up trumps. However, enclosed with her now dog-eared manuscript, with the occasional brown ring from a teacup, which meant at least that someone had read it, was an encouraging letter, handwritten by the fiction editor of her chosen magazine.

Don't give up! Some rewriting is required, as suggested in the pencilled comments. A bolder plot, an intrepid heroine, caught in a seemingly impossible situation at the end of each chapter – you'll need ingenuity and imagination to extricate her from trouble!

It seems to me that the character with whom you have most empathy, is not Angela, but her youngest sister. Like your writing, Pat grows in confidence and could be the true heroine. She's not glamorous like Angela, but she's more real to the reader – all she needs is a strong dash of romance!

Do have another go!

'*I will*,' she said aloud. Reading through the suggestions, she realized it was quite a daunting project, but the editor's first three words made her determined to succeed. DON'T GIVE UP. I won't, she promised herself.

She spread the typed sheets on the kitchen table, sharpened a pencil. How had she described Pat? Quite simply: short, skinny and red-haired – a girl with a hidden ambition, revealed early to the reader, who would, she hoped, be willing her to succeed right to the very last paragraph.

Pop finished work unexpectedly early. The staff car was proving a boon in the inclement weather, so he decided to motor up to Strand House to see Jean, as Leo had asked. It was tricky negotiating the patches of ice on the drive; clearly, no vehicle had been in or out since Leo's car.

A figure hurried towards him across the grass, as he parked the car. He realized it was Jean, wearing an old coat, stout boots and head scarf.

Without make-up her face was pale, fine-lined, her eyes shadowed. 'Pop! How nice to see you! Leo rang this morning to say they'd arrived safely, and I wondered how to let you know, I didn't think I ought to ring you at work.'

'Probably there's a letter from Roma at home,' he hoped.

'Yes. Do come in; I've been out for a walk, hardly the weather for it but with Moray still brooding I felt in need of a break.' She pulled off her boots.

'You're breathless,' Pop observed. She'd run to meet him, he realized, as Millie Mae had long ago, when he returned from the Front. A fleeting illusion of course, but he seemed to feel the warmth as she hurtled into his arms.

'Take off your coat – I'll make some tea. Edith and Agnes have gone home for a few days. They both have elderly parents: they'll be back after the New Year. Barclay comes in to see to the fires. No driving for him to do, no car. I hardly think *we'll* be celebrating here, so I insisted we could manage.'

He followed her into the kitchen. 'Where's Moray, Jean?'

'In the sitting-room. Why don't you have a word with him, it might help? I'll follow on.' She looked around the cavernous room. 'There must be a tray here, somewhere; I don't need the trolley, no cakes left, I'm afraid.'

'I'll be having my supper when I get home.' He added, 'I'll wait, it's a chance for us to have a few words, eh? You were a good homekeeper once, Jean, though like Millie Mae you believed there was more to life than dusting and polishing. You vied a bit with one another to copy the latest fashions—'

'We shared my sewing-machine . . . I was very fond of her, you know.'

'She thought a lot of you, too. You were both right behind Leo and me when we joined forces. It was a bit of a come-down for you, after' – he spread his hands expressively – 'all this. Times were hard, but you stuck by Leo, as Millie Mae did me. Seeing you now, I realize that you haven't changed so much.'

Her hands shook, as she spooned tea into the pot. 'You mean, I'm minus lipstick, my hair's a mess, and I feel a nervous wreck.'

He ignored that, took the kettle and filled the teapot. 'Cups and saucers? You were caught in the crossfire, in the marsh days – I was never against *you*. Looking back, perhaps it would have blown over, maybe I was too hot-headed, nothing happened after all – can you call it betrayal in that case?'

She shook her head. 'Not then, perhaps – though if Leo wants something, he's not usually deterred. His pride was badly hurt, Pop. You actually spurred him on to success. He couldn't help falling for Millie Mae. She was a such a lovely, lively young woman – very like Roma is, now.'

'Leo's let you down since?' Pop prompted.

'Oh, yes. It's partly my fault. I – I was cold towards him; I felt I couldn't trust him with other women, after—'

'You were right, obviously.'

'We haven't . . . shared a room for years, not since Sally was born,' she stated baldly. 'I made him pay for his infidelity: the Surrey house, the entertaining, expensive clothes. This war made me see how superficial all that was. I don't want that life anymore, that's really why I returned home.'

'You didn't consider divorce?'

'No, because of the children; even though they are officially of age now. They still cause resentment between us, particularly Moray. He and his father have never got on, though Leo spoils his daughter.'

Pop cleared his throat 'You didn't have to tell me all this.'

'It's cleared the air, hasn't it? We can be *real* friends again, can't we?'

'I believe Millie Mae would want that,' he said quietly.

Moray sat hunched and gloomy in his chair, patently not pleased to see a visitor. 'No biscuits, Ma?' he complained.

Jean, flustered, went back to the kitchen.

'You shouldn't expect your mother to wait on you,' Pop said bluntly.

'She expects that from other people!'

'It's just the way she was brought up, Moray. She's also kind and good-mannered – attributes which you obviously haven't inherited.'

'That's not nice!'

'Nor are you, my lad.'

They glared at each other for a moment, then Moray smiled reluctantly. 'All right: I don't *feel* nice right now. I'm taking too long to heal. I've always been impatient and I want to get back in the thick of things. I thought I'd see more of Roma, in Surrey – how often does she visit here, after all?'

'Roma: ah, that's the real reason, is it?'

'No, of course not. I'm determined to fly again – look at Douglas Bader! Roma would chivvy me along—'

'She's like her mother, that's why.'

'Soggy shortbread, Moray,' Jean said apologetically, holding out a tartan-patterned tin. 'You were talking about Roma? Well, she's *there*, but Tess is *here*. Do ask her to come soon, Pop, and sort out this miserable son of mine.'

'I was going to suggest,' Pop said, on the spur of the moment, 'that you come to us on New Year's Eve. We could ask Swindon as well; there's an even chance he'll be able to join us, for some of the time, anyway. He's a good chap: he was rather impressed with Roma, too, it seems.'

'He hasn't got a chance,' Moray said firmly. 'And, Ma, you're forgetting that Tess is already spoken for—'

Jean looked at Pop. 'I wouldn't be too sure of that,' she said.

CHAPTER NINE

Tess despatched Barney to Dougie's on the afternoon of New Year's Eve, where she suspected the minister's wife, with the Watch Night service at the kirk in mind, had already cooked any celebratory spread, thus unlikely to be bothered by another boy whizzing round on his bike in her garden.

She scraped balsa cement from the table. Trust Pop to say casually as he left, 'Oh by the way, Tess, can you knock up something tasty for supper tonight? We'll be having a party after all. Old Swindon's fetching Jean and Moray: they'll be here about seven-thirty. We've still got that bottle of sherry haven't we? Pity I finished Roma's whisky. She paid ten bob for that bottle; I should have spun it out, but – it was good while it lasted.'

She opened the door to Mrs Munro, unaware that her face betrayed her mixed emotions: relief that here was someone who could advise her how to stretch a small tin of pink salmon and a larger tin of pineapple chunks, and apprehension, because she hadn't seen Gregor's mother since he left.

'Are you well, Tess?' Mrs Munro asked. 'You look vexed – not because of me, I hope – we are still friends, surely?'

'Of course we are!' Tess said quickly. She pulled out two chairs from the table. 'Have you heard from Gregor yet?'

'I have not, but it's maybe too soon. Now, you have a problem?'

'Well, it's Pop: he's just sprung it on me that we'll be six for supper tonight, and the cupboard's bare after Christmas and Roma being home. What's traditional fare for New Year here – haggis?' she guessed.

'Aye, well, you'll no be able to manage that: you need to be brought up on it to appreciate it. What's in that big can, the one you're using as a doorstop?'

A dented tin held the inner door open for Fly. He seemed in a world of his own these days, poor old dog. Tess felt him all over fearfully for lumps and bumps. He slept away most of the day. Old Age, she told herself, but knew that when Fly was gone it would be another link lost with the marsh.

'That? Oh, it's iron rations. I suppose I didn't like to use it before.'

'But you could now: isn't this an emergency, lassie?'

'We-ell,' Tess smiled, 'yes, I believe it is!'

Mrs Munro retrieved the tin of corned beef and considered it. 'Not marked enough to be blown. Hash, Tess, that's it. You'll need to cook up a few pounds of tatties, and an onion or two – got those?'

'Mmm. Shall I get started on them?'

'That's so.' Mrs Munro nodded. She carefully furled the lid with the key provided. 'Lucky you hadn't lost this. Pass me a bowl, so I can shred the meat, will you – in the bottom cupboard you'll find a great baking dish.'

When the hash, meat layered with baked beans and topped with oniony mashed potato, forked into tram lines, then dotted with margarine, was in the oven, Tess and Mrs Munro sat down to a welcome cup of tea.

'I must go, my brother will be wondering where I am; ready for his own supper, no doubt,' Mrs Munro said finally.

'I've kept you too long, I'm sorry,' Tess exclaimed contritely.

'No, no, my dear.'

'Why don't you both – join us?'

'Enough for six, Tess. The table seats that number. We'd rather be quiet, thank you, with Gregor away. We have the service to go to, later on.'

That was all she said about him, but Tess remembered Gregor's words to her: 'She is not against you', and was glad that they were true.

'Thank you,' she said in her turn, meaning it.

Pop arrived, shortly after Mrs Munro left. 'Something smells good!' he said appreciatively. 'I thought I'd have to eat humble pie, expecting you to make something out of nothing.'

'No humble pie tonight, Pop,' she murmured, and she gave him a sudden, unexpected hug. 'Thank you, Pop.'

'What for?' He sounded bemused.

'It really doesn't matter, if you don't know!'

Tess was upstairs changing, and Barney sent to scrub off the mud from his knees when Pop opened the door and welcomed Jean inside.

'We're a little earlier than expected, I'm afraid. We had to leave the motor further down the street, so Swindon's calling in the pub for bottled beer, that's if it isn't all under the counter, then he and Moray will bring up the rear.'

'I'll have to close the door – the wind blows through from back to front.'

She unbuttoned her thick plaid cape, revealing a wine-coloured crepe dress with elaborate gold buttons. Pop hung the cape up. 'Don't I recognize this?'

'I've had it years, not much call to wear it in Surrey but, I thought, just right for the weather.' She handed him her soft leather gloves, then glanced in the hall mirror, to reassure herself her hair was unruffled, her lipstick unsmudged. The vulnerable look of their last meeting was banished. He fingered his own top lip ruefully. Barney had certainly blunted the razor edge.

'When Roma was born,' he recalled, 'we were all in the one house. Millie Mae and me – I was home on compassionate leave because my father died, not dreaming Millie Mae was about to go into labour; you and Moray, a few months old – it was bitterly cold and snowing, and Leo was out in France.

'Millie Mae had a rough time with the baby – the nurse had to hurry off to another confinement. While you and I were sweating from all the rushing around, she was shivering away in our bed, even with the fire roaring up the chimney. We'd no spare blankets, so you spread your cape over Millie Mae.'

'Her teeth stopped chattering; she was so young and Roma coming early was a shock to her system,' Jean said softly. 'She gave such a sigh, then she said, "Now I'm warm I can go to sleep", and she did.'

'She told me later that she had that on our bed for ages – how did you manage without a coat?' he asked.

'Oh, I had a mackintosh, and the next winter after the war, we moved to our own home, when you and Leo started up the garage with the money your father left you, and my mother sent me a fur coat. I think she equated the marsh with Siberia. Leo rudely remarked that it smelled like wet dog!'

'Talking of dog,' Pop said ruefully, 'old Fly pongs a bit – he'd better stay in the kitchen. This way, into the parlour.' He paused, as they heard footsteps and then the knock on the front door. 'You go ahead, and I'll let them in.'

'Pop,' she turned to say, 'I've just realized, you've shaved off your moustache.' She smiled at him. 'A slip of the razor?'

'Grew it when I joined up, got married, thought then it made me look more mature like Leo, him being five years older than me,' he said matter-of-factly.

Aunt Peg's iron rations provided generous helpings of steaming hash. The company was appreciative, and Tess was pleased that Moray was in good form, cracking jokes with Barney and Swindon. Maybe the beer had something to do with it, or someone had said something to jolt him out of his gloom.

'What's this, Tess?' he asked. 'Pineapple only for boys – and chaps under twenty-five, I hope?' Pop said he was too full and Jean politely declined to partake. Tess was rather obviously counting the chunks in the bowl.

'Say, that let's me out,' Swindon grinned.

'Sorry, Swindon,' she blushed. 'There's enough for you, it's just that—'

'Three's an odd number,' Swindon obliged. 'Well, I would have politely eaten up, but fortunately I don't have to; you see, I don't care for pineapple.'

'I do; I'll have your share!' Barney put in quickly.

'Those without afters get to wear these,' Tess said firmly, dishing out the fruit into two bowls, then producing hastily concocted newspaper hats.

They grouped round the fire; Barney bagging the shove-ha'penny game. 'I wanted a dart board, but Pop said if we didn't throw straight and made holes in the walls, we'd have to pay for the damage. See, Swindon, you shove the edge of the board with the flat of your hand and try to get the coin between the lines, not on 'em – that round bit at the top stops the ha'penny flying off.'

'Rather like hopscotch, only played with hands, not feet,' Swindon thought, jolting the board vigorously.

'No hopping,' Barney decreed. 'Now we'll have to start again.'

Pop and Jean sat on the sofa. Tess was thankful that Barney hadn't commented on Pop's shaven lip. What had made him do that? It would take a while to get used to his new look.

'Tired, Tess?' Moray said in her ear. She sat on the footstool by his chair.

'Just a bit,' she answered. 'The meal went off well – that was a relief.'

'I was relieved when you discarded your pinny! You look very nice.'

'You didn't notice when I wore this outfit on Christmas Day.' She was aware of sounding childish.

'I'm being really nice to everyone tonight, haven't you noticed?'

'I'm wondering why that is.'

'Oh, something Ma said the other day: it made me think . . . I guess you're missing Gregor – isn't that his name?'

She nodded. 'Though if he was at home, Moray, he'd be with his mother this evening, not me.'

'It's not that serious between you, then?'

'Why do you want to know?' She surprised herself by challenging him.

'I think you know the answer to that.' She looked up to see him grinning.

'Stop teasing me,' she said crossly, rising. 'Anyone fancy a cup of tea?'

No one commented as the nightly roar of the planes began.

Pop and Jean nodded off on the sofa. 'Well, they *are* old,' as Barney said. He showed no signs of flagging, as he and Swindon played Newmarket, a card game, with Tess and Moray, for matchsticks rather than money.

'Almost midnight – I'll nudge the weary ones and you charge the glasses, Tess, eh?' Swindon said, gathering up the cards despite Barney's protests.

Sweet sherry for the ladies; beer for the men, the last of the American soda for Barney. They toasted the new year, 1941, and absent family.

'May I?' Swindon asked Tess, as he saluted her with a smacking kiss on the lips. 'You're safe, Barney, no one wants to kiss *you*!' he joked.

'Oh—' Tess exclaimed, blushing.

Then Moray looked at her speculatively. 'I can't get to my feet, but *you* can come and kiss me, can't you?' he said.

She found herself on his lap, his arms firmly around her waist, and knew she could not escape. 'Happy New Year,' he murmured. She thought, I can't help myself – oh, Gregor I didn't mean to be disloyal to you.

Pop drained his glass, glanced at Jean. 'Am I so unapproachable?' she said drily. 'You may kiss me, you know, it's traditional, after all.'

Their heads slowly inclined together. Pop hadn't been so close to another woman, except for his girls, since Millie Mae. Her perfume was obviously expensive, her skin soft as he cupped her face with his work-hardened hands.

'I'm glad you got rid of those bristles,' she said softly, as they kissed.

Barney, embarrassed, escaped to the kitchen with the empty glasses.

'*Tess!*' His anguished cry had her dashing to find out what was wrong.

Barney bent over Fly, lying motionless in his favourite spot by the stove.

'He's gone, poor old chap, I'm afraid,' Swindon told her.

'I thought he was asleep.' Tess was shaking with shock.

'He likely was, Tess, it's a good way to go.' Swindon tried to console her. 'Come on, Barney, nothing to be done tonight, let's tell Pop, eh?'

Tess turned, as she heard Moray manoeuvring himself into the room. She almost knocked him over when she flung herself at him, sobbing.

'Hey, hey,' he said soothingly, 'you're making my shirt all wet . . . and I can't even take advantage and hug you back, can I?'

'Moray,' Jean was behind him, 'I think it's best we go home now. I'm so sorry about the dog, Tess.'

'I'm sorry, too,' Moray said. 'Come and see us, soon, won't you?'

'I will,' she promised through her tears, for how could she keep away now?

CHAPTER TEN

Tess and Moray walked in the grounds of Strand House on a bright, breezy spring afternoon. Moray limped along determinedly, with a single stick. He said almost diffidently, 'I'm raring to go. Swindon and I are driving back to base, tomorrow.' They paused by the pines, and the astringent perfume induced Tess to tilt her chin, inhale deeply. He looked at her searchingly, then: 'Your hair, Tess, is really fiery where the sun catches it, and you've a few more freckles . . .' He traced them with a finger. It was an intimate gesture. She willed herself not to blush.

'I'm glad for you,' she managed. 'You've had such a frustrating wait.' She couldn't say how she really felt, though she shared in the general belief that the battle of the skies was perceptibly diminishing, the threat of invasion receding. However, they were all aware that the struggle was intensifying on many other fronts, including what was now called the Battle of the Atlantic. She had not heard from Gregor in weeks; the last time his mother heard, he had intimated that he might transfer to minesweepers.

'Now I shall discover what Roma has been up to,' Moray said, 'with all those dashing Polish and Czech air aces vying for her favours, eh?'

'Roma says we couldn't have seen off the Luftwaffe without them. Shall we sit on the grass for a few minutes?' she asked. 'It's sheltered here.' She didn't want to turn back yet, especially now she knew he was going away. 'You know,' she added, 'I couldn't help thinking that if you didn't get the go-ahead soon, you'd take off in the *Spirit of Millie Mae* again.'

'They'd have shot me down as an unidentified aircraft,' he joked. 'Anyway, Dad made sure I'd never fly her again when he gave her to

Barney, didn't he?' He wasn't revealing whether that rankled or not.

He lowered himself carefully. 'Aren't you going to admit you'll miss me? You've kept me at arms' length since I got too close to you on New Year's Eve. I'm grateful to you, Tess, for buoying up my spirits these past months.'

'Thank you for saying that,' she said quietly.

'Oh, Tess, you're such an innocent: don't you know what I *really* want?' His face was disturbingly close to hers, his gaze intense.

'I can guess, but I – I don't think you're sure yourself,' she faltered, making to rise, but his hands on her shoulders lightly restrained her.

'You sound bitter.' He looked puzzled.

'Maybe I am. It would be so easy, you see – for me to—'

'Fall in love with me?'

'Yes. But it would be *wrong*, because I promised Gregor—' I assured Gregor, she thought, that I'd be here when he came "back on the tide". I couldn't, nor could he, promise more, then. Seeing Moray is wrong, because of the way I really feel. . . . 'Please let me go!' she added, unconvincingly.

'D'you mean that?' He drew her, unresisting, closer. He threaded his hands through her hair, lightly caressing the nape of her neck. 'Relax, Tess.'

'You'll make me cry,' she said sadly. 'I don't want you to leave, Moray.'

'You want me to kiss you, to squeeze the breath out of you, don't you?' he asked softly. 'I wouldn't mind at all, but I'm positive you want me to commit myself much more. Well, I can't do it, Tess, I'm sorry. It wouldn't be fair to you, even if it's what Ma hopes for. I'm too restless to be tied down to a nice girl like you. You'd regret any reckless moments of passion – unlike me. Does it shock you, that I find you desirable? Don't worry, I'm not about to surrender to my baser instincts . . . and, as you reminded me, there is Gregor.'

'Just hold me tight,' she choked. She clung to him, as she had to Gregor, before he went away. He gently kissed away her tears.

Back at the house, Jean looked at them searchingly. Tess's face betrayed her upset; Moray was subdued. 'He's told you then? You'll still visit me won't you, Tess? I appreciate he's very busy, but – tell Pop I'd be pleased to see him too.' She hadn't seen him since the New Year's party.

'Of course I will. I must get back; Barney will be home,' Tess said. 'Goodbye, Moray, good luck – give my love to Roma when you see her.'

'I'll keep in touch,' he promised, as he had when she was a skinny little girl.

'You're very quiet,' Pop said later, when they'd chivvied Barney off to bed. 'What's up? Anything to do with Moray going back to his squadron?'

'You know then?'

'Had a farewell drink with Swindon at lunchtime. He told me. It's probably for the best, Tess.'

'I know. By the way, Pop, Jean asked after you—'

'Oh, did she?'

'Yes. She looked different today. She's got her hair really short. The housekeeper cut it, she said, because she can't get to the hairdresser's.'

'Don't crop *your* hair, will you Tess?'

'Why would I want to do that?' she asked. Moray said nothing about loving me, though he admitted that he, well, *wanted* me, but he did admire my hair . . .

It was Jean who came to Pop. Tess was right: she looked youthful with her bobbed hair. He'd not seen her in slacks before, not even in the old days. Being tall and slim, they suited her. 'Barclay looked over Sally's bike. I haven't ridden for years so I expect I'll be stiff tomorrow. Finish your bread and cheese, Pop; where are the others?'

'Tess popped round to Mrs Munro's: she had a letter from Gregor this morning, and they share their news. Barney ate at Dougie's. I imagine he's now endeavouring to put the knees out in his first pair of long trousers. Did you' – he cleared his throat – 'have any special reason for coming here?'

'Yes: I'm glad you're by yourself. Have you heard from Leo recently?'

'We only talk about work, on the telephone at the base. Why, is there something wrong?'

'I've asked him for a divorce,' she stated calmly. 'I've had enough of his philandering. This latest woman friend isn't much older than Sally.'

'It's not too late,' Pop said slowly, 'to find someone yourself, Jean, is it?'

'A few months ago I'd have said that was the last thing I needed.'

'How did he take it?'

'He says he's "surprised but agreeable".'

'Jean—'

'Look, I know you can't replace Millie Mae, I don't expect you to, but – I need a friend, someone to talk to, while this is going on. It'll be a slow process, but Leo won't contest it.'

'I'm here for you,' he promised. Friendship: yes, he could cope with *that*.

'Forty-eight hours' leave,' Sally said, snapping open her case. 'Bliss! Home to Virginia Water, hot baths and square meals courtesy of Dad, who'll be elsewhere, with his present paramour – and Swindon and Moray willing to take us to town on Saturday night. Looking forward to seeing Moray again?'

'I suppose so.' Roma was stretched out on her bed, with a book and a cigarette. Swindon wasn't calling for them for a good half-hour yet.

'He's mad about you, I can tell.'

'Well, Swindon's attentive to you, too,' Roma countered.

'I wish that was true. When we're together he talks about *you*!'

'I wonder why he's never married' – you don't think—'

'No, I don't!'

'Take your chance, then, captivate him.'

'I intend to! He may be older than me, but I get the feeling I'm the experienced one. And you, Roma? You and Moray, last Christmas. . . .'

'A dangerous attraction, Sal, for both of us, and one I intend to resist.'

'Then why did you pack that slinky frock with that provocative neckline?'

'Because I hardly get a chance to air it these days.'

'So you say,' Sally grinned.

The cinema was packed for the late performance, foggy with smoke; uniforms; younger girls and older women in dresses with exaggerated shoulder pads; hair released from factory turbans; mingled perfumes. All were putting on a bold face as usual, with bright, greasy lipstick and often-replenished powder. Bodies in close proximity produced suppressed anticipation on a warm evening. In the back rows, not many eyes were on the screen.

'Phew!' Roma wriggled out of her jacket, with Moray's assistance. He kept his arm round her shoulders.

'Enjoying the film?' he whispered. It was Howard Hawks's *Bringing up Baby* – the baby concerned was a leopard, leading to many comic mishaps and misunderstandings for the lead players.

'Seen it before,' she admitted truthfully. 'But I *do* like Cary Grant.'

'And I'm *mad* about Katharine Hepburn. She's playing hard to get; she's tantalizing, like *you*, Roma.'

'I don't know what you mean,' she pretended.

The oft-repeated theme was echoed around the cinema: *I can't give you anything but love, baby* . . .

Sally, on the other side of Roma, snuggled up to Swindon, but she sensed he was more alert to the whispering of the couple beyond.

The alarm had them filing without panic along the aisles to the exit. Then they headed to the nearest shelter. Hopefully, the raid wouldn't last long, and they could get back to Surrey and a comfortable bed for the night.

'Home on the milk train,' Roma yawned. She slumped at the table, kicking off her shoes. 'Any volunteers to cook breakfast?' she asked.

We ought to get some kip first, Sally thought. 'I'm off to bed.'

'Good idea,' Swindon agreed. 'Need a push up the stairs, Moray?'

'Nope. You go, I need a drink – fancy a cup of something, Roma?'

'A glass of milk?'

'Good idea; don't have to boil a kettle. Sweet dreams, you two,' he said.

Swindon and Sally parted company at the top of the stairs.

'See you in the morning,' they said, then smiled sheepishly.

'Later in the morning,' Sally amended.

'Might as well take our glasses upstairs,' Moray said to Roma.

'I'll carry the tray,' Roma offered. She slung her bag round her neck.

'Aren't you going to tell me how the film ended?' he asked at her door.

'You want me to do that now?'

'Suddenly, I feel wide awake. Can I come in for a bit?'

'Five minutes, that's all.' I'm courting danger, she thought. *I can't give you anything but love, baby* . . . I can't get that tune out of my head.

*

The undrunk milk clouded the glasses on the bedside table. It was past midday, but the curtains were still closed.

In the kitchen, Sally, who had looked in her brother's room had noted the empty bed. Accordingly, she tiptoed past the room next door. Swindon was frying bacon and eggs and had put four plates to warm. He was whistling cheerfully. 'Lovely day, pity to waste it,' he told her.

'Breakfast for two, I think,' she said. No need to say more.

'Why?' he said huskily. 'He's taking advantage of her; he's no doubt crazy about her, but – he doesn't love her, Sally, as I do.'

She turned abruptly, so he wouldn't see that she was hurting just as much.

Roma folded the blue dress slowly, selected clean clothes from her case.

Moray watched her from the rumpled bed, still half-asleep.

'I'm taking a quick bath now,' she said. 'I heard the others go downstairs a while ago. You'd better go to your own room, I think.'

'Come here,' he said softly.

'*No.*'

'I suppose you think I should make an honest woman of you now.'

'I don't think anything of the sort. It wouldn't work, Moray; we're both too volatile. You wouldn't be faithful – I can't practise forebearance, like Jean.'

'I don't regret what happened,' he parried. 'I believe it was inevitable.'

'Look, Moray, it's best forgotten.'

'If that's the way you want it.' Giving up too easily, she thought sadly.

'It is. And leave Tess alone; please don't break her heart.' Then she went before she blurted out the truth.

CHAPTER ELEVEN

June 1941 began well, for Tess was now a published author. She went around in a happy daze, for the news had spread. She wrote a long, joyful letter to Gregor. She hadn't confided her secret ambitions to Moray: she hadn't heard from him anyway. She couldn't know he had taken Roma's plea to heart.

She even merited an inch of print in the local paper, cut out carefully and passed on by Mrs Munro. 'For your scrapbook, lassie.'

'Who talked to *them*?' she asked Pop, surprised but pleased.

'Ah,' he said.

'It's – gratifying, Pop, but I can't believe anyone round here will want to buy a magazine for *girls*!' Reading the item yet again, she added, 'Miss Tess Rainbow of Silver Strand, doesn't that sound grand?'

'Sounds like a character for your next story. Are you going to frame your cheque, Tess, or spend it?'

'Neither; I'm going to open up a bank account with that ten pounds! I hope it's just the start of wonderful things to come, for all of us, Pop.'

'You never know,' he said.

They found a table in a corner of the pub. Swindon joined the crush at the bar. Roma rubbed idly at the damp beer rings on the wood, oblivious to the noise and people around. There wasn't the excuse now for flyers to drink too much after daytime sorties, the Luftwaffe had been withdrawn and the threat to the capital and other great cities had ceased, for a while, at least. There was cautious rejoicing, for the war overseas was escalating. The accepted way of life here was rationing, black-out, bomb sites, women working at heavy manual tasks, a steady trickle of evacuees returning home, if that place still existed.

'I said, what's up, Roma,' he repeated. She hadn't touched her drink. She blinked at him. 'Sorry, Swindon, I didn't mean to be rude.'

'You can tell me your troubles,' he said lightly, but looked concerned.

'If you really want to know,' she suddenly burst out, 'it's the old, old story. Before you ask if he's going to do the decent thing – I haven't told him, and I'm not going to. It wouldn't work out, Swindon, it just *wouldn't.*'

'Are you sure?' he asked gently. No need to ask who was responsible.

'It's too early for that yet, but—'

'Then why don't you marry me? A family right away, well, that's just fine.'

'I like you so much, I really enjoy your company, but I don't—' she faltered. His proposal had come out of the blue. She had persuaded herself that he and Sally were becoming close.

'Love me? Liking me a lot, that's a good start. You know, I never thought I'd get the chance to tell you that I fell for you, whoosh! when I hung on while you were air-sick. I applaud your free spirit: I wouldn't stop you achieving what you want, but I'll there, especially when things go wrong, like now.'

'What about Sally?' The last thing she wanted was to hurt her friend.

'She's young; she'll fall in love again, in time. I haven't led her on, Roma, you know. But, maybe you consider me too staid for you?'

'No! You're a pilot, aren't you? You're steady, Swindon – no, *steadfast* – and I guess that's the kind of partner I need – like Millie Mae with Pop.'

'Are you saying "yes" in a roundabout kind of way?'

'D'you know, I am!'

'Then let's get a special licence, and get on with it,' he said.

'I won't be here, Roma, when you get back from leave,' Sally said evenly, on the wedding morning. 'I've asked for a transfer, now things aren't so hectic.'

'Sal!' Roma bit her lip, 'I accept you won't come to the registry office, even though that hurts – but I hoped we'd still be friends when—'

'When I get over my best friend marrying my chap? I find it hard to forgive, like Ma. I don't understand why you are in such a hurry, unless—' She looked at Roma, in the one-piece masquerading as a suit, with its flared peplum; a style sometimes jokingly referred to as 'hiding a multitude of sins'.

Roma said nothing. One suspicion could lead to another. Perhaps it was as well they were going their separate ways. *It's my fault, no getting over that.*

'He's a damn fool, my brother . . . oh, you needn't worry, I promise he won't ever hear it from me. Duty calls. Goodbye, Roma.' She hesitated. 'Good luck.'

It was more a boarding-house than an hotel, in Dover, some way from the white cliffs and the barricades of the siege.

'I'd have liked to bring you somewhere more grand,' Swindon said.

'I really don't mind,' Roma reassured him. She giggled when she opened the wardrobe cupboard and the door almost came off its hinges. 'Whoops! The whole place is falling to bits.'

'Let me see to it.' He steadied the door while she hung up her wedding outfit. She stood there in stockinged feet, in a pink rayon petticoat, with a miniscule edging of lace curving round her bust. The Alexandra rose he'd plucked in passing from a garden hedge on the way to the registry office, was still pinned to her hair. She'd insisted, 'No hat. I've had quite enough of my service cap, let alone that heavy tin 'po' which I wore day in day out during the raids.'

'Not exactly trousseau material,' she said ruefully, aware of his bemused glance. 'Creases, and it'll be too tight soon, if – you can close the door now.'

She sat on the bed. 'We ought to send a telegram to the family, I suppose. I don't know whether they'll be shocked or surprised.'

'Pleased, I hope.'

'Aren't you going to get changed?' She swung her legs up on the bed. 'Think I'll have a lie down before the wedding breakfast.'

'I doubt whether it'll be worthy of that name; spam fritters proba- bly,' he said, unbuttoning his jacket slowly.

'Can I just say something important?'

'Sure, go ahead.'

'I'm really not *that* sort of girl, Swindon. It's important you believe me.'

'I never had any doubts.'

'There's a couple of months to go, before I need to call it a day at work, I hope. Remember what you said, about letting me have all my own way?'

'Did I really say that?' As his face emerged from pulling off his shirt, she saw that he was smiling ruefully. In his singlet, his body was revealed as firm and well muscled. She'd never really thought of him as attractive before; just as Old Swindon. It gave her a bit of a jolt.

'We-ell . . . another thing I should've made clear to you, was that this needn't be a marriage in name only – I know you wouldn't *presume* – is that OK?'

'You bet,' he said. 'You know something? We haven't even kissed properly yet; what'ya say we do something about that?' He plumped down beside her, which set the mattress springs groaning. She giggled.

It was an unexpectedly satisfying kiss. He released her gently, gazing at her. 'Your skin is so smooth,' he said, in wonder. 'You're *beautiful*, Roma.'

It was up to her now. 'Don't keep a lady waiting,' she whispered.

They read the message in disbelief.

JUST MARRIED! WRITING. ROMA & SWINDON.

'He's so nice, but, I never thought,' Tess said to Pop.

'Nor did I. She's made a good choice; he'll let her have her head.'

'You make her sound like a horse, Pop!'

'Well, isn't she a flighty filly? I was going to add, he'll also know when to keep a tight rein on her, eh?'

'You'll be next, Tess,' Barney suggested innocently. 'Can I go and tell Dougie? After all, I might be an uncle before you know it, like he is.'

'Wartime marriages,' Pop said enigmatically. He looked at Tess. 'Reckon we'll hear soon enough, if so. Barney, don't rush off, son, I've got some news, too; might as well tell you both, now. I'm wanted down

90

south at the works as they've got a huge new contract. It could well be a permanent move, for all of us. How d'you feel about that?'

'I don't want to go,' Barney almost shouted.

'You didn't like it here, at first; you'd settle down again; it's your home ground, after all. What about you, Tess? I'm not sure how it is with you and Gregor. As I recall, distance is no barrier, if you're sure about each other.'

'I could stay here; get a job.' Tess actually sounded defiant. 'He'll expect me to be *here* when he comes back.'

'So could I, Pop! Tess would look after me,' Barney insisted.

'I'm not leaving either of you behind,' Pop said emphatically. 'You haven't really got a choice; I'm sorry, but I must make myself clear. Anyway, you might feel happier, when you hear the rest of it: our old place on the Romney Marsh is available for rent – the garage isn't a going concern, naturally, but it could be, in the future. It might still be our last stop. Things have quietened down and it's a good time to go. Don't let's row about it, please have a good think about things and you'll see I'm right.'

The postman was early: Tess took Gregor's letter back to bed to read.

Darling Tess

I am thrilled for you. I knew you could do it! One of us will be famous, eh?

My own imagination is working overtime: I dream we are together, rebuilding my grandfather's house; that the war is over; that we are walking along the strand together, arms around each other's waists, towards the blowhole. Dreams cushion reality, Tess, and reality at sea is grim and cold; still, I can report, "all's well". But one day soon, I promise, I will come back on the tide. I love you. Hold on to that.

Gregor

This was too personal to show Gregor's mother, but she'd go round to Mrs Munro's to tell her she'd heard from him, that all was well, and also to break the news of their imminent departure, before Pop called to pay the rent, plus an extra month in lieu of notice.

*

Mrs Munro took a long time to answer the door; when at last she opened it, Tess knew, from her ashen face, that something terrible had happened.

'Shall I come in?' she prompted gently.

'Aye.'

The stark message lay unfolded on the table, the envelope crumpled.

'Gregor – gone down with his ship – no survivors.'

'I had a letter from him this morning,' Tess said helplessly.

Five days later, they were ready to leave. Jean cycled over to see them.

'I'm so sorry it had to end like this for you, Tess.' She took her hand.

'Excuse me,' Tess said numbly. She turned and went upstairs.

'She's still in shock,' Pop said, checking the luggage in the hall.

'I packed up some food for the journey, I hope you don't mind.' Jean indicated a carrier bag which she placed on top of the cases.

'It's good of you, Jean,' Pop said.

'I'll be in touch, that's if you want to, when the divorce is through.'

'I do want you to, very much. Before Barney gets back from Dougie's.' He hugged her tightly to him. 'You never know, Jean.'

'You never know,' she repeated. 'Give my love to Roma.'

'They didn't waste any time, they're expecting a baby in the new year. Swindon wants her to move in with us.'

'That will be good for Tess, as you will be away during the week.'

'Heard from your two?'

'From Moray, yes. He didn't mention Roma's wedding. He must know. Sally will have told him surely.'

They moved back hastily, as Barney pushed open the door. 'Taxi's here, Pop! Shall I carry some of this out?'

'I might as well wait and wave you off.' Jean's voice was husky.

'Tess!' Pop called. 'Time to go.'

Tess finished off the note to Gregor's mother.

I know you said I could take any of Gregor's books, but I think they should stay here, where they were written. Thank you for all your kindness to us, particularly me. I shall think of you often.

I told Gregor once that I would never forget him. I won't. He was a very special person. It was a privilege to love him, and to be loved in return.

God Bless.

Affectionately, Tess.

'Coming!' she confirmed. There was nothing now to keep her here.

PART TWO

THE ROMNEY MARSH

CHAPTER TWELVE

The Last Stop Garage was not as they had left its four years before – shabby and forlorn. The pumps were shrouded; with signs proclaiming NO PETROL and B&B, with a note attached NO VACANCIES.

The house was painted marine blue, the door flanked by two huge pots embellished with a rainbow arc, planted with scarlet geraniums. Above the lintel the theme was repeated, with a ceramic plaque: RAINBOW POTTERY. This was unexpected: for a long moment the returning family were speechless.

'We're home,' Tess said simply, for all of them. She thought, Millie Mae would have approved the transformation.

Roma and Swindon had met them at King's Cross, and driven them here. Swindon was returning to his station tomorrow, but Roma was staying, at least until after the baby was born. She was vague about the date it was due. Following Pop's lead, Tess didn't dream of prying.

The men dealt with the luggage while Barney swung the knocker. 'Glad we're here,' Roma sighed. Her loose dress was creased.

'D'you feel all right, Roma?' Tess asked anxiously.

'Blooming: *blooming* big! Yes, I'm OK. You mustn't fuss, I can't put up with it. I'm like Millie Mae in that respect – but unlike her, little Frankie will be quite enough for me.' She'd told them they were sure the baby was a boy. He'd be called Franklyn after Swindon's grandfather. It was also the name of the US president, which might augur well, only Mr Roosevelt spelt it with an 'i'.

'You'll change your mind; Millie Mae did, twice. Oh, here's Mrs Crisp—'

Their landlady came round the side of the house, smiling and rubbing paint-smeared hands on her oatmeal-coloured artists' smock.

She was in her middle forties, with salt and pepper hair twisted into an untidy knot, and bright eyes looking over half glasses, which had slipped down her nose.

'Sorry to keep you waiting. I'm Penny Crisp. When I'm working I lose all sense of time, especially now I've removed myself to the studio flat we built on the back.' She had a breathless way of talking. She inserted the familiar oversized key. 'Please come in and we'll introduce ourselves properly.'

Milky tea was served in bowl shaped cups handpainted with corn-flowers. Flapjack, oddly shaped, with a sticky toffee consistency, was handed round. 'Made that with honey from the marsh bees,' Penny told them proudly.

The living-room furniture was more comfortable than the hard stuffed chairs they had abandoned to the house-clearance man. They sank down on feather-filled cushions. The atmosphere was permeated with the heady scent of tiger lilies, not the lingering odour of oil, which Tess recalled. Sitting on the windowsill was a fluffed-out black cat, regarding them suspiciously through one green eye. The other was clouded blue. His kinked tail twitched.

'I hope you don't mind cats. I'm not sure if Moses has agreed to move out with me, you see – it took him long enough to decide this was his home.'

'We never had a cat,' Pop said, 'because our old dog would have chased it, but if he doesn't try to sit on my lap, I'm sure we can tolerate his presence.'

'Oh, I can promise you he won't do that! When he knows you, you'll be allowed to tickle behind his ears, or under his chin – never on his tummy, unless you want to get bitten and scratched. He's not completely domesticated, although he's had his credentials curtailed. Moses sleeps in the barn, plenty of nightlife there, to deal with. He's giving you the once over, I imagine.'

'Why Moses?' Barney asked, emerging from his big sulk at last. He'd moaned in the car, 'I don't suppose I'll ever make another friend, and I definitely don't want to go to another school.'

Pop advised the others, 'Give him time, he'll get over it.'

'Care to finish off the flapjack?' Penny asked Barney. 'I found him in the bullrushes, when we first moved here. I was sketching by the Military Canal. He was in a bad way; he'd obviously been run over. His fur was matted with blood. He'd been struck on the head, and blinded in that eye. I put my jacket over him, before lifting him up, because he still had some fight left in him.

Jack had a way with animals, so he cleaned the cat up, took him to the vet. No one claimed him, and he was Jack's cat, until my husband died last year. Now he's my companion – not of the constant kind, but it helps.'

The bedrooms were easily allotted: Roma and Swindon had the biggest room, with space for a cot; Tess was next door; Pop took the room opposite; and Barney, the single bedroom, Pop's old office.

'This is very nice,' Tess remarked appreciatively, to Penny. 'Thank you; we didn't expect you to make up the beds.'

'Oh, it was no trouble; we always had a houseful of visitors before the war, the kind who preferred quiet and a fishing rod. Then the barbed wire put the beach out of bounds, young families were evacuated – we stayed because Jack was a special constable and involved with local defence and I am with the Red Cross. We had soldiers billeted with us for some time and the garage had to close. But, I always thought you'd come back, you Rainbows.'

'Is that why you called your pottery that?'

'I suppose it was. The Last Stop bit, sounds – so *final*. It's the first place Jack and I ever owned. I heard about you all, especially your mother, Millie Mae, from your old friends and neighbours, Tess, so I felt I knew you. When I was able to rent out the house, I wasn't surprised to hear Pop had contacted the agent. When he said it might be a couple of months before you could come, I said I'd wait, because I had my ideal tenants.'

'It was meant to be,' Tess mused.

'I hope you don't mind, but Pop briefly mentioned your loss, Tess; I understand . . .' They were sitting companionably side by side on the bed.

Tess nodded. It was going to take time, she was aware of that, for her sadness to dispel, but already Scotland, Gregor, and all the rest of it, was beginning to take on a dream-like quality, now she'd returned to her roots.

Roma plaited her hair and secured it with a rather limp rubber band. She looked distastefully at herself in the mirror. She had appropriated one of Pop's shirts, as her nightwear. Her face was pallid. Her figure had naturally thickened; she turned sideways to regard the bulge, which threatened to eclipse the curve of her breasts. Was she bigger than normal for four months? The baby had been moving for a while now, which meant she must actually be more than halfway through the pregnancy. How was it possible for her skin to stretch any further – would it slacken, like the rubber band, after the birth? Her lips trembled.

'Come to bed,' Swindon said. He'd been watching her face in the mirror.

'I'm *ugly*,' she sighed.

'You're beautiful. Come on, lights out; I've got to rise early.'

'I shan't sleep. Too many memories.' But she climbed in obediently.

He plumped the pillows behind her. 'Millie Mae?'

'Ye-es. Not only that. . . .' *Moray*, she thought, landing here, in that little plane. But I have Swindon, and I've grown to care for him, depend on him, in a comfortable sort of way. I'm very lucky.

The baby was most active at night. She sighed, as the gymnastics began.

'Let your mum sleep, Frankie.' Swindon patted her writhing stomach.

Roma giggled. Her arms went tightly round his neck.

'Are you throttling me, or inviting me to cuddle you?' he whispered.

'I'm going to miss you,' she said. 'You'll be a great dad, Swindon, and you'll need to be, as I guess I'll be far removed from the perfect mum.'

You're OK by me,' he said, '*very* OK.'

Pop opened his bedroom window, then got into bed, opened the newspaper. The curtains rustled, parted slightly, and he sat still, waiting. Moses launched himself from the windowsill, landed safely, crouching at the foot of the bed.

He turned a page, wary, but not making eye contact. After a time, there was a rather rusty purring. Pop refolded the paper, turned out the light.

'You're a strange bedfellow. Be gone before morning, that's all I ask.'

Barney had begun a letter to Dougie, but sleep had overtaken him. Ink leaked from his fountain pen, fortunately only on the writing pad.

Dear Dougie

I am back in our old house at last. I wish I was still in Silver Strand, shaving the hedges, as your dad says, and eating your mum's fish and chips. Take care of the Gladiator, it took me long enough to make. And if you get a chance, please can you make sure my real plane is still there at Strand House. . . .

Tess, looking in to say goodnight, carefully shifted the paper, and capped the pen. She couldn't help seeing what he had written, by the light of her torch. She felt the familiar constriction of her throat, tears welling.

As she tiptoed back to her own bed, she could hear low voices from Roma and Swindon's room. It was obviously an intimate conversation.

Roma is lucky; things always turn out well for her. I won't think of Gregor tonight, she told herself firmly; I have to put away thoughts of love and loving. Maybe I'll never experience those again. Maybe I'll stay single, who knows? That's not so bad, because I have family still to care for, and my writing, which means a lot to me. Scotland was a mere strand in my life, a *silver* strand.

She actually fell asleep quite quickly, but the dreams were back, more delusions really, because she was with Moray, and he was telling her he loved her and that she mustn't ever leave him again.

'I didn't mean to oversleep!' Tess exclaimed, next morning. The others had breakfasted an hour ago, and Swindon had already departed. Roma was unpacking in her room, and Pop and Barney had gone for a walk.

'You must have needed it, Tess,' Penny observed. 'What d'you fancy for breakfast? They left you a rasher, and I have plenty of bantam eggs.' They were standing in the kitchen. The walls throughout the house were whitewashed, and in here there were blue and white delft tiles.

'Oh, I don't expect you to cook for me, Penny – that's my job – I don't mean to offend you—' she floundered.

'I know what you mean! But you might be glad to have me around today.'

'We are! Thank you. I'd love a boiled egg, then.'

They talked while Tess dipped her spoon in and out of the yolk, and ate several pieces of bread and butter.

Penny rubbed ruefully at the red mark on her nose. 'I keep meaning to fix my glasses to a cord, leave them dangling round my neck, so they're handy when I need them for close-up work. Where have I left them now, I wonder?'

'They're sticking out of your top pocket.'

'So they are. Jack said it was like hunt the thimble most days here.'

'You must miss him terribly.'

'I certainly do – sometimes I find myself having a one-sided conversation with him; his presence remains very strong.'

'We still feel like that about Millie Mae.'

'Jack was twenty-five years older than me, Tess – he wasn't so young when he had the heart attack. It's tragic to lose someone the age your mother was, and, oh, forgive me! like your young man.'

'His name was Gregor. I didn't know him for long. And the worst thing is,' she paused, then continued, on seeing Penny's look of kindly concern, 'there was someone else, you see, whom I knew first, but he didn't love me, as Gregor did. I was really confused.'

'First love is always complicated,' Penny said wisely. 'You can't begin to understand it. It's over with the other chap, is it?'

'It never really began. He had a thing about Roma, you see, but she married Swindon and so I don't suppose we'll see him again.'

'I'm dying for a cup of coffee,' Roma said evenly, coming into the kitchen. 'Here' – she held out a large jar – 'Swindon appropriated it for us from the stores – it's the real stuff, from America.'

CHAPTER THIRTEEN

Things were not the same, of course. Tess missed her walks along the shore, and the marsh sheep, evacuated to safer pastures in the emergency. The canals, dug to deter Napoleon's army, were not accessible; the dykes, the land reclaimed from the sea were even more vital now. There were military manoeuvres, mysterious goings-on after dark. Yet it was good to be home.

Barney cycled off to school each morning, then it was a house of women during the day, from Monday morning to Friday evening when Pop returned home. When his arrival was imminent, Moses appeared like a sentinel between the rainbow pots on the porch, his eyes luminous in the dark. The cat shadowed Pop discreetly until it was time for him to depart. Penny said generously that she forgave his defection, because Moses had bonded with Pop, like Jack.

Tess was closeted in her room in the mornings, having been invited to submit regular short stories to the magazine which had published her serial. She had to be disciplined about her writing. She fitted in the chores when she could, as Roma ignored the carpet sweeper and meal preparing. Two afternoons a week, Tess accompanied Penny to Red Cross meetings in the nearby village, to learn the rudiments of emergency first aid and elementary nursing. She rolled bandages, tied slings, fixed splints, practised artificial respiration with dedication. She felt she was doing something for the war effort, even if it was just a drop in the ocean. 'In a couple of years' time I'll be twenty-one,' she told Penny, 'and if the war's still on, perhaps I can join up after all – Pop couldn't stop me then, as Barney'd be more or less grown up.'

Swindon came whenever he could, not often since he transferred to Bomber Command and went up country. Roma was thoroughly fed up;

she missed the stimulation of her WAAF duties, and leaves spent in London.

Penny suggested Roma help with decorating plain white china, crates of which she had wisely accumulated during the spring of 1939. That was how she'd started herself, she said: when she'd discovered her artistic flair. Roma painted a few blobby yellow daffodils and then abandoned the brushes. 'Too tired,' she sighed. She couldn't concentrate on knitting for the baby either, but fortunately the aunts were busy making woollens and tiny garments on her behalf, although Roma ungratefully pronounced their efforts 'old-hat'. She passed the flannel nighties to Tess to shorten. However, she approved of the rompers sewn by Penny, who was already a good friend, particularly to Tess, despite the age difference. She was more like one of the family.

Roll on March, Tess thought privately, finding it difficult to be patient with her sister at times. Though when their first quiet Christmas here had come and gone, she couldn't imagine how Roma would last out that long.

Swindon, on a precious week's pass, one Thursday evening early in February, 1942, endured a hazardous journey on icy roads, crawling along in a car with muffled headlights. He arrived around nine to find Tess cooking his supper, Barney finishing off his homework on the kitchen table, and Roma gone to bed.

'I don't want to worry you,' Tess said, turning the slice of liver among a pile of sweating onions in the pan, and wondering if it was as rubbery as it looked, 'but Roma had some pains earlier on, and Penny phoned the midwife to ask her advice. It might just be the baby shifting down, she said, so not to worry unduly, but be vigilant for any other signs, and to report back. She was just off to a confinement, but she's not far away, so one of us could run there in an emergency, and Penny's around of course. She did her midwifery bit, even if it was twenty-five years ago. Glad you're here at last, and I know Roma will be.' Quite a speech from Tess.

'Is she asleep?'

'I don't think so; she was reading to take her mind off things.' She hesitated. 'She told me to go away when I looked in on her a while ago, she said she'd shout if she wanted anything.'

'She does plenty of that, recently,' Barney said, in his newly gruff voice.

'She can't help it,' Tess said, making excuses as usual.

'I'll go and see her right away. Tess, sorry, I can't eat anything.'

'Oh, Moses can have the liver, I'm not sure it's edible anyway. A nice cup of tea? Off to bed, Barney,' Tess told him, 'it might be a busy night.' Barney didn't argue, but gathered up his papers, his protractor and pencils.

Roma greeted her husband petulantly. 'Ugh! Did Tess need to fry onions tonight? And the smell from that paraffin stove Penny brought in.'

'She was only trying to warm the room up for you,' he said. His lips brushed her cheek, which was chilly, but slippery with sweat.

'How do you feel?'

'How do you think I feel?' she asked crossly, then gasped. When the pain subsided, she stretched out her arms to him. 'Don't look so glum. I don't mean to upset you. I'm so glad you're here – oh!'

He held on to her, instinctively rubbing her back.

'That was close,' she murmured, with feeling, 'or it might have been the tail end of the last one. Nurse thinks, it could be a false alarm.'

'Doesn't look like that to me.'

'Oh, you're an expert are you?' she groaned, with a vestige of a smile.

'I was around when Mom produced my younger sisters,' he told her.

'Haul me out of bed; Nurse said it might help to walk around the room.'

'Fancy a route march, eh?' He kept his arm firmly round her.

She stopped abruptly, gestured at the bed. 'It's no good, I'll – have to—'

'*Tess!*' he yelled.

Tess was there, and Penny, summing up the situation, advised her to fetch the nurse. 'Get some water boiling, Swindon, while I take a look at what's happening – I'll need you, and Tess, if Nurse isn't able to come right away.'

Roma was breathing fast now, trying to tell Swindon something.

'What did you say?' he asked, returning quickly to her side.

'I . . . said . . . I was born in this room . . . Millie Mae—' she clutched at his wrist. Don't go away, *please!*'

105

*

'It might have been quick, but don't you dare say it was easy,' Roma told her husband, as they watched the nurse, who had arrived in time for the actual delivery, suspend the baby in a folded, pinned nappy, from her balance scales.

Tess and Penny had gone away discreetly to give Barney the good news, to telephone Pop, and to brew more tea.

'Just over six and a half pounds,' Nurse said, satisfied. 'Not bad for a bit early: nothing missing! A quick clean up tonight, and a proper bath tomorrow morning for the little dear and a blanket bath for you, Mrs Swindon. It's lucky you followed my advice and made up the crib. It's advisable the last month—'

'That was Penny,' Roma said, 'it's hers, a family heirloom, I think.'

'Ah, poor thing: *her* baby was still-born, I understand.'

'I – didn't know.'

'Some twenty years ago, but she won't have forgotten. Now, have you a name for your daughter?'

'Franklyn, we'd decided – Frankie for short, but—'

'That's nice, unusual,' Nurse beamed. 'Well, Frankie, you're half presentable, so Daddy can hold you for five minutes while I clear up here. Mummy can enjoy her cup of tea, then try to nurse baby before I tuck her up.'

Swindon sat beside the bed, cradling the baby in his arms, while Roma rested. 'Welcome to the Rainbow clan, Frankie . . . but don't forget you're a Swindon, too,' he told her.

'Has she got the Rainbow hair?' Roma asked quickly.

'No, and she isn't fair like you, although she has your blue eyes, I think – she half-opened them just now – she's got a thatch of jet-black hair.' He touched it gently with a finger. 'All damp and oily.'

'Most babies are born with dark hair,' Nurse put in, taking Frankie from Swindon and settling her in her mother's arms. 'Here, get comfortable . . . the first hair rubs off, and the new hair may be quite different.'

'She's certainly got more hair than me,' Swindon grinned ruefully.

Roma looked down at her baby, nuzzling uncertainly at her breast. She wasn't too sure about this, fearing she might not regain her figure. She knew instantly of whom that little face reminded her.

*

Tess didn't get to hold the baby until next morning. All had been quiet during what remained of the night; Swindon had assured them he could cope.

After breakfast, kindly seen to by Penny, she braced herself, she couldn't say why, and knocked on their door.

'Oh, good, it's you, Tess – I thought it might be the midwife; can I seize this chance to get washed and dressed in the bathroom? Breakfast was good, by the way, nothing like porridge with brown sugar, after working hard, eh? That's Roma, of course, not me!'

Roma looked pleased to see her sister. 'Thanks for everything, Tess – I mean it. Can you bring the baby over here? Swindon actually changed her nappy when she woke first thing, I haven't a clue.'

'You'll soon learn,' Tess said, gently lifting her up. 'Time for her feed?'

'Again, I haven't any idea, except Nurse says there won't be any real supplies, as she puts it, until the third day – *then* I'll know it, and be only too glad to nurse her! I thought the motherly instinct was inherent, but it's not working yet. However, her daddy knows exactly what to do. You cuddle her for a few minutes, that's what she seems to want, more than anything.'

Tess seated herself carefully. 'Hello, Frankie. May I give her a kiss?'

' 'Course you can, on top of her head. You're her auntie, aren't you?'

'She's wonderful, Roma. You and Swindon, you're so lucky . . .' She felt a rush of love for Roma's baby.

'I guess we are,' Swindon said, returning, freshly shaved and dressed.

'You look like a lumberjack in that checked shirt,' Roma told him.

'Thought it'd be warm for Frankie to snuggle up to. So, you approve of our first-born, d'you, Tess?' He held out his arms for her.

'I love her,' she said softly, relinquishing the baby.

As the baby opened her mouth to mewl in protest, Tess, watching, caught that likeness, too. *No she said to herself, that can't be so.*

CHAPTER FOURTEEN

In May, Frankie was three months old, and they picked spring flowers for Millie Mae's birthday. She would have been forty-four, a grandmother. It was nearly ten years since they had lost her. They walked to the church where she was baptized, married and laid to rest, when her family stood in the rain as the minister observed the old hudd would have helped. These, like sentry boxes, sheltered the clergy at gravesides in inclement weather in centuries past.

Tess carried Frankie on her hip as they brushed through the long grass, busy with insects. Roma arranged the flowers in the stone pot; Barney cleaned the moss from the headstone. *Millie Mae Rainbow, Beloved Wife and Mother*. Pop wielded the shears in silence as he cleared the ground around.

The baby chewed at the strings of her sun bonnet and kicked her bare feet as the sun warmed her legs. She hadn't lost much hair; it was still as black as a crow's wing, with what Pop referred to as a peacock's perch in the front. Millie Mae always said approvingly that sounded nicer than a widow's peak.

It was peaceful here, and now there was cautious optimism as the lull in the bombing continued. Of course there were shortages, with which mainly women had to cope as the men fought in alien places overseas. America had been catapulted into the war following Pearl Harbor, which boosted confidence generally – particularly in the Pacific, where soon decisive victories would be won. Russia, Japan and North Africa were in the news.

'Better get back,' Pop said. 'You'll want tea before Scouts, Barney.'

Barney had made friends after all. He was fourteen years old, already taller than Tess, and his stammer had all but disappeared.

'Want me to carry Frankie back to the pram?' he offered.

'Don't let him,' Roma said. 'Have you seen his hands?'

'I can manage, thanks, Barney,' Tess hoisted her up more firmly. 'Anyway, I'm telling her a story.' She was aware that Roma and Pop were grinning. 'I'm stirring her imagination,' she added lamely.

'Tess,' Roma said, as they settled Frankie into her pram by the church gates, reminding her it was afternoon nap time, 'can we have a chat tonight, just us? I don't want Pop putting his oar in. It's something I've already discussed with Swindon.' Pop and Barney were walking on ahead.

Tess shot her a wary glance. 'Who's pushing?' She adjusted the canopy to shade the baby's head. Some of the fringe was missing. Everything was second-hand: pram, cot, playpen, clothes, she thought. A beautiful baby like Frankie should have only the best, but there, at her age, she couldn't care less.

'You, if you want to. You know when it comes to crossing over, or going on and off the path, I never know how to manage the wheels.'

'You're not going to ask me to keep a secret from Pop, I hope, Roma.'

'No, of course not. I'll tell him myself, if you agree.'

The baby was passed around at feeding time. She had been bottle-fed since she was a month old. She was quite equable about it all. When Pop was home it was his prerogative, but no one else got a look in when Swindon was around. Tess mixed the formula and sterilized the bottles. She prevailed upon Roma to wash out the baby's clothes and bibs when her sister used soap flakes extravagantly to wash her own nice things. At least she tossed the nappies in a pail to soak, but then left them to Tess to boil and hang out. Tess had hardly written a line since Frankie was born. There just wasn't time.

Now, they sat on Roma's bed, Tess rocking the crib, Roma ready to talk.

'Tess, I'm not sure you'll understand, but it's not enough for me, this mummy business. I'm restless; I never really wanted to come back, like the rest of you. Remember how I longed to get away when I was younger – after Millie Mae? Pop says we're alike, but I can't give up on things like she could, always putting family first.'

'You don't love Swindon – Frankie, like that?'

'Don't be disapproving, of course I do. Maybe you guessed I married

109

him on impulse, but I don't regret it. However, what with a honeymoon baby, much as I love her, and living apart, there's no time to, well, feel like a *couple*. Swindon's right for me, like Pop was for Millie Mae.

'I want us to be together. I know it's selfish, when so many are apart, but I'd get a job on his base, or rejoin the service. We'd come here whenever we could. I'm sure it would work. That could be your war work, Tess, looking after Frankie, freeing me to do what I really thrive on.'

'I'm not sure . . .'

'You want what's best for Frankie, don't you?' Roma urged.

'Yes.'

'Well, then.'

'I'll have to give it some serious thought.'

'You've got until tomorrow night, when Swindon comes home.'

'I must talk to Pop first.'

'I said I would.'

'No, I will.'

'Pop, mind if I come in?' He had gone to his room after Barney went out, and she knew that he wanted to be quiet, to think of Millie Mae on her special day. 'I'm sorry to disturb you,' she added, as she closed the door behind her.

'I'm sure you've a good reason.' He stood by the open window, and she saw Moses on the sill, half concealed by the fluttering net curtain.

'Yes, I have. It's Roma; she's restless. She wants to join Swindon – that's natural, I suppose, not being married long, and not living together.'

'You don't have to defend your sister to me,' Pop said heavily. 'She wants to leave little Frankie with you, is that it?'

Tess nodded. 'Yes. What d'you think?'

'It might surprise you to know that I think it's a good idea. Roma's not the maternal type, but she wants the best for Frankie. I'm sure Penny would help you, as Millie Mae would have done. It's your decision, Tess: you're young to take on such a responsibility, but then, Millie Mae was younger when Roma was born. Also, you have to bear in mind, if things get hot again on the home front, we might have to leave again in a hurry. Or Roma might miss the baby so much, she'd take her away.'

'You mean, I might not want to let her go, in that case, don't you Pop?'

'Yes. I know you're not ready to meet someone yet after Gregor, but it would be difficult looking after a baby, particularly when it isn't your own.'

'That's not a consideration right now. I suppose I want your blessing.'

'You have it. I hope Roma appreciates what a wonderful sister she has.'

'Put her down, come and kiss me,' Roma told Swindon. It was late the next night, and she had awoken, even though he had tiptoed in. He couldn't resist lifting Frankie up and holding her, all warm and drowsy, for a moment.

'Anyone would think you're jealous,' he told her, but he tucked the baby up. Roma looked full of promise in her flimsy nighty, she'd certainly regained her voluptuous figure. He kept his distance, at the foot of the bed.

'Well?' she challenged him.

'Tess said yes? You're sure this is what you want, Roma?'

'I'm sure. Are you happy?'

'If you are.'

'Prove it then.'

He lay awake for ages, still holding her with her head comfortable against his shoulder. In the crib, Frankie gave a little hiccup in her sleep. In an hour or two, she would need her bottle. Roma would expect him to see to it, despite the hours of driving, and the busy day before that.

If only, he thought. The moment he held Frankie in his arms for the first time, he'd known. It made no difference to his feelings for her; she was his daughter, and he adored her. As he did, her mother.

Pop was out early, walking over the marshland where once they had kept their sheep; Moses oscillating at his heels, tail waving, fur stirring in the breeze, revealing the rust colour beneath. Pop was glad of his jersey, there was a definite reminder that the sea was not far away, though out of bounds.

He'd been foolish to believe Roma had returned to the family fold, that things could be as before, carrying on as Millie Mae would have

111

wanted. Roma was going, with their blessing, and entrusting them with her daughter.

He almost cannoned into Penny as he turned to retrace his steps. 'I'm so sorry!' he apologized. He seemed to see her properly for the first time; the pretty, untidy hair, the engaging smile – without glasses her eyes were revealed as amber-coloured, with laughter crinkles at the corners.

'You're out early.' She was a little breathless, as if she had been hurrying.

'So are you. Going further!'

'No. Might as well walk back with you, if you don't mind.'

'I'll be glad of the company.'

'Good.' She bent to stroke Moses. Head lowered, she said, 'Tess was up at the crack of dawn, too. We had a cup of tea together. She told me the news; said she'd heard you go out.' She straightened up.

'So you decided to come after me?' He sounded almost teasing.

'I – thought you might be worrying. Jack kept things to himself. It doesn't always do, you know. I don't suppose you really want Roma to go, do you?'

'We haven't always seen eye to eye.' He caught at her arm as she stumbled over a large stone in the grass. 'Here, hang on to me.'

'Haven't been arm in arm with a man for ages,' she giggled. 'Feels nice.'

'Good! Roma's made up her mind. Perhaps Swindon can damp down some of her wilder schemes. She wasn't ready for motherhood, Penny, or marriage. Age doesn't always come into it, does it? She can maybe make a go of one, if not the other. Thank heavens for Tess – what would we do without her?'

'You'll have to let *her* go one day; that time almost came a while ago, eh?'

'Somehow, I don't think she and Gregor would've married. It might be a solution if I found another soul mate – then we could take Frankie on.'

'Roma mentioned the name Jean.'

'She's married to my boss.'

'Oh, I'm sorry.'

'You needn't be. There's rather a tangled relationship between our two families.' They were at the house. 'I'll see you before I leave tonight, Penny?'

'I hope so. Pop, I'll support Tess, I promise.'

'I know you will, bless you.' On a sudden impulse, he embraced her. 'Just putting the seal on our friendship,' he told her, sounding almost boyish.

'I'll leave the studio doors open, then I can listen out for Frankie in the garden, while I paint,' Penny insisted. 'You've got a story to finish, haven't you?'

'Yes, but—'

'No buts! It's my pleasure. You had a sleepless night, I believe?'

'The first of many, I expect. Frankie's cutting her front teeth. Thanks for the reviving cup of coffee.'

'The last of that jar. We'll have to drop a heavy hint to Swindon.'

'Roma sounded very happy when she rang last night; back in uniform and driving the big brass around, no less!'

'And you? You're still happy with your lot?'

'Yes; it's good having you to back me up. Pop says you're wonderful.'

'Does he?' Penny sounded bemused.

'Penny, I don't mean to be nosy, but you really like him I can tell, and, well, Barney and I – would approve, be happy, if you two got together . . .'

'So would I, Tess, so would I. Now, retreat to your typewriter before I say too much! And don't you dare say anything to your father!'

CHAPTER FIFTEEN

Tess trundled the pram home after a first aid session. It was a hot July afternoon with a threat of thunder, which prompted brisk walking with a way to go. Penny cycled ahead to take in the washing, in case of a downpour.

As soon as Frankie's old enough, she thought, I'm going to look out for one of those little seats for my bike. You can't get up much speed pushing a pram.

Frankie jigged in her harness. She was crawling now, backwards rather than forwards, but, as Pop observed, you had to start somewhere. Tess tied the cord of the canopy to the pram handle and exhorted her to stay under its shade. Frankie blew a rude raspberry; coached by Barney, no doubt.

'Mumma,' Frankie said, parting the canopy fringe and looking out.

'Mumma's not here, and if she was, she'd say, behave! Oh, it's raining, we'll have to make a dash for it.' She pulled up the raincover.

It was nearly ten minutes before Tess put the key in the door and pushed the pram inside. She hadn't noticed the sports car at the side of the house.

'Phew!' she exclaimed, looking ruefully at her rayon dress, clinging to her legs. Her feet were squelching in her canvas plimsoles.

'Tess?' she heard, as she lifted Frankie from the pram. 'Your landlady said to come in out of the wet when she found me waiting on your doorstep.'

'*Moray*,' she said weakly, aware how awful she must look. 'How—?'

'I didn't fly here, or belly flop in the meadow – I hope that doesn't disappoint you! A *baby*, Tess, I didn't imagine you to be married, especially as—' He broke off. His hair was cropped short, but he was as good-looking as ever. 'I heard about Gregor. I didn't write, I'm sorry,' he added.

'This is Roma and Swindon's baby, she—' Tess was floundering now.

'Ah, I see. Ma did tell me they were spliced, months after the event, and that you were back here. I don't know why Sally kept it secret. Roma here?'

'No. She's rejoined the WAAF; I look after the baby for them.'

'Aren't you going to introduce me to the infant? Your friend mentioned tea. D'you want to change out of your wet things? I think I'm capable of holding the baby, though I have to admit I have no experience.'

Tess put Frankie in the playpen in the corner. 'She'll be all right. Her name's Franklyn, Moray, Frankie for short. Excuse me for a minute, then.'

Perversely, she didn't put on anything special, just a cotton top and skirt. She bunched her hair with a ribbon, and returned bare-footed.

There was a tray on the table, but Penny had gone, discreetly. Frankie amused Moray as she pushed a felt elephant through the bars, chattering busily.

'She's a honey, Tess,' he said. 'She's got Roma's wide blue eyes; pity she hasn't got your gorgeous hair.'

'It's the bane of my life.' Why did he always make her feel gauche?

'Roma's happy, I hope?'

'Yes, she is. How's Sally?'

'Oh, she bounced back after Roma bagged Swindon. The Yanks are here and Sally's snared one! He's of Scottish descent; finds the family pile fascinating.'

'And Jean?' Tess wanted to divert his attention from Frankie.

'Ma? She's not too happy, what with divorcing Dad at last. She must be lonely in that big house. She suggested I come and see you when I visited her last. You know, she always had hopes that you and I would get together.'

'You're back in action now, are you?' she said ignoring his last remark.

'I certainly am. The old leg's bearing up, thank goodness.'

'I think Frankie needs her nappy changed,' Tess began, rising.

He caught at her sleeve. 'Roma warned me off, Tess. The last time I saw her, she said to leave her little sister alone. What d'you think about that?'

'I think you've probably got two or three girlfriends in tow as usual,' she returned smartly. 'Blonde and busty, which I'm not.'

He released her instantly. 'You're not joking – you're over me, aren't you?'

'Yes. Anyway, I haven't time for flirting, I've Frankie to look after now.'

'I hoped you might put me up tonight. I'd like to see Barney again, he must be due back from school soon, eh?' He sounded almost pleading.

She knew it was foolish to fall for this. 'You can have Pop's room, but don't expect a lot to eat, this end of the week.'

He was smiling now. 'While you do your bit for the baby, I'll fetch a few surprises from the car; fancy a nice illicit piece of fillet steak?'

Tess persuaded Penny to join them, but she needn't have worried: Barney monopolized the conversation with all his eager questions.

'Hope the war lasts out until I'm old enough to join your lot,' he said ingenuously. 'And one day, I'll fly the *Spirit of Millie Mae* back home here, only *I'll* make a decent job of landing her.'

'Barney!' Tess remonstrated.

'Don't worry! Hope he won't be as irresponsible as I was, at that age.'

'Pop'll see to that,' Barney told him. 'He lays down the law, weekends . . .'

'It's quite a responsibility being a father. One I don't intend to take on for a good many years, if ever.'

Roma was right, Tess thought, she and Moray are too alike. Even if – well, I'd still have been left holding the baby.

'Lovely steak, can't remember the last time I enjoyed a meal so much.' Penny sighed with satisfaction, spooning up the last of the gravy.

'Your good cooking, Mrs Crisp,' Moray said gallantly.

'Oh, do call me Penny – everyone does.'

'Thanks for taking charge of the frying pan, Pen,' Tess said.

'I enjoyed tackling a decent piece of meat for once; the last large steak I had was with Jack, wild goat – poor thing met a sticky end on the minefield.'

'I remember the goats, they were around the fishermen's cottages.'

'They weren't considered a nuisance,' Penny recalled. 'Some became almost domesticated; the locals made goat's cheese. They reckoned the milk and meat might have a strong taste but there was nothing they liked better. Good, nourishing food, when people struggled to make a living. I doubt whether either the folk or the goats will return after the war.'

'The war, the defensive measures have changed the marsh way of life, but not, I hope, for ever. You don't see all that wire, so many warning notices in our part of Scotland,' Moray said.

'No, but you hear the drone of big bombers. Your turn to wash up,' Tess reminded Barney. 'Then you two can talk aeroplanes to your heart's content, because I must feed and bath Frankie and put her to bed.'

'And I must search out old Moses – I suspect he's lurking in the barn, keeping out of the rain – and give him his grub. So, I'll say goodnight to you all, and thank you again for my supper,' Penny said.

It was well after nine before Tess returned, and reminded Barney that he had school tomorrow. 'If you've got any homework to finish, you'll have to do it in bed, just don't get blots on the bedclothes.'

'But we were having a great discussion, Tess.'

'I'll be here tomorrow night, if you'll have me – I'd like to see Pop.'

'OK then,' Barney sighed. ' 'Night.'

' 'Night,' they said in unison.

'Sneaky,' Tess reproved Moray. 'Want to go in the other room?'

His apologetic smile disarmed her. 'I'd be glad to put the leg up, Tess.'

'I'll make a cup of tea, shall I?' she asked, escaping again.

When she returned, he was dozing on the sofa. She sat down opposite, weary herself, sipping her tea. How did she feel about Moray turning up? She was relieved that Roma would not be home this weekend. Was it possible he hadn't seen that distinctive, stubbornly parting hair, in Frankie as on himself?

The cup being removed from her hand, startled her. 'Sorry, Tess, I could see you dropping it – I drank my tea, by the way.'

'I suppose we'd better call it a day.'

'Oh, why? We're both alert now, and I feel like talking.'

'You look happier than the last time I saw you,' she said softly. 'Are you out of pain now?'

'Mentally, yes – physically, it comes and goes. I'm not aware of it when I'm flying. I'm at peace with myself, even if I'm at war like the rest of the world . . . *Come here*,' he said, as he had to Roma, only Tess didn't know that.

With his arm comfortably around her, he said, 'I've missed you, Tess, more than you'll know. Ma was right; there's something about you I just can't resist.'

And I can't resist *you*, she acknowledged to herself.

He seemed intent on kissing her, when he abruptly drew back. 'Tess, there's something I must tell you. You might want no more to do with me when you know: you could say it was the fulfilment of a youthful passion, or the conclusion of a love affair which never was. Roma and I, we made love, it was only once, I promise you, but—'

'I know,' she said, almost inaudibly.

'She told you?' he asked disbelievingly.

'No, she didn't have to.'

'Sisterly intuition?'

'Something like that. Moray. I'm not ready for what I think you're suggesting: I'm committed to Frankie, and Barney still needs me. Can't we be just friends, as we agreed in Scotland?'

'Don't look so worried, I'm not nearly as hot-headed as I was. A warm hug, that's all I ask, to show you're glad to see me! Tess, you're not the only one who's grown up, only it took me much longer than you.'

She was glad he kept his word, because one kiss was not nearly enough.

'If that was merely a friendly kiss, well . . .' he said.

The shrilling of the telephone in the hall made them literally jump apart. She rushed to answer it, before it woke Frankie.

'Sorry I'm late.' It was Roma's voice. 'A quick call to say tell Frankie we love and miss her – and is everything OK?'

'Everything's OK,' Tess repeated. 'See you next week, Roma?'

'Hope so. Hectic here. Swindon sends his best. Love to you all. Bye!'

Moray's arms encircled her from behind. He rested his chin on her head.

'Time to turn in?' he asked.

She moved away. 'Yes. Goodnight, Moray.'
'Tess, you haven't, you know.'
'Haven't what?'
'*Got over me at all, and I'm glad,*' he said.

CHAPTER SIXTEEN

'**C**oaxed another half-pint from the milkman,' Penny said. 'Thought you might need it, with Moray here, and Pop home tonight.' She looked searchingly at Tess, holding on to Frankie's slippery little body as she splashed merrily in the sink. 'You look bleary-eyed – bad night with young Frankie? Keep the bath water and wash out yesterday's bits.' They were conscientious in saving water, and re-using it if it was hot and soapy and not too grey and scummy.

Tess yawned. 'I didn't get much sleep, I must admit, but I dropped off when I should have been getting up. Frankie snoozed again, too, after her early bottle. Barney must have got himself off to school.'

'That's why you're still in your pyjamas? Moray's lying doggo?'

'I suppose so. Waiting for the call to rise, maybe.'

'Kettle's boiling; I'll make the tea while you dry Frankie and get her dressed. Then you'd better make yourself decent, before your friend catches you in Barney's cast-offs. Wear something nice today, Tess.'

'Why?'

'You *know* why. He came here specially to see you, didn't he? He's your very first love, even before your dear Gregor, isn't he? The one who hurt you and went away – whom you can't forget?'

Tess managed to get the little vest over Frankie's head. The child thought the process of dressing a big giggle. 'Is it so obvious?' she asked ruefully.

'To another woman, yes. I don't really know Moray, of course, but I'd guess he's definitely aware of the attraction between you, and intends to do something about it, this time around. Ready for your tea?'

'I certainly am! Keep still for a moment, please, Frankie!' Tess buttoned her rompers. 'There! Behind bars for a play while I mix your Farley's rusk.

'Sit down for a minute, have your tea. I'll make Frankie's breakfast.'

'Thanks, Pen, I don't know what I'd do without you.'

'Same here. You and Barney – *Pop* – Frankie: you're like the family Jack and I always hoped for. I intend to make the most of fussing over you all. Now, you haven't commented on my assumption, have you?'

'That's all it is, Pen. Moray's not the marrying kind – though he hints that he's finished sowing his wild oats. Yes, I'm afraid I do feel the same as I did and the worst thing is, he knows it.'

'Why? Why is that so terrible?'

'Because it can't – mustn't come to anything. It's the way it has to be.'

'It's something to do with his father, isn't it? With Millie Mae – Pop didn't tell me the ins-and-outs, but something in the past clouded your two families' friendship. If you love Moray, Tess, you'll find a way. I *know* you will.'

'*Mumma*,' Frankie demanded, banging her rattle on the playpen.

'She's hungry,' Tess said, 'and I really must get dressed. I'm sorry, Penny, there's much more to all this than a family feud. I really wish I could explain things to you, because I believe you'd understand, but I can't. There's still a barrier between Moray and me, although it's an invisible one, as far as he's concerned. But, it's not up to me, you see, to well, pull the plug . . .'

'*Dadda*,' Frankie protested, trying the other word in her vocabulary.

They strolled in the garden which was still Penny's really because she did the planting and weeding. Frankie slept in her pram under the apple tree, and Tess fastened on the fine mesh cover which guarded against stinging insects and cats. Not Moses, though, who kept his distance from drowsy infants. Frankie made him skitter whenever she tried to clutch his fur – she was fascinated by his funny tail, but wisely, he kept his sharp claws sheathed.

Tess wore a sun-top she'd sewn from a remnant of blue cotton, and there was enough left for a triangle worn gypsy style on her head. The top tied in a jaunty bow exposed her pale middle. She felt self-conscious, but Moray complimented her on the outfit. He indicated her midriff. 'Don't get sunburnt.'

They sat on the bench after removing the odd snail. It was overhung with pink mallow, a shady spot, away from the house. Not that Penny would have dreamed of spying on them, Tess thought. An early

121

memory resurfaced of her smaller self escaping from her bed and a scary tale by Roma, to find her parents relaxing here. 'I thought you'd run away,' she wailed. Millie Mae embraced her, smothered her with kisses. 'Darling, you *know* I'd never leave you.'

There being no back to the seat, he slipped his arm casually around her waist and she found herself unable to demur when he lightly caressed the strip of soft, bare skin. It was an exquisite but almost unbearable sensation.

'I want you, Tess,' he said, urgently. His lips brushed the naked nape of her neck. She shivered violently, as if it was cold.

'Want, yes, but you don't *love* me.'

'Who says I don't?'

'I do!'

'You're wrong. I suppose I went on thinking of you as that solemn little girl in a long black coat . . . When I left Scotland, you, I was intent on retrieving my old exciting life: flying, and, yes, I admit it, gorgeous girls, but, you were always at the back of my mind. Don't reject me, as I so cruelly did you. I'll even marry you, if that's what you want.'

'It isn't,' she said forlornly.

'I don't believe you. You don't think I'm a reformed character, is that it?'

'No: I don't know! You didn't ask *Roma* to marry you, did you?'

He hesitated. 'Are you referring to the confession I made last night?'

When she didn't reply, he looked searchingly at her. 'I'm not going to give up, Tess. You never know what tomorrow might bring.'

They didn't have to wait until then, for Pop brought bad news later in the day. 'So this is where you are!' he exclaimed, when he saw Moray. 'They've been frantic at the works, trying to locate you, but I never thought you'd be *here*.'

'Why – what's wrong?' Moray demanded anxiously.

'Leo – your father, collapsed this morning. He's been rushed to hospital; they contacted your sister and she sent for your mother, which is only right. You'll need to leave straight away for Surrey. I'm sorry, Moray, really I am.'

'How serious is it?'

'He's had a severe stroke, that's all I know.'

Within ten minutes, Moray was slinging his bag in the back seat of his car. Tess stood back, with Frankie in her arms, while Pop and Barney saw him off.

He reversed the car, drew alongside Tess. 'I'll be in touch,' he called, over the noise of the engine.

'God bless; *goodbye*,' she said, not sure if he could hear her.

Then he saluted her, and drove away. Fast.

'I'm glad you came,' Jean said to Pop, as they walked away from the graveside, leaving Moray and Sally, supported by her fiancé, Hank, to thank the personnel who had attended the funeral, and who were now returning to the aircraft factory. 'You'll join us, won't you, at the house? Just a small reception for close friends and family, of course, if I still qualify in that way.' She didn't sound bitter, just vulnerable and sad.

He took her arm, his clasp slipping on the silk sleeve of her black dress. The sombre feathers on her hat brushed his face; he was always surprised by how tall she was. 'Of course you do,' he said gently. 'You can't wipe away nearly thirty years together. In a way, that applies to me, too. I guess I'd begun to think of Leo as a friend again – he was a good boss. Yes, I'll stay for an hour or so, for your sake, and his. Then I must go back to work – catch up – before I drive home to Kent for the weekend.'

'I know it's not the time to ask, does this . . . make a difference, to *us*. Pop?'

They went through the kissing gate at the side of the church, taking the short cut to the big house beyond, which fronted the village street. The other mourners were departing through the main gate and they were on their own.

'I'm sorry; the truth is, I don't know.'

'Is there someone else?'

'Why on earth should you think that?'

'I didn't – not until I said it, saw your face.'

'I suppose you could say that, after all this time, I realize if I don't do something soon, I'll be left on my own when Tess and Barney have gone.'

'I don't think Tess will ever leave you, unless you're happily settled.'

'Nor do I. I need to find that special someone, you see, for her sake as well as my own.'

'And that's not *me*, is it?'

'Jean – please; when we were in Scotland – well, for the first time, since Millie Mae, I wondered if we . . . I really feel a great deal for you, you know.'

'But not enough. Oh, don't feel upset – you are dear to me, and always will be, but Leo really was the love of my life, Pop, despite everything.'

'I know. I understand. We'll stay good friends?' he asked.

'I do hope so, yes,' she said, as they turned into drive. But they both knew it was the end of an era.

Moray, pale and taut, poured Pop a generous measure of whisky. 'What happens now?' Pop asked bluntly, as an old friend.

'To Ma? He didn't change his will you know. She'll be very comfortable, no worries, thank God, for the rest of her life. She'll go back to her house – that's entailed in the female line, so eventually it will pass to Sally. I understand that Dad has provided generously for her, too.'

'And you, Moray?'

'I'm to have this house, which I'll sell eventually because I can't afford to run it; anyway, I don't need a place as big as this; and shares in the company, which will carry on under the same management. Money's all tied up, wisely, I suppose. Dad always thought I should make my own way in life, as he did.'

'He could be obstinate: you were his only son, after all.'

'Yes, we didn't always get on, but that doesn't mean I'm not devastated now he's gone.' Moray downed his own drink. 'What I need right now, and I never thought I'd hear myself say it, is a family of my own. It's the wrong time, of course, but when is it right?' he appealed to Pop.

'You're thinking of Tess, aren't you? Don't rush things, boy, that's all I ask. We're not ready to relinquish her yet. And, don't forget, there's Frankie.'

'*Roma!*' Moray said vehemently. 'How can she be so selfish? I'm sorry, I shouldn't have said that, she's your daughter, too.'

'Yes, she's my daughter, too,' Pop repeated slowly. 'I'm proud of them both, and Barney of course, so please don't expect me to take sides, Moray.'

Penny, far from glamorous in a faded old dressing-gown was waiting up for him, kettle steaming. 'Tess went to bed with a tummy ache: I shoo'ed her off with a hot-water bottle, then I saw to the baby, and settled her down, hopefully until the dawn chorus. Barney's staying the night with his friend Ray, hope that's all right? How did it go, Pop? You look really tired.'

'I am. Thanks for being here, Penny, I appreciate that.'

'You'll want to get off to bed.' She bent down, scooped up Moses. 'Not tonight, old feller. He's had a day of it; let's leave him in peace.'

'Don't go. I need to talk.'

She sat down, released the cat. 'Jean?'

'I – we decided to leave things as they were. She's going back to Scotland. It wouldn't have worked – us – we both knew that. She married beneath her, as they say, which made Leo even more deter- mined to prove himself, to succeed in business. Millie Mae and I, well, we were happy with our lot, with each other, with the children, any small successes.

'Driving back here in the dusk, I thought, I'm going home to my family, and that includes you now, Penny. I really am too tired to beat around the bush.'

'Would Millie Mae mind?' she asked obliquely.

'Millie Mae always followed her heart. She'd say not to hesitate.'

'Then we won't,' Penny said softly. 'Would you like me to be with you tonight? It needn't lead to anything more,' she added diffidently. 'That side of it'll take time, for both of us, I believe.'

'We'll get there,' Pop said positively.

'You don't think the kids'll object?'

'They'll wonder why it took me so long to propose.'

'Propose?' she teased. 'You? I rather think it was *me!*'

Then they were actually laughing and shushing one another as they crept off, like bashful young lovers, to bed.

Penny woke with a start. 'Tess'll be bringing your early morning cuppa any moment, now.'

Pop put out a restraining hand. 'I don't imagine she'll be *too* shocked.'

'She will! I don't want her to think badly of me.'

'Lie still. She'll get used to the idea. Anyway, we'll be mister and missus as soon as it can be arranged.' He pulled her to him, cuddled her close.

125

Tess tapped on the door as she always did, opening it almost imme-diately. Her eyes widened when she saw two heads on one pillow. She stood there uncertainly for a moment, then she said, 'I'll get another cup.'

'Tess,' Penny called impulsively 'I'm sorry; we didn't mean to surprise you – it just happened, well, *nothing* really. Anyway, we're going to get wed.'

'You don't have to explain,' Tess said quickly. 'I understand, I really do. And I'm really happy, you know, for both of you. You don't have to rush off, Pen, it's Saturday morning, after all, and I'm going back to bed myself, to make the most of it, while Frankie's still asleep. I'll leave the tray outside the door for you.' She felt as if she was blushing all over.

Tess wept silently, thoroughly dampening her pillow. Pop and Pen, they're right for each other. Maybe it won't be a big romance this time around, but it's still a wonderful outcome to our coming home. But what about me? I can't be with Moray because he is Frankie's real father, and I can't tell him that because not even Roma is aware that I know.

CHAPTER SEVENTEEN

'**K**eep still, Pen,' Tess said, in mock severity. 'You fidget as much as Frankie does when I'm washing her hair.'

They were bending over the tiny bathroom basin in the studio, while Tess lathered Penny's long tresses with Amami shampoo, mixed to a gritty, greyish paste in an old cup.

'I nearly decided to use the henna, but it's years old. I thought my hair might turn out rusty, rather than red.'

'You made the right decision. If you rinse this enough, you get a lovely shine, and a nice fresh smell and, anyway, you have such pretty hair.'

'Even if it's fly-away, eh? Even on my wedding day?'

They could hear Frankie shouting exuberantly in the background. 'Don't worry about her,' Tess said. 'Pop bribed Barney to do the amusing uncle bit, he's flying paper aeroplanes.' She poured over a jug of tepid water.

'Ouch! That's almost cold, Tess.'

'Sorry. No more hot water. There, let's wrap your head in the towel; open your eyes now. Sit down, while I rub your hair. Only three hours to go, Pen.'

'Don't I know it,' Penny said with feeling. 'Think my dress will do?'

'You know it will. You'll be a beautiful bride. Pop will blink because you're wearing purple, but being a mere man he won't realize it's curtain brocade. It really suits you, and I won't clash in my old but best pink dress.' The dress I wore for both Gregor and Moray, she thought.

'Tess, you know there's one thing that makes me feel sad,' Penny put in.

'Millie Mae? She wouldn't want that.'

127

'I know. It's probably too late, you see, for more little Rainbows. Anyway, wouldn't that be embarrassing for you all, particularly Pop? I'm forty-three, Tess. I had a baby once, when Jack and I were first married. Our little boy was still-born and no one seemed able to tell us why. Later, we tried again, but it wasn't to be. When Frankie was born, it brought it all back to me.'

'Oh, Penny, I wish I'd known.'

'No long faces today, Tess! I'm so lucky to have found another good man. What did Roma's telegram say? *Congratulations Granny and Grandpa! we'll be there!*'

'I thought that was a bit cheeky,' Tess smiled.

'I took it to mean they've accepted me, like you and Barney have, and that I'm now Frankie's granny – so you see, there's a baby in my life, after all!'

'Boo!' Roma said, coming up behind Tess as she stared into the mirror. She was immaculate in her uniform, with her hair up and a curled-under fringe.

'Lo, Roma. Seen Frankie yet? Where's Swindon? D'you think I ought to wear a hat? Too bad if you do, my old panama's squashed to bits.'

'Well, you can guess the answer to the first two questions: Frankie saw her dadda and that was it. Bye bye Mumma! As for the hat, well, I wouldn't – it's really windy out, not much September sunshine.'

'Did you want to ask me something?' Tess asked warily.

'Now why should you imagine that?'

'Because I'm the one with the imagination, or so you always say!'

'You're right, of course. I'm about to wheedle. Can Frankie stay in your room tonight? We haven't had much time to ourselves lately. Swindon's been away on a course, and it seems an opportunity for—'

'You don't have to spell it out.'

'And you don't need to sound so cynical; sympathetic would do!'

'All right, I will. Our pink dress – remember?' She wore her own underpinnings these days, she smiled to herself. Although she would always be slightly built, the mirror revealed pleasing curves in the right places. All those home-grown extras, plenty of eggs, provided by Penny to supplement their rations, she supposed gratefully. She was nearer eight stone than seven now – confirmed when she sneaked on the Red Cross scales last week.

'Should I? Tess, isn't this – the wedding – happening in a bit of a rush?'

'I seem to remember you and Swindon surprised us, too.'

'We really like Penny, of course we do, and Pop looks years younger and happy, and he won't need to buy the property back from her now, will he?'

Tess's smile vanished. 'It's their business, Roma, but Pop reminded us that naturally Penny still owns the place. She wants to stay on in the studio flat and feel welcome to come in and out our side as usual; he'll pay rent as he does now and they'll sort the rest out, after the war. Anyway, they'll have privacy in the studio at nights, when Pop's home at weekends.'

'You don't need to give me a lecture.' Roma sounded aggrieved, adding, 'We heard about Leo, of course. Swindon wrote to Jean on our behalf. Pop said Moray came to see you, just before—'

'Come on you two,' Swindon said from the doorway. 'The best man, me, has a damp patch bestowed by an over-excited daughter on the knee of his trousers; Barney's rustling up a nappy. As bride and groom are dressed up, too, Frankie's in the pen and expressing displeasure.'

'I'll see to it,' Tess said, making her escape from Roma's questions. It didn't matter too much about the pink dress, although she wanted to look nice for Pop and Penny, but who else was there to impress?'

The gusty wind billowed skirts, flapped trouser legs, tousled hair, unsettled hats. They emerged from church to threads of sunlight blinking in grey clouds. No bells, the invasion signal, but the wheezing and sighing of an organ attacked by enemies of its own, dust and church mice. After the war, the rector promised, funds would be raised for the organ's long overdue refurbishment. It sounded more like a croaky lullaby than wedding music. At least the church had escaped the raids of 1940, unlike the great church at Lydd.

Pop and Penny held hands in the porch, while Swindon snapped them. Then he joined Roma, Tess, Barney and Frankie for the family group while the rector fiddled with the camera then took a couple of photographs, admonishing them, 'Get the baby to smile! Penny, display your bouquet.'

'Is *that* what it is?' Penny whispered to Pop, but she obediently raised

129

the bunch of mauve Michaelmas daisies so that their sunny yellow centres showed, and tweaked the centre bloom, the last pink rose of summer, hastily plucked from her garden. A petal or two drifted down on to her sensible brown shoes.

They scooted for the motors, as a fierce spattering of rain, which ceased almost as soon as it began, showered them instead of confetti.

The table was ready laid. There were white candles in rainbow candlesticks, tinned salmon sandwiches, courtesy of precious points and under-the-counter tactics by their kind grocer; tomatoes ripened on the windowsill; sausage rolls; Penny's flapjack and a sponge cake dribbling last year's bramble jelly. A solitary strawberry, the very last one from Penny's patch, placed to conceal a bird-peck, decorated the centre of the wedding cake. That was for Frankie.

Barney wound the gramophone, ready to lift the needle when it stuck in a groove. Most of their collection had not survived their moves, but Judy Garland still soared *Over The Rainbow*. Pop put a match to the fire as it was decidedly chilly, then he uncorked a bottle or two of something to warm them up. 'And me?' Barney insisted. 'I don't see why I should drink Frankie's clinic orange juice!' The arrival of this thick syrupy stuff from the US had more-or-less coincided with Frankie's own arrival to their world.

Tess fastened the blackout. She suddenly longed for cindery cheese and seemed to hear the echoes of Millie Mae's voice, saying wasn't that the best treat ever? Pop had not mentioned her today, but she guessed she had been in his thoughts. She caught the lingering look exchanged between Penny and her father; it was easily interpreted. They needed to be alone after all the excitement of the wedding. She was sure now, as she blinked back happy tears that this was a real romance, if a quiet one, between two mature people.

The party ended at ten when Tess took Frankie off to bed at last, and Roma and Swindon closed their door firmly. Only Barney protested, but Pop let him take the wireless into his room, on the promise he would keep the volume low.

They relit the candles and carried them through to the studio. They didn't need, or desire, to switch on the light in the small bed-sitting room.

'Never slept on a put-u-up before,' Pop observed, as he pulled out the couch. Penny took the bedding from the pine box and made up the bed. Then she undressed in a shadowy corner, hanging up the purple wedding frock.

'You looked lovely in that, did I tell you?' Pop asked, turning away discreetly as she donned her night attire.

'No, but I knew you approved.'

He was in bed already. Penny looped her hair round her raised left hand, secured the topknot hopefully with a couple of hair pins. 'There, will I do?' She wore a silky creamy-coloured slip, which left her shoulders and neck bare; she wouldn't tell him it was the petticoat she had worn under her first wedding dress. She had been thrilled to find it still fitted her, banishing the rueful thought, 'blow the salt cellars'!

'Glad to be Mrs Rainbow?' he asked. She didn't look like Millie Mae at all, but there was something about Penny which reminded him of her. Her optimism, her cheerfulness? More than that, her indomitable spirit, he realized.

'You know I am. Shall I blow out the candles?'

'Mmm. Which side d'you like to sleep?'

She giggled. 'Move over . . . on the outside, because I reckon you expect me to make the tea in the morning – Tess has spoilt you.'

He shifted, but not very far. He enfolded her in his warm, strong embrace. Now was – now. To love, to be loved in return, was surely natural, good. The impetuosity of youth was past, but that didn't mean passion was spent.

Moses suddenly sprang from the end of the bed to the windowsill, his good eye luminous in the dark. The soft little sigh didn't appear to emanate from either of them. Maybe the spirit of Millie Mae was leaving: for that particular moment, anyway.

Tess was awakened by the phone. Sighing, she shone her torch on her watch face. Nearly one in the morning, who on earth could it be?

'Tess?' breathed a decidedly tipsy voice. 'Is that you?'

'Moray! Where are you?'

'Confined to base. Why haven't you written?'

'Shush! I did write, you know I did, when Leo—'

'Not since. Tess, you do love me, don't you?'

'You know the answer to that. You're drunk. Don't spoil a lovely day.'

'Two good friends – down in flames – blown to bits – *over there.*'

131

'That's terrible: I'm sorry, Moray. But it won't help, hitting the bottle . . . I must go back to bed, before everyone else wakes up. Please, you mustn't ring again tonight.' She replaced the receiver, hands shaking and sweating.

'Who was calling at this unearthly hour?' Roma said sharply, feeling her way towards the flickering flashlight. 'No one for us, I hope? Surely we can have one night off, even if there is a war on.'

'That's why we're allowed the phone. Wrong number,' Tess mumbled. There was a sudden wail. 'You've disturbed Frankie,' Roma said accusingly.

'I'm sorry, but you can see to her this time, can't you? She's yours, after all. I've had quite enough!'

'Tess, what on earth's wrong?'

'What d'you think? All right, that was Moray.'

'Did . . . he want to speak to me?'

'No! Believe it or not, he believes he's madly in love with *me*, now.'

'He's not the right one for you, Tess, any more than he was for me.'

'Don't you think I know? But, it doesn't make it any easier to bear, especially when I have to reject him, and can't tell him why, when he needs me most. I've let him down. That hurts more than you'll ever know.'

CHAPTER EIGHTEEN

In October, Tess was stricken with a mystery illness. It began with a sore throat and soaring temperature, then a rash and swollen glands. It was several weeks before the doctor diagnosed glandular fever. There was no real treatment: the patient must rest as much as possible, drink water copiously and keep to a light diet. The blinding headaches were treated with aspirin, the hot sweats with cool sponging. There would be a slow recovery period. She found it impossible to concentrate on her writing, or on reading.

Penny moved back into the house to nurse her, to look after Frankie and to keep an unobtrusive eye on Barney. He had transferred Frankie's cot and paraphernalia to Roma's room without being asked, and did his bit when he was home from school, as Penny told Pop, knowing he would feel proud.

Roma and Swindon expressed concern on their next visit, especially when Penny said bluntly that the illness usually struck those who had been under some strain, working too hard.

'You mean, looking after Frankie, I suppose?' Roma asked anxiously.

'Maybe. Mothers do it all the time, of course. Look, I'd be glad to share your daughter's care in future, with your approval. I'll talk to Tess, when I feel she's up to it, but I must admit I've already discussed the situation with Pop.

'You see, the real reason I didn't move in here after we married was because I didn't want Tess to think I was taking over, interfering. I also thought that Barney might feel I was trying to take his mother's place. But we all get on so well together it seems the obvious solution now.' She added tentatively, 'When you next have a longer leave, it might be a good idea if you took Frankie for a few days, so you were on your own for once, as a family.'

Swindon spoke for them. 'I think that's just what we should do. We're both very grateful for all you're doing in the meantime, aren't we, Roma?'

'Yes – thank you, Penny,' Roma said, still bemused by events.

Pop tried to cheer Tess up. 'You know it's called the kissing disease?'

Tess mustered a wry smile. 'Chance'd be a fine thing, Pop, eh?' She was sitting out of bed in the wicker chair, but still cocooned in blankets.

He was serious now. 'Yes, but you've had plenty of upsets, to put it mildly, over the last couple of years. It must have lowered your resistance. Moray wrote, asked me to apologize' for phoning you late at night. When was that?'

'It doesn't matter. I didn't handle it very well. Did he say anything else?'

'He said he'd leave it to you to contact him, if you wanted to see him again. Wait until you're well, I should.' He betrayed his misgivings.

'At this moment, I don't think I'll ever stand up again without coming over all woozy and weak.'

'Christmas is coming,' Pop said, 'and we intend, Pen, Barney and I, to make it a good one, especially for you.'

They missed Frankie, away with her parents for three days, but late on Christmas Eve Pop brought home an unexpected guest from the works.

'This is Nick, life and soul of the works' canteen. He's a bit of an artist – all the girls bring him airletters to illustrate with a sketch of themselves to send to their boys overseas. Nick joined us as a draughtsman earlier this year.'

'Almost my whole history in a couple of sentences,' Nick Nicholson said ruefully. 'Please don't get up; heard a lot about you,' he told Tess. 'Glad you're better.' He reached out to shake her cold hand.

'Thank you.' She regarded their clasped hands. 'You have nice hands,' she blurted out, immediately wondering what on earth had prompted her to make such a remark, even though it was true. He had long, tapering fingers.

'So I'm told by the ladies,' he told her, smiling widely without a trace of embarrassment. 'My one attractive feature, they add rather too quickly.'

She felt at ease after that, because being a few years her senior, of average height, with thick, untidy brown hair, furrowed forehead and snub nose, he was not the type to make a girl's heart miss a beat. More the universal brother, the sort played by Mickey Rooney.

Barney cheered up: he'd said earlier that Christmas wouldn't be much fun without Swindon and Frankie around to liven things up, though he couldn't say the same for Roma who was always telling him off for leaving things around which Frankie could get hold of, now she could stand and wobble-walk a bit.

'You're a writer, so Pop says.' Nick looked directly at Tess and she could tell that he was genuinely interested. There was an unexpected solemnity about those brown eyes belying the cheerful smile.

'She writes girls' stories,' Barney put in. 'And she even gets published!'

'Good for you, Tess,' Nick approved.

'Can you do any card tricks?' Barney asked hopefully.

'Let the poor chap unpack first. You're in our room Nick; hope you won't mind the cat-in-residence. We'll move into Roma's room while they're away.'

When he had gone, Barney asked his father, 'Hasn't he got any family of his own to go to at Christmas?'

'No.' Pop shook his head, kept his voice low.

'Why isn't he in the forces, Pop? He looks fit enough.'

'Things aren't always what they seem; he was turned down by the army. He's doing his bit for the war effort, anyway. Don't go asking him a lot of embarrassing questions will you, Son?'

' 'Course I won't,' Barney said stoutly.

Tess, absorbing this information, only wondered aloud how they would find him a present at this late stage?

'Leave it to me,' said practical Penny. 'Cup and saucer do? Hand-painted by Roma when she was fed up and pregnant, or by me?'

'You know the answer to that one,' Pop told her. 'Wrap it now, before he comes back, eh? Barney, there's a brace of pheasants outside, never mind where I got 'em, or what they cost me, and you and I have a job to do—'

'I can guess.' Barney made a face. 'They need to be drawn and quartered, and I jolly well hope they're not high – but now you won't have to catch one of Pen's hens and wring its neck at dawn.'

'Where did you acquire your finesse, boy?'

'From you, I reckon.' Barney dodged a mock cuff round the the ear.

'Shut the kitchen door,' Tess called after them. 'I don't want to see those birds until they come out of the oven tomorrow!'

'Oh, on your own?' Nick sat at the other end of the settee. 'You look tired.'

'I don't know why. Penny hasn't let me do a thing, today.'

'I understand how you feel: when I was in hospital as a youngster with TB, anything out of the ordinary exhausted me.'

'But you got better in the end?'

He tapped his chest. 'I learned to cope, to pace myself . . .' That warming smile was directed at her again. 'So will you. You'll recover fully, I'm sure.'

'Thank you,' she said simply. She looked at the clock. 'I don't believe it! Almost eleven, I haven't been up so late in ages.'

'Don't go yet,' he said, 'We're just getting acquainted.'

'What do you see, when you look at me?' An impulsive question: would he think she was fishing for compliments, when she really needed reassurance?

'I see an attractive girl, twenty years old – Pop let me in on that little secret. Pale, because you've been ill, and your eyes have dark rings round them, but they're green at the moment because of your jumper, and you wouldn't look right with anything but auburn hair. I sense you're unhappy, despite your loving family. I don't expect you to say why, until we know each other better.'

'Are we going to do that?'

'We are. I know a real friend-to-be when I meet one, don't you?'

'I have to admit I do.'

'I didn't say boyfriend, just friend. What we both need right now, isn't it?'

'I do. We do,' she said.

Early on Christmas morning, Roma and Swindon lay in their comfortable hotel bed in Sevenoaks, with Frankie, asleep at last after the first bottle of milk of the day, lying contentedly between them. Her head rested on Roma's bared breast; plump and pearly white in the shaded light.

'Undo your buttons,' Swindon had suggested, 'or they might mark her cheek.'

Roma stroked her baby's dark hair. Her lower lip suddenly trembled.

'I believe I'm coming over all maternal at last. D'you think she'll forgive me, later on, for leaving her, pursuing my own interests all these months?'

'Don't reproach yourself, darling; it's all been in a good cause, surely.'

'It wasn't just that – I wanted to prove to you that I . . .' she faltered.

'Didn't just marry me because you were expecting another man's child?'

'Swindon! We don't know for sure.'

'Be honest with yourself, Roma. We both know it. Darling, don't cry, you'll wake her up. Nothing's changed, no one else needs to know. Frankie's my daughter, and I love her. Just as I love you. Here, let me lay her back in the cot. She doesn't realize there's a stocking full of surprises hanging from the bed knob, eh? You might get another couple of hours' sleep yet.' His hand lightly brushed her breast as he lifted Frankie up. 'If that's what you really want . . .'

'I love you: it didn't take me long to realize that, did it? Isn't that what you deserve to hear?' she said softly. If you repeated something enough it just had to be true, she thought. It was a habit of hers from childhood.

'That's all I want to know,' he said.

'I've got something to confess myself,' he whispered later, as Frankie began to stir. 'I've been asked – promised, to confirm acceptance when we go back – to return to Canada in the spring to train more pilots there . . . 1943 is going to be a year of preparation. I hesitated, because I don't know how long I'd be away. I don't have any option, really. I can't bear to leave you and Frankie behind.'

'You don't have to,' she said instantly. 'I don't care what strings have to be pulled, we'll come with you; we can put the past behind us then, can't we?'

'You've made my day—'

'Then hooray! Happy Christmas!' She felt awash with sheer relief. Surely any disturbing thoughts of Moray would fade away, along with the memory of the shaft of jealousy she had felt when Tess said that he loved *her* now.

*

'Come on, Tess,' Penny coaxed, 'just a spoonful of Christmas pud.'

'Plenty of carrots; you'll be able to see in the dark,' Barney teased. 'If she doesn't want it, I'll have her share, Penny.'

'In that case, I'll have it,' Tess told him. 'Or you'll turn into Billy Bunter.' She had given him one of the *Greyfriars* books this Christmas. Then she giggled, because these days her brother was a long streak of lightning.

'You haven't laughed like that for ages,' Pop approved.

'Make the most of today's feast,' Penny reminded them. 'We've enough meat for sandwiches tonight, then it's tinned ham, thanks to Nick, tomorrow.'

'All I could prise out of my landlady. I believe she counts the corn-flakes for breakfast. We lodgers call her Minnie Meanie. Poor old girl, we shouldn't really, she has to battle with the rations, after all.'

'My landlady's very kind,' Pop began.

'Not too kind I hope,' Penny put in.

'She doesn't make me as comfortable as you do, Pen.'

'Good! Who's for coffee, courtesy of Swindon?'

'May I have mine in my new rainbow cup?' Nick asked.

'Why not! Barney, Pop, coming to help? You can start the washing up whilst I watch the coffee bubbling.'

'Last mouthful,' Nick encouraged Tess when the others went out.

She put down her spoon with a clatter. 'I can't—'

'You're crying. Why? You were laughing a few moments ago.'

'I was remembering Christmas in Scotland two years ago, when—'

'When your fiancé was home? Pop told me about him, too.'

'Barney fell out of a tree and winded himself, and Gregor ran up the hill to us, and we didn't expect to see him, you know – and he'd knitted me a lovely warm scarf while he was at sea, and we walked along the cliff top all buffeted by the wind. But it wasn't perfect because there was someone else, too . . .'

'You still feel guilty, don't you?' he asked quietly. 'You mustn't. You have to let those regrets go, Tess. I lost a girl I loved, too.'

'Were you married?' she wiped her eyes.

'No. I was a fool, I hesitated. I'd known her all my life; we were brought up in a children's home together; then, we thought of each other almost as brother and sister. Our feelings changed while I was in the sanitorium, which prompted Dawn to become a nurse. When we both qualified in our chosen professions, just before the war, we talked about marriage, but I held back.'

'Did she go away?'

'No. We stayed good friends She was killed in the blitz. We missed a precious time together, before— You have to forgive yourself, let the past go.'

'Still at the table?' Penny asked. 'Coffee's come.'

'Thank you,' Tess said, to both of them.

'We're giving you plenty of time to adjust to it,' Roma said defensively, at a family meeting a month later. She had come on her own this time.

'I know, but it's still a bit of a shock. We're glad for you, aren't we, Pop, but have you thought how all this will affect Frankie?' Tess looked anxious.

'Oh, she's easy-going, you know she is – much more like Swindon than me! We'll be staying with his oldest sister to begin with; she's used to kids, got six of her own. I'll be working, that's the only way I could get out there. They're turning a blind eye to Frankie coming too.

'You'll all miss her, of course you will, we know that. But Tess can get on with her writing, Penny with her pots, and Barney won't need to fear for his model aeroplanes and Pop—'

'Pop'll be lost without his little girl,' he said.

'We'll be back, you know we will, and she won't forget you.'

Tess looked at the cot, stripped of bedclothes. She picked up a bib from the floor, held it against her face; it smelled of baby, of Frankie. 'Maybe we should give it to someone in need, as Roma suggested,' she said to Penny. Not the little crib though, she thought, that was Penny's treasure.

'No, we won't get rid of things, Tess – you see, well, they might be in use again sooner than you think.'

Tess looked at her, eyes wide with surprise. 'Pen, you don't mean—?'

'I do. Haven't had a chance to tell Pop yet, keep mum, as they say, eh?'

'I will! When?'

'Not quite sure; September, probably. Doctor pooh-poohed my suspicions at first. He confirmed it yesterday, says I'll need to take extra care at my age, and I have to face the fact that the baby – I don't have to spell it out, do I? Even if it was affected in some way, we'd all still love it, wouldn't we?'

'Of course we would! Pen, how wonderful!'

'You're not embarrassed, are you?'

'Not at all. Just thrilled for you and Pop – and over the moon at the thought that the crib will be occupied by a new little *Rainbow*, this time.'

CHAPTER NINETEEN

Pop didn't say much after Penny imparted the news in the privacy of their room, the following weekend, but, hurt at the remark 'I imagined we were past all that', she took it that he was more dismayed than delighted.

'You might be, but I'm not!' she flashed back.

'Pen! I didn't mean—'

'Didn't you?' She marched out, adding, 'Supper's ready.' You couldn't call it a tiff, more a catastrophe, she thought, sniffing loudly as she ladled out the stew in the kitchen. If I had an 'added ingredient', well, I'd add it to his plate. That actually made her laugh. She was so rarely angry, she'd get round him, make him believe it was all his idea to have a baby, eh?

He rustled his paper after supper, ostensibly reading, while Penny silently signalled to Tess, 'D'you think he's all right?'

She began clearing the table. 'Your turn with the dish mop, Barney.'

'What's up?' Barney asked bluntly. 'Have you and Pop had a quarrel?'

Penny put the plates down with a clatter, dashed from the room.

Pop lowered the paper at last. 'You've upset her.'

'No, *you* have, Pop!' They glared at each other.

Pop rose. 'Had a shock, that's all – it'll take time to sink in.'

'What will?'

'Penny's – going to have a baby, Barney.'

'Gosh!'

'What exactly does that mean?'

'It means – it'll be golly-gosh if it's a boy! I always wanted a brother.'

'Pop,' Tess urged, 'go after her, tell her.'

'I know what to say. I've had some experience, after all.'

Penny was curled up on her couch. 'Millie Mae,' she wept aloud. 'Help me! please.' Then Pop sat down heavily beside her, gathering her up in his arms.

'I'm sorry, Pen, it was so unexpected – an old buffer like me.'

'And me!' She clung to him. 'But we weren't too old, were we, to start a baby, and who cares what others think – apart from family – and I want it.'

'I want it, too,' he said. 'Isn't that all that matters?'

She didn't need to say it this time, anyway she couldn't because they were too busy making up, and being old buffers didn't come into it at all.

Nick spent a week with them in June. When Penny was resting in the afternoons, her only concession to pregnancy, he and Tess went walking, where defences permitted, or sat in the garden, among the weeds, as Penny ruefully pointed out, flourishing now she couldn't bend and touch her toes.

Barney monopolized their guest in the evenings, and Nick didn't seem to mind. He couldn't impress with flying stories, only general aircraft design, and then nothing specific because of the nature of his work; but he really was quite an artist, as Pop said. His lively, lifelike sketches entertained them all.

'I must frame that one of Moses stalking some poor little creature in the long grass,' Penny said. 'How about a Moses design for my mugs, Nick?'

'Give him matching eyes,' Barney suggested, 'or you'll frighten the customers away.'

'I can't catch the essence of your colouring in 3B pencil,' Nick sighed to Tess, tearing off the latest attempt from his pad.

'Don't throw it away – I'll post it to Frankie, so she won't forget me.'

'Who could ever do that?' He winked. 'Your turn, Penny. Pop said I was to be sure to draw you, to pin up among the spanners at the works.'

'Not like this, surely?' Penny plucked at her smock, streaked with paint.

'Particularly like that.'

'Oh well,' Penny looked pleased. On an impulse she pulled the pins from her hair, 'Will I do? Or do I look like the wild woman of the woods?'

'You look beautiful, Pen – big and beautiful – honestly,' Tess said sincerely. It was true: Penny's angles had filled out and she carried all before her proudly.

'Never mind big; draw me, Nick, I can't sit still for long, you know that!'

Tess, Nick and Barney went to the Saturday night hop, rounding off a lazy week, as he put it, with a lively full stop.

It gave Pop and Penny an opportunity to spend some time together, for baby-talk – he was still a bit bashful in that respect in company. They sat close together on the sofa, and Penny tried to knit despite the distraction of Pop's hand resting gently on her tumultuous tummy.

'What a kick!' he marvelled. 'Reminds me of Barney before he was born – Millie Mae was sure he was a boy. Sorry, love, that was tactless.'

'I didn't poke you with my needles, did I? I don't mind, really. I've always felt the spirit of Millie Mae here. If it's a girl, shall we name it for her?'

'It's a boy,' Pop was positive. 'And you can choose his name, just as she did with Roma, Tess and Barney.'

'My first little son, he would have been Jack, for his father—'

'Jack, then?' he offered generously, in turn.

'No, I was going to say, how about Paul? Goes with Penny and Pop.'

'So long as you don't insist on Percy for his second name!'

'I just thought, Jack was your age when our – and, here you are, with your eldest daughter married, with a baby herself . . .' her voice trailed off.

'Mmm?' he prompted.

'He – he wasn't too interested in that side of married life. I gather his first wife, who died before we met, put a damper on it. Oh, he was sad about the baby, but he accepted the loss better than me. I was free to help him in the business, he liked that, just the two of us. It was different to the way I feel for you, but I did care for him very much. I just want to say, I feel so blessed to have you, your lovely family; this unexpected second chance, your baby—'

'*Our* baby, Pen. Yours and mine.'

It was noisy in the hall. Outside, it was a lovely summer's evening; inside, the pianist thumped out the latest tunes with a limp Craven A seemingly glued to her lower lip and her hat askew on tight curls peeping through a holey hairnet. Barney and his pals scoffed most of the lemonade and provided percussion with spoons, a tribal drum brought back long ago from Africa by the vicar's missionary father, washboard and dolly stick and occasional squeezes of an old car horn, which evoked cries of '*That's it, boy!*' from the stamping dancers.

Tess, in the pink dress, giggled her way through the *Paul Jones*, captured by schoolboys, a solitary soldier, and older men dodging their better halves on duty behind the urns and serving rock cakes, which lived up to their name.

She whirled at last into Nick's arms. 'Gotcher!' he said, with satisfaction. 'I nearly got knocked down in the rush!'

'Phew!' she said, as the pianist riffled along the keys to show that it was refreshment time, no tea for her, thank you, something a bit stronger than that. 'Fancy a cuppa?'

'Fancy a breath of air: shall we sit outside for ten minutes?'

They nipped out of the fire door, at the rear of the hall where there was a bench. A scuffle in the bushes beyond, then a couple emerged sheepishly. Pretending not to see them, they inspected the splintery seat. No roses here, just an odorous flowering currant.

'I've never been to a real dance, with a real band,' she confided. 'See? I'm not much out of breath: I'm not on the mend, I'm mended!'

'What could be more real than this? We're having fun, aren't we?'

'Got a hanky? I've blown in mine, and I need to mop my forehead.'

'Let me do it.' He carefully applied a clean cotton square to her damp brow.

The sky was darkening; pinpricks of silver stars appearing. He cupped her face with his smooth, sensitive hands, looked at her thoughtfully.

'Just friends, you said,' she reminded him softly.

'That was six months ago. I didn't reckon on—'

'Being stirred? Nor did I.'

'Still hankering after *him*? The other one, I mean.'

'We – didn't – did you?' she blurted out.

'No.'

'Do you regret it?'

'Does it matter now?' he asked.

'No. I've accepted that's how it was for us. You can kiss me. I'm not

144

promising anything, Nick, I can't.'

'You don't have to. I'm patient. I'll wait.'

I can trust him, she thought, as she slid her arms tentatively around his neck. I reckon sly old Pop had just this in mind when he brought Nick home that first time. Who knows where this will lead to? *But not yet.*

A roll on the drums, the door opened and Barney peeked round at them.

' "Ladies Excuse Me", Tess – have you had enough of what you're doing?'

'Brothers!' Tess said with feeling. 'Who'd have 'em?'

September: Penny was, as she laughed, making her nest. She and Pop had taken over the larger bedroom, and the crib was ready, just as it had been for Frankie, twenty months before. Penny wasn't having a home birth, in view of her past history and her age, and would go to hospital when the time came.

'Ridiculous,' she said to Tess, one morning, with less than a week to go. 'Look how well I am.' They were checking the contents of the baby basket: cotton wool, zinc and castor-oil ointment, Vinolia baby soap and talc, nappy pins, tiny, soft-bristled hair brush, when they heard the rattle of the letter box.

'Letter from Roma,' Tess called out, retrieving it. She read it out:

Waiting for news of that baby! Meanwhile, hope this doesn't come as too much of a shock, we have a new baby, too! Her name is Evelyn (Evie for short) and she arrived on 9 September, three days ago, in the base hospital. I had my suspicions that I was pregnant again (though the very last thing we intended) before we left for Canada, but, of course, I kept quiet about it, or we, Frankie and me that is, would have been told the trip was off. I didn't even tell Swindon until I was almost four months gone, and I played my part so convincingly that they refused to believe me at work at first, and said I was in line for promotion!

Hope you are not too cross we kept this a secret. Anyway, I didn't want to upstage you, Penny. May your labour be like mine, swift and easy this time. Swindon says he can't believe his luck – two beautiful daughters and a gorgeous wife (I had to prompt him to add that) when not much more than two years ago he had no hopes in that direction at all!

I wish I could pass Evie over to you to hold and admire; she's not much like Frankie – what little hair she has is very fair (or tinged with red?!) except for the big, blue eyes. Frankie isn't too sure if she approves of this little thing who has taken Mummy away from her, but she'll come round, and Swindon wangled leave so he could look after her himself.

So it looks as if we will be in Canada for quite some time yet, maybe even until after the war, maybe eventually for good – I love living here – so who knows? Will keep you posted with pictures and news!

This time, I'm going to do the mothering bit, because I want to, and I'm ready for it, you see.

Love you lots, from us four,

Roma, Swindon, Frankie and little Evie.

'There goes my moment of glory!' Penny smiled ruefully. 'What d'you think about Roma's little surprise, Tess?'

'I really don't know what to say!' What did she think? Trust Roma to mention so casually that they might stay in Canada for good. Now, there was nothing to stop her seeing Moray again, except that she and Nick were sort of walking out together and this time she knew she had the family's full approval.

146

CHAPTER TWENTY

Barney held the baby and remarked nonchalantly. 'They improve, don't they? Well, Frankie did. Anyway, he's a boy and I'm glad he hasn't got the Rainbow hair; you don't know how I've suffered with *that.*'

'I do,' Tess said. 'My go, Barney, I think.'

'You can have him, he's wrinkling his face, that means he's going to cry.'

'I'll walk him up and down the room then, OK, Penny?' Tess held the baby against her shoulder, feeling the warmth of his face nuzzling her neck.

Penny nodded. 'I can trust you to do that, eh?' She struggled up on her pillows, wincing at warning twinges. She was still shaky.

Pop put out a restraining hand. 'Lie still, Pen, you know what the hospital said – they only let you come home because they needed the bed.'

He had stayed with Penny until the actual birth, when he was firmly escorted from the labour room by the midwife. It seemed a very long time to him, before the call came, '*It's a boy!*' Pop was allowed to see his wife and baby for two minutes, before he was banished again while Penny was well and truly stitched-up. His new son had been in a hurry on the last lap, it seemed.

Almost seven pounds, young Paul was quite different in appearance to his older children when newborn. Pop pronounced, 'Looks just like you, Pen darling.' Most importantly, the baby was fine.

'Come on, Barney, Penny must be weary after the journey,' Tess said tactfully, handing the baby back. She realized she missed Frankie still.

'If I was twenty years younger, I'd be up and about,' Penny sighed.

'Make the most of the next few days,' Pop said wisely. 'I intend to; I saved my holiday for this, after all.' He stretched beside her.

'Have you got your shoes on?'

'Slippers. Anyway, who cares? I'm sleeping in here tonight, too, whatever Nurse says – who's paying for her services after all?'

'Did – did you do that, with Millie Mae?'

He nodded. 'I wanted – *want*, to be close to the baby, like you. I want to look after you both while I can, until Tess takes over.'

'I don't want Tess to take over,' she said vehemently.

Startled, he looked at her. 'I meant, surely you'll be glad of her help?'

'Of course I will. Don't take this the wrong way, Pop. She needs to be given a gentle push in a short while, and told to go off and do what *she* wants to do, while she's young – that's still possible even in these times, isn't it?'

'You mean, get married, have a family of her own?'

'Perhaps, but not yet. She has to find the right person first, you know.'

'What about Nick?'

'She may have other ideas.'

'He's a good chap; he'd look after her.'

'Is that enough? She's looked after others herself, since she was a child; that habit may be hard to break. Anyway, loving someone and having them love you, is what most of us aspire to, isn't it? Like us.'

'I advised her once not to fall in love with love, Penny.'

'Didn't you really mean, with Moray Tann?'

'Women!' he said fondly. 'You know all the answers.'

'*Come and collect your twenty-first birthday present in person,*' Aunt Peg wrote to Tess in November. '*We've time for visitors now we're retired. Ida hasn't been too well. We often talk of the happy times with you and Barney.*'

'If Peg says Ida isn't too well, she's pretty poorly,' Tess told Penny.

Penny was nursing the baby, after his bath. Sometimes Tess felt like an interloper, seeing this. Because he was breast fed, she was not as involved with him as she had been with Frankie. He was Penny's baby, and he would be her only one; help must be unobtrusive, or it could be construed as interfering.

'You should go, before the weather gets bad,' Penny said, gently dabbing at the baby's mouth. 'Stay a few days, eh?'

'Maybe.' Tess thought, Pen can manage perfectly well, and Barney's there at nights. 'We didn't see our time there, in the same way,' she added.

'I understand. You missed your home, Pop and Millie Mae, still.'

'I know.' She made up her mind. 'That doesn't mean to say I would-n't enjoy being in town for a bit, even if there's not much on offer in the shops.'

'Send a telegram, then, say you'll go. Why not tomorrow, Friday?'

'Nick's coming, with Pop, remember? Nick's out of petrol.'

'Ring Pop tonight; he'll give him a message. Tell Nick to catch the train to Bromley on Saturday, spend the day together there.'

'You've made my mind up for me, but expect me back for my birth-day the following weekend! I'll bike down to the post office right now.'

Peg looked much the same, hastily divesting herself of the bottle-green overall, which Tess remembered her wearing behind the counter in the shop.

The aunts still lived in the flat above, and that, too was unchanged: the furniture in its place, the airer draped with steaming linen.

'Here she is, Ida,' Peg said. 'All grown up, our little girl, as you can see.'

Tess hoped that she didn't reveal her shock, as she greeted Ida. Both aunts had been big women, but Ida appeared to have shrunk, her face drained of the high colour Tess recalled. The wavering smile, her obvi-ous immobility, the appeal in the red-rimmed eyes told Tess what Peg had not. Ida had suffered a stroke.

'She's so pleased to see you,' Peg said gruffly. 'Tell her all your news, while I make the tea. You can hear and understand all right, can't you, Ida?'

Tess held Ida's cold hand and talked about Pop, Penny, young Paul; about Roma and family in Canada; how well Barney was doing at school. She babbled on, until Peg motioned her to move by the fire, while she fastened a napkin round her sister's neck and helped her to drink her tea. She mopped her mouth as gently as Penny did with her baby.

'And what about you, Tess? You've got a suitor, so Pop hinted, last time he called, before Ida had her funny turn.'

'I suppose Pop meant Nick – he's a good friend, that's all, Aunt Peg.'

'That's what I used to call my young man who went off to fight the Boers. Our dad made sure he was no more than that as I was the one to stay at home. Maybe I'd have rebelled if Bob had come back, but we'd lost Mother by then, our sister Mary married Pop's father, Ida was at school and Dad needed my help in the shop. When poor Mary died in childbirth, we took little Percy – Ida couldn't become a teacher. Time slipped by. Don't let it happen to you, Tess.'

Ida was trying to say something. Peg patted her cheek, removed the cup. 'What's that, dearie? She's agreeing with me. Tess, you're free to live your own life now Pop's married and Barney's almost off hand.'

'You always said I had to take care, my health—'

'We were over-anxious, I suppose: it was a good excuse not to let you venture far afield. We weren't used to girls of your generation, with much more freedom than we had, at that age. You children had run a bit wild on the marsh and you might have become wilful, like Roma. But now – seize the moment, as they say, Tess!'

The advent of the steam railway changed Bromley from a market town into a thriving suburb, with the imposing Royal Bell hotel, embellished with leather strapwork, in the High Street; historic buildings like the almshouses with their iron gates bearing the date of the Great Fire of London, mingled with the new.

Tess, with the aunt's generous gift of coupons – 'We've got a good stockpile of clothes; anyway, we don't go out,' and £20 counted out from the old black cash box, went shopping for a special outfit.

There it was, on a mannequin in the plate-glass window in a big store, among the utility clothes with their military styling – a back-less, long taffeta dress, halter-necked, in a striking shade of tangerine. A dress for dancing on a sprung floor with a real band, not on splintery boards to an out-of-tune piano. Too small for most of the young ladies who coveted it, as the vendeuse confided, infected by Tess's excitement, when the dress fitted. It came with its own half petticoat, and the top was shaped cunningly to eliminate the need for a brassiere. A drawn thread or two, from all those strugglings-into, and a mark you'd need to look hard to see, meant the dress was a bargain.

It was not at all what Tess had intended to buy, and eight guineas was still a great deal to pay. When would she get the chance to wear it? It went to her head, for in a happy daze she purchased silver dancing shoes, then went to the jewellery counter to try on thin gilt bangles. There was just enough birthday money left to buy a sensible costume for the cold months ahead.

She rushed back to the aunts' place to see if they approved, anxious that they might advise her to go back to the store to say she'd changed her mind.

'Ida says, try it on, show us,' Peg said, 'then you must hurry to the station to meet your Nick: we're having boiled ham and pease pudding in his honour.'

'You don't think . . .' Tess ventured, twirling so they could see how the skirt swirled. She hoped they wouldn't be shocked at the expanse of back revealed.

'Hang it in my wardrobe,' Peg said gruffly. 'He may not know it, but your Nick is going to take you out for a meal and dancing tonight, in the best hotel, and if he can't afford it, we'll pay. He can stay the night, if he'd like, in Barney's old box room. We want to see if he's the one.'

Tess kissed them both impulsively. 'He's really nice, but I don't know about that! Your plans for this evening are exactly right. I hope he agrees!'

'He hasn't any option. Look at the time – get going, Tess!'

Get going, Tess mused: that's just what I intend to do from now on! Who would have thought of the aunts as fairy godmothers? But they are. Millie Mae would approve: it's just her kind of dress.

The dress was not wholly revealed until she left her coat in the cloak-room. Nick looked up, startled, as she came towards him, and then he indicated his own attire ruefully. 'You deserve more than my best suit. You'll cause a sensation in that frock, Tess! No wonder Aunt Peg insisted we come here.'

'You don't mind, d'you? The aunts—'

'I know, they would have contributed to the cost. It's very generous of them, but I can afford a treat like this once in a while. Take it; we're celebrating your birthday a bit early, eh?'

They ate a glistening fish mousse, waxy potatoes dotted with butter and sprinkled with parsley, apple tart and cream and drank bitter black coffee from tiny cups. The nice waitress apologized for the lack of choice, but Tess appreciated the linen tablecloth, the handwritten menu, the single glass of red wine poured into sparkling crystal.

For a while they watched the other diners rise, take the floor to the nostalgic music provided by the band of elderly but accomplished musicians on the dais. Nick asked, 'Care to dance, Tess?'

'Thank you for asking me, yes,' she answered demurely.

'As you know, I'm not the world's greatest dancer,' he said, sweeping her boldly into the dancing area. It was a waltz; both were relieved at that.

'Well, you don't tread on my toes,' Tess returned.

'Who taught you to dance?'

'Actually it was Roma. She forced me to practise steps with her when she was in her teens. I took the male part, but I was so much shorter I had my view cut off by her bosom – she was all curves even in those days,' she giggled.

'You're not so bad yourself.' He slackened his hold across her back. 'I should be wearing gloves – sorry – it's warm in here, my hands keep slipping.'

'Don't be sorry!' The wine had relaxed her.

'I was going to wait until your birthday. It seems the opportunity to—'

'Ask me to marry you, Nick?'

'Yes. You'll turn me down, of course?'

'I'm not sure . . .' The music ended with a clash of cymbals. 'If I said yes, I'd want a long engagement, I do know that. I've decided, you see, to look for a job, there must be *something* I can do for the war effort.'

'You'll be leaving home?' he asked, pulling out her chair at their table.

'Probably. I haven't said anything to the family yet, so don't you tell.'

'No, of course not. Tess – I'm really fond of you.'

'I'm fond of you, too. I'm asking for more time, that's all.'

'*Tess?*' a voice said. 'I thought it must be you, but I certainly didn't expect to see you here.'

Moray Tann stood there, with a beautiful blonde girl in a black dress.

'Moray!' Tess exclaimed.

Nick rose, held out his hand. 'Nick Nicholson.'

'Moray Tann. May I introduce you to my fiancée, Sylvia Field? Sylvia, this is a family friend, Tess Rainbow.'

'Nice to meet you, Tess,' Sylvia said. 'We'll join you if we may.'

'Of course,' Nick said. 'Have you eaten?'

'We're just here for drinks and dancing. Sylvia's in the WAAF; we're on a weekend pass visiting her parents in Hays Common – they were playing bridge this evening, so they told us to scram.'

'They didn't put it like that, darling,' Sylvia smiled.

The band struck up with a smooth foxtrot. Nick made a rueful face at Tess. 'Waltzes, quicksteps, old-time stuff, that's about my limit.'

'Why don't you dance with Tess?' Sylvia prompted Moray.

'D'you realize this is the first time we've danced together?' he asked, as he guided her awkwardly because of his stiff leg, through the complicated sequences of the dance.

Don't let him realize I'm trembling, Tess prayed.

'I couldn't believe it when I saw you, all sophisticated. We should be gliding to 'Tangerine' – thigh to thigh, so to speak – damn my leg.'

'You need a split skirt for Latin dancing,' she said primly.

'I did try to get in touch with you, Tess: old Pop put the barriers up.'

'You got over your disappointment eventually, I see.'

'Sylvia's fun.'

'You're engaged.'

'Neither of us has mentioned marriage, though.'

'*Still* not committed!'

'You sound bitter. You couldn't expect me to wait around for ever. *You* obviously haven't. Seems a good chap.'

'He is.' She resisted his attempt to draw her closer.

'Pop approves?'

'Yes.'

'Then I hope you'll be very happy. Here we are, our table.'

She saw Nick off at the station, hanging on to him until the last minute.

'Hey,' he observed, 'does this mean you've made up your mind?'

'Nick, ask me again next weekend.'

'You're still carrying a torch for Moray Tann, aren't you?'

'It's too late, Nick. He's engaged, after all.'

'D'you know what Sylvia told me, when you were dancing? That she was aware of your existence – Moray's mother thought she should know. Sylvia said, "I believe he's still in love with her, and she feels the same way, doesn't she?" And I, well, I just didn't know how to reply . . . Whistle's about to blow, Tess.' He hugged her tightly to him. 'Just remember I care for you, too.'

CHAPTER TWENTY-ONE

Four days, she thought, when she woke on Monday morning: I've got four days to find employment, so I can go home on Friday with something positive to impart. She'd confide in Aunt Peg, get her backing.

'What about the General Hospital?' Peg scraped butter on and almost off her toast. 'You ought to use any experience—'

'Oh, Aunt Peg! Rolling a few bandages, learning first aid, how to treat shock; it takes years of training to become a nurse, though I *was* considering it, before—' She broke off. Before Roma asked me to look after Frankie.

'Compassion: you've plenty of patience, Tess. There must be jobs in hospitals, not just nursing, where those qualities would count. What other accomplishments do you have, eh?'

'A way with words? Writing's still my passion, but I feel guilty I'm cutting myself off from all that's happening in the world right now. These days they're looking for practical people, not those who let their imagination run away with them, as Millie Mae used to say about me.'

'Who took on her sister's baby? Isn't that practical enough? That protective nature of yours, Tess, would enable you to look after the elderly as well as the young. Get going, my girl. Time I saw to dear old Ida, I reckon.'

'General health?' the senior nurse interviewing her asked.

Tess didn't hesitate. 'Good,' she replied. She brushed away the memory of how ill she had been a year ago; surely that didn't count?

'Not afraid of hard work?'

'No.'

'You'll forgive me for being blunt, but you are not pregnant now, or likely to be, during the next few months?'

'No, I'm not married,' Tess stated decisively.

'You and I both know that these things happen, regardless of marriage lines. We need dedicated staff, continuity. Still "no"?'

'Yes.'

Sister tapped the form Tess had filled in. 'You were ill quite often as a child, I see. The heart murmur doesn't appear to cause you any significant problems. The doctor who conducted your routine medical here believes that you are not likely to keel over at moments of stress. You've handled family responsibilities with maturity. I'll be frank: we're not sure you would have the physical capacity to be a nurse, however determined you are. I see that you registered as required, for essential work in the past, but were exempted. Still, your health has obviously improved and your circumstances have changed.

'We have decided to offer you a trial period as a ward maid; in many ways, just as demanding a position. If you prove to have the stamina for that, well – but I can't promise anything, you understand. What do you say?'

'I'll take the job. Thank you!'

'When can you start?'

'The week after next? Would I be able to live-in?'

'Crowded quarters. Could you stay with your aunts, I wonder?'

'I'd . . . rather be independent, Sister.'

'Then I'm sure we could fit you in somewhere. Any more questions?'

'Is this considered essential work?'

'It most certainly is. It doesn't confer the same status as nursing, of course. I believe you'll do well, Miss Rainbow. Well, good luck!'

'You'll wear it for our little celebration tonight?' Penny jiggled the baby as Tess held the folds of bright material to her, so that Penny could get the effect. The colour seemed to attract Moses, staring inquisitively from his windowsill perch.

'It's hardly warm enough for November blasts; I suppose I was too impulsive,' Tess said ruefully.

'My cashmere shawl, that would do it! And a brooch to keep it in place at the front. You're only twenty-one once, Tess, and it's just what I would have chosen at your age, and it's a Millie Mae sort of dress, isn't it?'

'That's just it. Can't you picture Roma in this, too?'

'She'd burst out of it!' said Penny candidly. 'Pop'll love it, so will Nick—'

'He's seen it already. He took me out on the town and we danced and dined – not at a British restaurant either!'

'How romantic!'

'It was, until Moray turned up at the hotel out of the blue.'

'Oh, Tess . . .'

'He had someone with him, too. Her name's Sylvia. They look well suited.' How banal that sounded, she thought.

'Then?'

'We danced, and Moray paid me extravagant compliments to make me blush, then he said he hoped I'd be very happy with Nick, and that was that.' Then: 'Why can't I shut him out of my life, *why*?'

'Pop and I were hoping for an announcement tonight.'

'Sorry to disappoint you. I have plans for the future, which I'll tell you all when Pop and Nick are here; I'm going to need your support, Pen, please.'

Pop couldn't hide his dismay. 'Why couldn't you apply to the Cottage Hospital, near to home?'

Penny busied herself with repinning Tess's shawl with the brooch with which Nick had presented her on his arrival: a piece of glowing amber, set in filigree silver. 'Much nicer than my old Woolworth one, eh? Pop, be happy for Tess; it's her choice.' She gave her husband one of her expressive looks: 'enough said Pop', but which he chose to ignore.

'I want to do this, before the war ends – the Italians have surrendered—'

'It's not the end by a long chalk,' Pop said heavily, 'I know, having been involved last time. What d'you think, Nick? Or is this a surprise to you, too?'

Nick was perched on the arm of Tess's chair. He gave her shoulder a brief caress, then let his hand rest there, reassuringly.

'I had an inkling . . .'

'Thank you, Nick. For that, and for this, it's lovely.' She touched the brooch, then reached up impulsively to kiss him. He smelled pleasantly of shaving soap.

Barney nudged Pop. 'You'll have to get used to the idea that if the war goes on, as you keep saying it will, I could be joining the RAF in a couple of years' time, and you won't be able to say no, because you did exactly the same in the Great War, didn't you? You even got married then, too.' He looked very much like his father at that moment, as he challenged him.

'Let's roll up the rugs,' Penny cried. 'There's room for one couple to dance at a time. Barney, put on one of Swindon's records, and, Tess, you're the one dressed for it, so you and Nick take the floor first for the supper dance!'

Glenn Miller's 'In the Mood': flickering flames from the fire throwing dancing shadows on the wall; Nick's arms hugging her waist; his lips brushing her hair as they swayed back and forth. Suddenly Tess was aware of the wonderful smell of cheese melting on toast under the grate. It was Pop's idea. Goodness knows where the cheddar materialized from. That made it perfect.

'Duty calls,' Penny yawned. 'The midnight chorus. That boy'll make a good sergeant-major in due course. Pop, wake up! Barney – off to your bed.'

'They're so nice, your family,' Nick said, when he and Tess were on their own. 'The sort I'd have chosen, given the chance.' There was more room on the sofa now so he made to move up. 'Sorry, I've been crushing your dress.'

'Don't shift – you're keeping me warm. No more coal on the fire tonight; we won't have another delivery until the new year. Nick, I know you were brought up in a children's home, but that's all.'

'Not much more to tell. My father, whoever he was, left before I was born. My mother struggled to keep me for six months, then she had to let me go.'

'Did she keep in touch with the home?'

'No.'

'Perhaps she couldn't bear to see you because she couldn't keep you.'

'Perhaps. I'm sure she did what was best for us both.'

'She must think of you, still. Haven't you ever wanted to find her?'

'When I was growing up, I did. Dawn was in the same situation. We discussed it endlessly. In the end we decided it might cause more hurt. You just don't know what you might turn up. And—'

'You had each other,' Tess said simply.

'And now there's *us*, or is there, Tess?'

'There's us. I'm positive we'll always be good friends.'

'Any hope of something more than that?'

She hesitated a fraction too long. Roma settled for Swindon, she thought, and they complement each other very well. Nick and I are two of a kind, even though he appears more confident on the surface than I do. He's had to be like that to, well, survive. 'I'll be back on the tide,' she heard herself saying.

'Did Gregor say that?'

'Yes. He didn't get to celebrate his twenty-first . . . I ought to write to his mother, but somehow, I can't.'

'I took Dawn to Lyon's Corner House, to celebrate her becoming an SRN. After . . . she'd gone, I spent my own coming-of-age in my digs, rereading her letters, and no one knew it was a special day, because I only had one card and that was from my house-mother at the home, or that I was hurting like hell.'

'Shush,' she whispered, then she kissed him to stop him saying more. He hasn't got over losing Dawn yet, she thought. He says he loves me because he wants it to be true. He'll make someone a good husband, one of these days, but it won't be me.

'She's a woman, now, your Tess,' Penny observed to Pop, as she tucked the replete baby in his crib. 'Night night, Paul, sleep tight, don't let the bed bugs bite.' She climbed back into bed thankfully.

'Wonder what they're doing out there. I can't hear any talking.'

'Pop! I'm surprised at you. Didn't you hear what I said just now?'

'Something gruesome about bugs?'

'No: that's just something I tell Paul when I want him to go to sleep, he doesn't know what a bug is, and I hope he never will. Didn't you get the message when you saw Tess in that dress?'

'Of course I did. I reckon Nick did, too. I was hoping—'

'So was I. But she's got something to prove, Pop, to herself, as much as us. You didn't stop Roma.'

'No one could stop Roma,' he murmured ruefully.

'You were right about the cheese supper, she loved that. If only Millie Mae could have been here, but then—'

'*You* wouldn't be, would you? I feel as if I've always known you, Pen.

I just wish I didn't have to be away from you, and the baby, all week.'

'It can't last for ever.'

'She said that. Millie Mae. There's something I must tell you about her, one of these days.'

'Oh, I feel I know everything there is to know.'

'Let's leave it there, for tonight.'

'Wake up, Tess,' Nick said, 'It's the middle of the night.'

'Oh, sorry! Did I go to sleep on you?'

'You did.'

'Did you mind?'

'I minded not being able to reach my sketch pad. I wanted to draw you as you are at twenty-one. So I just gazed at you instead. Time to say goodnight, I think. You go, and I'll turn the lights off here.'

'You're the best of friends,' she began impulsively.

'That's a great compliment. But you know what, Tess? You could do with a girlfriend, too, someone to exchange secrets with. I'm sure you miss your sister in that respect.'

'Roma and I were never really that close – the gap in age between us, perhaps. No doubt I'll make friends at the hospital, eh? Goodnight, Nick.'

CHAPTER TWENTY-TWO

Living in the hostel was a definite shock to the system. It could have been bleak, but here Tess met a girl of her own age, who knew all the ropes.

Connie Picton had been a working girl since she was fourteen, mostly in menial jobs, despite her quick intelligence. Her father was in the army, her mother, of Maltese parentage, was evacuated at the outbreak of war to Somerset with Connie's younger siblings. Connie was philosophical about the bombs. 'If one's got your name on it, that's it, ain't it?' She fended off 'any bloke what gets the wrong idea, even if he is in a hospital bed.'

Tall and attractive, Connie, with eyes the colour of dark chocolate and black hair in a bun. Her shrill voice led to reprimands from those in authority, but she was irrepressible. 'They won't sack me, they wouldn't dare!'

'Come in and shut the door!' she greeted Tess, on her arrival.

The hospital escort departed smartly, with, 'Cheerio, report for duty tomorrow at seven.'

There were iron-framed bunks, a small table, two chairs, a cupboard, a shelf, a basin, a gas ring. The shared lavatory was on the landing outside.

'We get most of our grub in the canteen; only supposed to use the gas for a kettle for tea and for washing ourselves – you're allowed to use the hospital laundry if you don't mind getting back others' stuff, despite having embroidered your name on yours – but you're sure it's clean, eh? I said to close the door quick, or Beryl, what brought you over, might tell I'm cooking you a treat – she's our supervisor, a bit of a snoop,' her room-mate informed her cheerfully. 'New to all this lark, are you?'

'Yes.'

'Don't worry, I'll look after you.' She dobbed a gooey mass on to two chipped plates. 'Get that down you, and unpack after. Me mum used to run a transport caff along the Great North Road – one of her concoctions that is – you might find more veg than mince, but it's tasty, ain't it?'

It was. And surprisingly comforting to a girl who had just left home.

Without Connie, she thought often, during the months ahead, she'd never have survived the hard labour on the men's ward. Sluicing floors, the reek of carbolic, unblocking sinks, cleaning lavatories, emptying then sterilizing bedpans; helping out when there was a new influx of patients by stripping and making beds; discreetly handling bottles under bedclothes; spoonfeeding some; shaving haggard faces, or, sometimes, razoring unmentionable places before urgent operations. She hadn't time to blush when she was busy.

She was so hungry the unappetizing food went down regardless. It was the only way to keep going. In bed at last, the writing ran off the pages of her diary as her eyes refused to stay open.

Twice a week they were allowed to use a staff bathroom, after a late night shift. The bath salts given by grateful patients came in handy then, though Connie reckoned they were coloured soda crystals, and too much might skin you. No false modesty here; to conserve water they sat one either end of the deep bath, and solicitously washed one another's weary, blistered feet.

'Ooh, my back!' was the cry, but not when Staff Nurse made her rounds.

Every few weeks, Nick visited on Tess's weekend off. They went to the pictures, for hostel rules decreed members of the opposite sex were not to be entertained in rooms. Exhausted, she went to sleep in her tip-up seat, with his arm round her, the packet of Butterkist, a sweet popcorn, untouched.

He heard a lot about Connie, but they didn't meet until the New Year. Tess was greeting Nick outside the main door, when Connie came up. 'Been stood up,' she said. 'Hello, you must be Tess's Nick. I'm—'

'Connie, of course,' he smiled.

'Come out with us,' Tess offered. 'You don't mind, d'you, Nick?'

'I'll pay for meself,' Connie said quickly.

'We're only going to the Regal.'

'That'll do! Thanks.'

Nick linked arms with them. 'Mustn't miss the start of the big picture.'

'Long and short of it, Tess and me.' Connie soon forgot her disappointment. 'You balance us up, Nick, in the middle.' She obviously didn't mind at all being the tallest of the three, topping Nick by a good three inches.

Later, after she clattered up the iron stairs, and they were saying goodnight before the curfew at 10.30, Nick observed, 'Cheerful soul. She's done you good – you're much more relaxed. She reminds me a little of Dawn – we surmised that one of her parents was of Mediterranean origin.'

'I'm fortunate to have known both parents, and their backgrounds.'

'No mysteries then? Not even with Millie Mae?'

She looked at him in surprise. 'No, I don't think so.'

He bent to kiss her, as they stood in the stairwell. 'See you soon.'

She thought: now why did he say that? I've never told him the ins and outs of the Leo affair, not that I know it all, and I don't suppose Pop has.

After that, whenever Nick came over, they went out in a threesome. Tess didn't consciously encourage this, but it was an agreeable arrangement. Three good friends, enjoying a night out; not just Tess and Nick, and all that implied.

The long wait was almost over in the spring of 1944; rumours were about to become reality; the Allies were moving towards invading Europe. There was definitely an air of optimism among the staff and patients at the hospital.

Just when Tess was feeling that things were going particularly well, following an interview in Matron's office when she was told she would be considered for probationary nursing training in September, there was bad news. Aunt Peg wrote that Ida was really very poorly, and she hoped that Tess would come to see them as soon as she could. It was the P.S. which alarmed her: *I have sent for Pop.*

She was meant to be working next day, Saturday, but managed to change her shift. 'The only thing is,' she remembered belatedly, as she waited to don the clean blouse Connie was kindly ironing for her on a folded blanket on the table, 'Nick might be coming – he didn't say for sure.'

'I'll tell him what's what, if he does turn up,' Connie said.

'If he comes, well, of course, you two can go out as usual, can't you?' Connie tossed the blouse to her. 'I'm not sure.'

'What d'you mean?'

'Well, to put it bluntly, he comes to see *you*, and I tag along.'

'Connie, he really likes you. You make him laugh.'

'I don't want to make him *laugh*,' Connie said, blinking furiously.

'Connie!' Tess gave her a quick hug. 'I didn't realize, I'm sorry.'

'No. I'm sorry; you're my best friend.'

'And you're mine! Don't you understand? Nothing would make me happier than if you two got together.'

'You mean that? I thought—'

'Nick and I wanted to believe we would be married one day, but that's just it – one day will never come. We'll always be close, but not in that way. You see, there's always been someone else, for me, he knows that. I must go.'

'Good luck, Tess.'

'Good luck to you, too!'

Connie waited for almost an hour. She deduced at last Nick wasn't coming. She went back to her room and decided to wash her hair. She flung off her finery, donned her nightie and the towelling gown which had lost its belt and was bald in patches. She wouldn't part with that; she'd had it since she was thirteen, when Mum brushed her damp locks and told her tales of the island that was Malta. Such brave people, she thought. I'm proud to half-belong to them, and one of these days, when the war is over, I'll go there.

She wasn't expecting a knock on the door, for even if he turned up after all Nick would be refused admittance. But, by a lucky chance, the door opened as he arrived, and was wondering what to do. 'Quick, love – you're after the girls in number twelve, aren't you? I haven't seen you,' the girl on her way out said, with a saucy wink.

He trod the stairs stealthily, feeling conspicuous despite the closed doors. He half-expected the girls to be out because he'd heard from Pop that he was going to see the aunts and that Tess might get time off to join them.

He knocked, then a startled Connie appeared at the door.

'Can I come in?' He glanced over his shoulder.

'Nick! ' 'Course; 'scuse the turban, washed my hair. She isn't here.'

'I guessed she might not be. Sorry I'm late, train was delayed. I might have scrounged some petrol for the car, but normally, the train's just as quick.'

She pulled the towel off, shook her hair loose, aware that he was staring at the sheer length of it, hanging well below her waist. 'Fancy a cup of cocoa? We're low on tea, and milk too, but we've got some sugar.'

'Please,' he said.

She put a match to the gas and, as she bent, the naked flame caught at a dipping lock of hair and flared instantly. Connie screamed, backing away, and the next thing she knew, Nick had seized the damp towel from the back of the chair and smothered the flame. Then he reached round her to extinguish the gas, which brought them even closer. 'Just singed that's all,' he reassured her. He turned her to face him, holding her firmly. 'You're shaking like a leaf. D'you know,' he added softly, 'there's more of you than meets the eye.'

'More *to*, you mean, don't you?' she asked.

'No, I meant what I said; you see you look so—'

'Skinny?' she challenged.

'Yes,' his lips were on a level with her throat. 'But you're all woman, aren't you, as I've just discovered . . .'

Connie closed her eyes, allowed the robe to fall away. 'D'you want to kiss me? Oh it's all right, Tess has given us her blessing.'

'She saw this coming? I didn't.'

'Nor me. I'm a fine one to say this, but shut up and get on with it!'

She was making the cocoa she'd promised him earlier, her hair safely tied back, when she realized the time. 'Nick! It's almost eleven.'

'You mean I've outstayed my welcome?' He was lounging on the lower bunk, the only place for sitting, apart from the hard kitchen chairs.

'No; the front door will be well and truly locked and bolted!'

'So, I'm your prisoner for the night?'

'It's not that funny! You'll have to kip on my bed, as you've mussed that up already, and I'll sleep in Tess's bunk, she won't mind. I'll have to smuggle you out with me when I go on duty in the morning.'

'Well, at least I won't have to catch the last train back to my digs.'

'Nick, don't spill any on my bed and, remember, I'm a good Catholic girl.'

'You told me that earlier.'

'Can I trust you?'

'If Tess was here, she'd vouch for me.'

'Well, she isn't.' She looked at him solemnly. 'And I'm glad you said that because now I know it didn't go as far as that, with you two.'

'Nor with Dawn, though I've always regretted that,' he said softly. 'I fell for you, you know, the first time we met, when you and Tess invited me to go to the pictures with you – I can't remember what we saw, because I was thinking, 'oh, if only', and what a lucky girl she was, but now I guess I'm the lucky one, and we mustn't make her feel out of it just because—'

'Because it's you and me now, Connie, not Tess and me, and you're right, she's a wonderful friend to both of us, and I'm sure she always will be.'

'You'll love my family,' she told him. 'Mum's got such a big heart. You must come with me to visit them when I get some proper time off.'

'You can't nod off yet because I must tell you all about me, and I want to know all about you, too. We've got a lot of catching up to do.'

'I'll stay here with you for a while, then,' she said simply.

Tess and Pop were sitting in a corner of Aunt Ida's room, while Peg talked to her in a low voice. It was dark outside now, and the blinds were drawn.

'I'm glad you could come,' Pop whispered. 'I saw Nick and warned him that you might be here, but he decided to go to the hostel anyway.'

'Good. Connie usually comes out with us, anyway, so he won't be lonely.'

There was a long silence after this. Peg said no more, either.

Around an hour later, she rose; stood looking down at the still figure in the bed. Then she turned, and said in what Tess could only think of as wonderment, 'She's gone. Peacefully, thank God. Will you stay tonight?'

'We'll stay with you, Peg,' Pop said.

Connie awoke with a start. She put out a hand, touched Nick. 'We've got just ten minutes to get going!' He tried to pull her back into the sleepy circle of his arms. 'Nick! Did you hear me? Have we been lying here together all night?'

166

'At least I won't have to get dressed,' he yawned ruefully.

'Well, I will! Nick——'

'All right I'm going, but I'll see you tonight.'

'Nick——' she repeated urgently.

'Nothing happened, honestly. Is that what you wanted to know?'

'You're making me blush, like Tess!'

'But unlike dear Tess, you won't keep me waiting, will you?'

CHAPTER TWENTY-THREE

A bright Sunday morning in May, almost deserted streets, the shops closed, apart from a newsagent's, but churches packed for matins, uplifting hymns and earnest prayer for what lay ahead – the great invasion, the liberation of Europe.

Tess, pale and drawn, answered Nick's knock. 'I didn't expect . . . come in.'

'Things not good?' She looked as if she too had slept in her clothes. She nodded. 'Aunt Ida passed away last night.'

'I'm so sorry. Perhaps I should go, unless I can do anything to help.'

'Everything is taken care of. The undertaker came first thing. Have you had breakfast? Pop's making tea and toast.'

He felt his stomach growl. It had been quite a walk, several miles, from the hospital, but he hadn't wanted to arrive too early. 'Sure? How is Peg?'

'Very calm. She'll be pleased to see you, I think.'

They were standing in the hallway. 'You've something to tell me, haven't you? I could tell by your face, before I gave you the news.'

'It doesn't matter now.'

'Yes, it does. You and Connie? Oh, I do hope so.' Even as she said it, she felt a further sense of loss; she and Nick had been very close for a year and a half, after all. Who was there now, for her?

'I'm still dazed, amazed,' he said. 'It's all so sudden you see.'

'You mustn't feel guilty. I saw it coming. Don't hang around this time, Nick. Connie – well, she's the one for you. I wish I could have been, but I was right to hold back, wasn't I?'

He hugged her. 'I hope your own love isn't as hopeless as you think it is. Dear Tess, you deserve to be happy, too. He's a damn fool '

'Yes, he is. But I can't help loving him.'

Peg was staying with Penny on an indefinite basis, when D-Day came at last in June. Penny cycled to the village for the papers with their jubilant giant headlines. They sat by the wireless and sucked their way through a quarter of boiled sweets to celebrate. It was just as well that they were unaware that there was a tempest ahead – literally, with regard to the weather – and that the casualties on both sides, would be great.

Swindon had returned earlier in the year, but they hadn't seen him yet. Now, they realized why. Roma and the girls had remained in Canada.

Barney made triple-decker sandwiches for supper: one layer of marmite, one of sandwich spread. It was an interesting combination, but there were no complaints, especially from young Paul who seized the opportunity to crawl over to the coal bucket and to distribute the contents over the kitchen floor, without the usual admonishment of, 'No, Paul!'

'Boys, who'd have 'em,' Penny said fondly, examining his grimy hands, while Peg swept up the precious dust, for Pop mixed that with cement to make briquettes to eke out supplies. 'Why couldn't I have had a dear little girl?'

'You've forgotten what Frankie got up to at that age,' Barney reminded her.

'Pop was a holy terror,' Peg said. 'Give him to me; sink time, I believe.' Wrapped around with the old shop overall, she was girded for drenching. Moses leapt from the drainer, where he caught the drips from the tap, scuttled under the table, glaring through the bobbled fringes of the chenille cloth.

Just a week later, terror struck nearer to home. The first flying bomb, with a ton of explosive, careening on course for London, spluttered ominously, cut out, then plummeted out of the night sky. It exploded a few miles from the hospital, which was immediately on full alert.

It was the beginning of the nightmare. A wave of these pilotless planes followed, soon dubbed doodlebugs by the Press: the very British way of caricaturing catastrophe. Croydon especially, on the pathway to the capital, and swathes of Kent and Sussex, were designated Bomb

Alley. Pop insisted on a temporary evacuation for his family on the marsh. Penny refused to go further than Hertfordshire, where Barney could finish off the educational year with some of the pupils and staff of his school, much to his chagrin.

Once again, the pilots who had flown and fought in the Battle of Britain, and their successors, rallied to the call, alerted again by radar; the ground battery guns blazed, the barrage balloons played an important role, and the V1 was effectively routed.

However, far worse was to come.

Another September. 'Take the key to the flat,' Tess offered Nick. 'I'm on duty this evening, but there's no reason why you and Connie can't spend a few hours together relaxing on your own without me. Peg wouldn't mind. You've all the last-minute wedding plans to talk over, after all.' She hesitated. 'Don't be late in the morning,' she added casually. The way the two of them looked at each other sometimes was quite transparent. They were to be married in less than a fortnight's time. It had never been like that between herself and Nick.

'Thanks,' Connie whispered to Tess. 'I'll make sure we don't waste the opportunity – because, you never know—'

'Don't say that, please!'

'Oh, Tess you must admit it'd be a good way to go!' Connie teased.

Tess, lingering at the door as they walked away, wondered: why these fearful feelings? The doodlebug menace was apparently over; news was good from the battlefronts – what rejoicing there had been when Paris was liberated – though there was still fierce resistance from the other side. But now there was to be a desperate, dreadful message from the enemy.

Unlike its predecessor, the V2 rocket, launched from the Netherlands, rose to a tremendous height and was jet-propelled at 4,000 miles per hour, ten times the speed of the V1. It was undetectable by radar. There was no time for advance warning before the excruciating explosion, immediately followed by ear-splitting screeching as the fireball spiralled inexorably to the ground. This new weapon caused widespread destruction and terror.

The first casualties arrived at the hospital. Tess, in her first week as a probationer, was despatched to help the experienced nurses, where she could. She bent over a stretcher on a trolley in the corridor, where a woman lay in obvious shock. Her injuries were relatively minor, although the uniform she wore was bloodstained; she could wait for assessment. Tess realized almost immediately that it was Sylvia, Moray's fiancée.

'Sylvia, you probably don't remember me: I'm Tess. Can you hear me? You're going to be all right, I promise.'

'Tess . . . I don't understand – why are *you* here?'

'I've been here for months; I'm training to be a nurse, you see. Is there anyone you want me to contact? Your parents. . . ?'

'I was with them when – I don't know, are they. . . ?'

'I'll find out. Try not to worry.' What a ridiculous thing to say, she thought, angry at herself.

Then a porter came and wheeled Sylvia away to the ward. It was hours before she saw her again. It had been a long night.

She stood by Sylvia's bed. 'Your parents are here, too; your mother has a broken arm, she'll be along to see you later.' Sylvia's father was in surgery at this moment. She hoped fervently that she would not ask about him, because she had not been able to ascertain what his injuries were.

'What was it, Tess, a bomb?' Sylvia sounded puzzled. 'We were out, I think – I just can't remember.'

'Don't try now. Go back to sleep, if you can.' Tess spoke soothingly.

'Moray – will you let him know?'

She tucked Sylvia's hands under the covers. No rings, not even an engagement ring. 'I don't know where he is.'

'That little book, on top of the locker – all the addresses – please.'

'Of course I'll try to get in touch with him.'

'Tess – we're still – good friends, you see, even though. . . .'

Like Nick and I, she thought, and then chillingly: *Where's Connie?*

She had been on duty for forty-eight hours, when Staff Nurse took her firmly to one side and told her, 'Go home. You've had a baptism of fire. Unofficially, I'm telling you to take time off. We're ready for the next emergency. To put it bluntly, we need experienced nurses at this time. That's not to say, we don't appreciate all you have done over this period.'

At last she managed to telephone Moray's number. She fed the coin box with pennies, while he was fetched from his bed, at the base.

'Hello?' she heard faintly, but even so she could tell he was almost asleep on his feet. Of course: he would have been involved in combat.

'Moray, it's Tess.'

'Tess! What's wrong?'

'Sylvia was visiting her parents, they were caught in the blast – cuts and bruises – but she's in shock. Moray, she asked me to ring – she's in hospital.'

'How on earth—?'

'Didn't you know? I'm a junior nurse there.'

'Wait for me there. I'm off-duty, catching up on sleep supposedly. I'll come as quickly as I can.'

'I can't. I'm going home,' she began, as the money ran out. She replaced the receiver.

First, she must go to the flat. Connie and Nick must still be there.

She sat in the train, with gaping holes in the knees of her black stockings, dust all over her clothes. She didn't recall stumbling along to the station, waiting on the platform, boarding the packed afternoon train to the nearest point to home. She was deeply traumatized. The shop and its neighbour had been reduced to a pile of smoking rubble. There were no survivors.

'Thank God your aunt was not here,' the local constable said, arm firmly around her, supporting her. He remembered her from her schooldays. He'd lifted her up, when she collapsed at the sight of the devastation. She had to tell him then, about Nick and Connie. He was kind and sympathetic, took down details, but he couldn't comfort her, no one could.

Now, she caught the bus to the village, set out to walk on to the Last Stop Garage. The original name was the one which came to mind, in her confusion.

Not until she reached the front door did she realize that she had come home to an empty house; her family, of course, were still away. At least they were safe; she prayed that was so.

A car door slammed on the forlorn forecourt, as she found her key. Thank goodness, Pop had had one cut for her 'just in case'.

'Tess, here you are! I've been desperate with worry, not knowing—'

'Moray, *oh Moray!*' she cried in disbelief.

*

He lit the fire with broken boxes, scavenged for coal, located candles. The gas was turned off at the mains. An unmade bed, but he pulled off her shoes, cocooned her in blankets, gently coaxed her to lie down.

'Don't talk now, wait until I've made some tea. I'll have to boil the kettle on the fire. Know where there's anything stronger?'

'The sideboard . . .' she managed. The next thing she knew, he was spooning raw whisky between her teeth.

'Pop obviously thought it wasn't worth taking this drop – swallow, that's a good girl, it'll warm you up.'

Later, as she sat up and drank weak, milkless tea, because the caddy was almost empty too, he told her, 'I saw Sylvia; they say she'll be discharged soon. I rang Pop; he directed me to the hostel, then the flat – it was my guess that you'd come on here. Can you tell me the rest of it, now?'

'It was my fault, if only I hadn't suggested . . .' she cried bitterly. Connie's prophetic words were spinning round and round in her head: '*If it's got your name on it . . . a good way to go.*' When she had finished and the hot, helpless tears were spilling, he stroked her hair until she was calmer. 'You mustn't blame yourself. Get some sleep. We need to leave here by four in the morning. I'm going to take you to Pop: he must decide what's to be done.'

'Don't go,' she pleaded.

'You mean, now?'

'Yes, now. I need you, Moray. But not—'

'I know. Anyway, I can't; I'm weary beyond belief,' he admitted honestly.

'So am I,' she said, as he drew her, unresisting, against the warmth of his body. I hope, she thought, as she succumbed to blessed sleep, I hope Connie and Nick were close like this when it happened.

A week later she was back on her ward, quietly determined to carry on. She insisted on this, against Pop's advice.

'You're becoming as stubborn as Roma,' he sighed, as he said good-bye in the car, outside the hospital. 'Like Millie Mae. Look, I've had my doubts in the past, but I wouldn't object, seeing he really cares for you, if you and Moray—'

'No, Pop,' she said. 'It's not the right time. I can't say why, it just isn't.'

173

'You love the chap, don't you?'

'Love's a torture, sometimes.'

Pop looked at her for a long moment. 'I know. I've never told anyone, not even Penny, yet. Millie Mae was leaving me, that time for Leo – she said she couldn't help herself, though she loved me dearly. I broke down and wept, said I couldn't live without her. Well, she stayed: we never spoke of it again. Leo, well, it was a knock to his pride. Are you shocked? Should I have let her go, find out for herself what he was like? It wouldn't have lasted, anyway.'

'You did what you thought was right, Pop.' Inwardly she felt sad because truth so often hurt. She couldn't marry Moray unless Roma confessed: was it worth the distress that would inevitably cause, to others too?

PART THREE

HOME, WHEREVER THAT IS

CHAPTER TWENTY-FOUR

Unhappiness, uncertainty, grief: the pain of these, the tragic loss of her friends; the only way Tess coped was through work. For many months, sheer fatigue at the end of each day failed to obliterate anguished thoughts. She didn't go home often, because she caught the worried looks exchanged between Pop, Penny and Peg. Barney steered clear of mentioning Nick, who had been his friend, too. The desolate feelings were even harder to bear than those she had experienced after Gregor was lost at sea; this time it was 'If only I hadn't said . . .'

She didn't expect to find such comradeship again: like giggling in the pictures at Connie's candid comments on the technicolour, escapist films of the day: 'Soppy ending – they wouldn't be prancing around with bowls of fruit on their head on a South Sea island, they'd have been chased off by wild men with spears.' Or, on their last outing, linking arms with the two of them, 'Doing the Lambeth Walk – Oi!' without, as Nick cheerfully commented, 'A single beer to jolly us up.' She'd related this, in floods of tears to Connie's mum, when she visited her. Mrs Picton hugged her tight, told Tess she must be consoled by the thought that Connie and Nick were real soulmates even though their happiness was cruelly curtailed. 'Some never find the right one; they did.'

As for Moray, Tess wrote a careful letter saying she intended to continue with her training over the next three years, that she would always be his friend, but if that was not enough, she gave him her blessing to look elsewhere.

She hit home with the last comment, she surmised, for there was no reply. Like Millie Mae, she was retreating from the prospect of a passionate but uncertain love affair. Yet how could she forget the night

177

he held her in his arms and comforted her? His gentleness, restraint, had disarmed her then.

Tess Rainbow SRN, with frilled cuffs, and a convoluted pretty cap which she made-up daily, pinning carefully to shorter hair which skimmed her collar, with a feathered fringe. The crackling of her starched apron was music to her ears, and reassuring to her patients.

There was a post-celebration chat with Matron. Was she happy to stay on at the hospital, now the war was over? She had an obvious empathy with children; how about the children's ward? Or a further midwifery course?

Tess thought of Connie, of Nick, Londoners both, and their less than privileged childhood, though in Connie's case, she was fortunate to be part of a loving family. She knew exactly what she wanted to do in the future.

'I would like to go out on the district, in a poor part of London. They need nurses there. I can ride a bike,' she added hopefully.

Matron held out her hand. 'Our loss, Nurse Rainbow, shall be the community's gain. Leave it with me. Good luck!'

Pop left the Tann Corporation just before Moray, newly demobilized, joined the board. When Peg received compensation for her property, she said in her usual forthright way, 'I'm passing most of it to you now. Set yourself up here again, concentrate on restoring your old planes, with my blessing. That's what you always wanted, the garage was your necessary bread-and-butter. You don't need that now we're better off. Penny and young Paul need you here.'

'Just when Barney believes he doesn't and is taking off for his National Service, eh? I advised him to request deferment and go to college first.'

'You think you know it all, when you're young,' Peg agreed, adding, with a twinkle, 'Mind, there's a condition – that I'm allowed to live out the rest of my days with the Rainbows!'

'I certainly don't want to lose my baby-sitter; how would I spend time in the pottery, then?' Penny asked, with a special warm smile for Peg, as she came to show them the first of many Moses mugs to come, Nick's design.

'Still miss Moses,' Pop sighed. He didn't need to say how much he missed Nick, a feeling they all shared. If things had been different, well, it could have been Tess, not Connie, who was with Nick when . . .

'Moses is back among the bullrushes,' Penny said.

Tess was writing again: despite her busy working life, the words flowed at the end of each long day. There was so much to record: Woolworth notebooks served as diaries – she didn't know if she would get around to typing it up – if it would be autobiography – or if she would use the notes eventually in a fictional story. It really didn't matter at this moment, she thought. But if this was ever published, she'd dedicate it to Connie and Nick, she was sure of that.

She pedalled round the district, to the slum areas decimated by the Blitz, climbing endless steps to dingy rooms with a bleak outlook, with her black bag clutched in her hand. 'Got a baby in there, miss?' a cheeky child enquired. 'We don't want it at *our* house, me mum says!'

'Bicarb, bedpans and boracic lint, that's mostly it,' said the senior nurse, nearing retirement, whose digs she shared. Tess also cleaned and redressed wounds and ulcerated legs, gave insulin injections, enemas and blanket baths where conditions were not ideal. However, patients were invariably cheerful; they knew the routine, spreading newspapers on the table, so she could lay out her equipment, and always had a kettle on the boil, for tea as well as medical purposes, for the friendly chat after treatment, was part of the service.

Tess did not blanch at unpalatable tasks, like cutting neglected toenails for the elderly, or showing a young mother how to fine-comb a toddler's nitty hair. She didn't become impervious to sour smells, but most of her patients tried hard to keep their homes clean, against the odds, the lack of proper sanitation.

Sometimes, she was allowed to accompany the midwives on their rounds. In the early hours of one Thursday in October 1947, she was unexpectedly called upon to deliver her first baby, as Dolly was laid up with her back.

When she arrived home, she was too excited to snatch a couple of hours' sleep before going back on duty. She sat at the flapped table in the corner of her bedsit, with a cup of coffee and a Rich Tea biscuit, and began to write, shifting the paper to catch the light from the table lamp.

The front door was on the catch. Despite the street lamp, I stumbled over the broken step. I was in a dark hallway, crowded with bikes and a pram or two. Straight ahead was a winding flight of stairs. A torch beam was directed down on me. As I shaded my eyes and looked up, a man's voice asked, 'Is that the nurse? We was expecting Dolly Day.'

'She's laid up with her back,' I said. 'I was with her on her last visit; Nurse Rainbow, remember?'

'Come on up, then . . . Mother!' he yelled over his shoulder. 'It's Judy Garland!'

Tess dipped her biscuit absent mindedly into her drink. As usual, it crumbled and subsided into a soggy mess. She spooned it up anyway.

I've been lucky, she thought, with an experienced mum, a quick labour and a bonny baby girl at the end of it. Dad knew what was required of him, disposing of the trappings of birth, making tea and looking in on the older children, asleep in the next room.

Tess yawned. It was all catching up on her. One last sentence or two . . .

'What are you calling her?' I asked, wrapping the baby in a shawl.

'Judy, I thought, miss – after you, to say thank you for all you done.'

Dolly Day was obviously having her first cigarette and her first cough of the day next door. Tess closed her notebook. More tea required, for both of them. Perching on the edge of her colleague's bed, after hoisting her up, Tess told her about her night's work.

Dolly grinned. 'Did I tell you about the time I was called to give a woman an enema in the middle of the night? Her husband pounded on my door. "She's in terrible pain", he insisted, when I asked couldn't it wait until morning. 'She's been suffering from constipation for days!' Well, I got there just in time to deliver a ten pound baby, much to their consternation. They'd been married for years, never wanted children and, as she told me, "We reckoned we were safe." A neighbour obliged with baby clothes, then I asked, "What are you going to call the baby?" They didn't care. They were just concerned with who could take it off their hands. I felt so cross, it was a fine baby boy. I muttered, under my breath, mind, 'Why don't you call him Constipation?' and the chap said, "We don't want to give it a name, we might get attached to it." '

'Then I can't object to Judy Garland then, even if it's not my name?'

'It's not your only nickname – I've heard you referred to as Ginger Rogers, and I get Dolly Mixture, like the kiddies' sweets, and some I won't repeat.'

'Want me to put a belladonna plaster on your poor old back?' Tess yawned. 'Might as well keep going, I reckon.'

Everyone was talking about the forthcoming royal wedding, imagining what Princess Elizabeth's dress might be like, and reading avidly about the handsome blond young man she was to marry, Prince Philip of Greece.

The family on the marsh were looking forward to a celebration of their own: after four long years, Roma and her children would be back from Canada, early in November. Swindon had returned there after the war, but was now taking up a contract with a civil airline in this country.

I hope you can find room for us for a few weeks until we find somewhere to rent? (Roma wrote). *We have so much catching up to do! Please tell Tess she must take some time off, too! I don't want to miss out on the wedding, of course: I intend to be among the crowd lining the route to the Abbey.*

So Barney will soon be in uniform; you will miss him, but at least you won't have to worry about his safety, will you?

Barney missed the Great Homecoming, as Pop referred to it, by a few weeks. He travelled north by train on a chill, fog-laden day, herded with other apprehensive young men into the back of a lorry and taken to the reception camp to be kitted out for National Service with the RAF.

The new intake were given numbers and informed laconically that no uniforms were yet available. As they had been instructed to wear light clothing, and to pack the bare minimum, the lads were soon shivering with cold. The stark wooden hut with corrugated roof had several broken windows and there was no coal for the stove. Barney was thankful he'd heeded Penny's advice and brought pyjamas, even though he, and others, were ridiculed by the majority, stripped to their underwear. The pyjama-clad few were envied when snow drifted through cracks into the hut, forming icy patches on the floor.

Barney was thankful that over the last year his lanky, skinny frame had filled out; he was now big and burly, like Pop. His red hair was not so noticeable once it was cropped, and his stuttering was long vanquished. 'Be one of the boys, by all means,' Pop advised gruffly, 'but not to excess.'

He soon became wise to the service dodges: to the sixpenny raffle for a prized watch, which was inevitably won by one of the NCOs who sold the tickets. The recruits discovered, once in uniform, they could buy the brass button sticks cheaper in the NAAFI than from this band of entrepreneurs.

One recruit stood out: a cinema projectionist who'd turned up in a green hairy suit and a pork pie hat, had a droll sense of humour. Initially, Barney liked him, until he confided his intention to get discharged as unfit for service as soon as he could. He planned to appear unhygienic, stubborn and slow-witted and to refuse to wash, to carry out his duties. Barney did not join in the baiting that shortly ensued, but later he would feel ashamed of standing aloof.

One freezing morning, the pork pie hat chap was publicly humiliated by some of his fellows, dragged out on the barrack square, stripped, forced into a tub of cold water, and scrubbed with a broom, watched by a shocked and silent crowd, none of whom were prepared to intervene. The perpetrators were caught, punished; the victim reflighted. Barney was relieved, for what could he say to him – he had brought it on himself? The chap was a fool, but he didn't deserve *that*.

Barney, like Tess before him, was learning what it was like in the world beyond home, the place he wished he had never left. Pop had tried to warn him, of course, but he'd also said,'It'll make a man of you.'

Roma, Frankie and Evie were on the final lap of their sea journey. Roma was unsure how she felt about meeting her family again after such a gap. She was coming back to a country still struggling with austerity, where, after the ice-locked winter which had not let up until well after the advent of spring, there had been the contrast of a heatwave summer. That was a false promise of better things to come, for while Barney spent his final school holidays watching the county cricket championships at Lords, where his idols Denis Compton and Bill Edrich did not disappoint, Tess, as a nurse, was all too aware of an epidemic of poliomyelitis mainly among children and that for this cruel disease there was as yet no cure.

There were still hard, anxious times ahead, despite the war having ended.

CHAPTER TWENTY-FIVE

'**P**en, they're here,' Pop called out unnecessarily, for Penny was already coming along the hall, divesting herself of her working smock as she did so, and behind her appeared Peg, still in her overall, so it was hugs all round on the doorstep for a daughter coming home at last, even though her own daughters dodged shyly behind her back. Roma's face revealed her pleasure at this warm welcoming.

'*Wonderful smell*, steak and kidney pie, it must be!' Roma exclaimed, sniffing the air like a Bisto kid, but not remotely resembling one in her beaver coat.

'Peg's doing, I was just putting the finishing touches to a little surprise,' Penny said. Mugs for the children, patterned with a maple leaf. She smiled at the solemn pair, now edging forward but clinging to their mother's coat sleeves. 'My, you're almost the same size, but you must be Frankie, eh, and you must be Evie.'

'And where's Paul?' Roma asked, in her unfamiliar Canadian accent. Her hair was more than fair now, it was ash blonde, bubble curled like the Hollywood blonde bombshell herself, Betty Grable, whose lissom image had been painted on many a wartime US plane. Roma's last appointment before embarking on the voyage had obviously been to the hairdresser for a perm she hoped would last a while.

'Taking an unaccustomed nap before dinner: I didn't try to keep him awake, because I'm sure the children won't go to bed at the proper time tonight, eh?'

'It's nice to be home.' Roma led the children into the sitting-room where the fire had been going since morning, to warm the place up.

'Excuse me, just the last minute bits to do.' Peg went back to the kitchen.

184

Penny hooked the coats on the hallstand. Roma's fur; thick, hooded plaid coats with quilted linings for the children. 'Must be really cold in Ottawa,' she observed. Paul's coat looked shabby hanging alongside.

'It actually feels chillier here, even without the snow, because it's a damp cold; and our houses are centrally heated, of course.' Roma was still tactless.

'It's just as well you weren't here last January, when we certainly had snow-on-snow, drifts and all; electricity cuts, low gas, and coal was like gold. Tess was rushed off her feet with so many ill.'

'No Tess here today? I should have thought she would make the effort.'

'Tess is dedicated to her work,' Pop said lightly, joining them after depositing the luggage in their rooms. 'Here's your – I was going to say cousin, but it's all a bit complicated, isn't it? Here's Paul, girls. He'll show you where all the toys are.'

Paul, like his mother, was lively and outgoing. He invited Frankie and Evie to play with his collection of Dinkie toys, inherited from Barney, and small brown rubber building blocks which fitted together, like snap fasteners. The floor was soon littered, and the three children getting on well together. Then Frankie discovered the wooden ride-astride train with two carriages, which Paul had lately outgrown; made by Pop and painted poppy red by Penny, being the colour she had most of in her studio. Frankie pulled the engine out from the cupboard, helped by Evie, who followed her lead in everything. 'What's it say? I don't know those words, Paul.' She pointed at the lettering on the side.

'*Romney, Hythe'n'Dymchurch*,' he said proudly. 'Pop didn't have 'nough room for the rest. He writes too big.'

'Is the little railway going again?' Roma asked her father.

'Took a bit of restoring, after being armoured by the military. It was hush-hush throughout the war, part of our defence system here, though rumour had it, it played its part in carrying the equipment for PLUTO, the pipeline under the sea supplying the troops after D-Day. Bit ironic, I suppose: German prisoners repaired damaged sections of the line, then it was back to business last year. Gave the marsh a real boost. The children must take a ride on our light railway next spring – d'you remember the time you three went on it, Roma?'

'Barney made a fuss wanting to be in the engine stoking the fire, and you took a snap of him yelling his head off, from the platform, and Tess and me looking embarrassed because the other passengers could hear him – and Millie Mae was calling to you to climb aboard before we chuffed off.'

'Who's Millie Mae?' Frankie asked curiously.

There was silence for a minute. Then Pop said, 'Shame Swindon had to go back to work, after we met up.' He ignored Penny's anxious look and added more coal to the already blazing fire. He'd seen Roma's exaggerated shiver.

'That's better,' she said, 'I can feel the heat now. He'll be here the day after tomorrow to stay for a couple of days, if that's all right with you.'

'Of course it is; plenty of room now it's just us four. Peg is kindly allowing Paul to share her room. If you're here when Barney gets his first leave, he won't mind sleeping in the studio.'

'Tess doesn't use her room much these days?' This was where Roma was sleeping tonight, while the little girls shared the single bed in Barney's small room.

Penny shook her head. 'She usually comes just for the day. She suggested we make it Paul's room a couple of years ago, when he graduated to a bed.'

'Come and get it!' Peg was hot cheeked from baking. 'I'm not sure it's up to dear Ida's standard, but this is a rare treat for us, too.'

'You look so different, Tess, still too thin,' she scolded affectionately, as they embraced. 'That stuffy mac and that district nurse's hat don't do you any favours – and you've cut your hair!'

'So have you,' Tess returned. She gave Roma's waist a crafty squeeze. 'And you, dear Sis, have put it on.'

'Oh Swindon likes me curvaceous, men do you know.'

'Well, I have to admit you're right.'

'I discovered a super dress hanging all forlorn in your wardrobe, you must have turned a few heads in that, but when did it last get an airing?'

'Not since I was twenty-one, and then I only wore it twice. My dancing days are over; remember I'm a sober twenty-five now,' she joked.

'Don't be silly! What does that make me?'

'A not-so-stuffy mum of two. Well, where are the children?'

'Out walking with Penny and Peg; they need to let off steam before lunch, and it gets dark too quickly in the afternoons. I said I'd stay and give you the news that we're sharing a bed tonight. All set for an early start tomorrow?'

'Yes, apart from catching the early workers' train. Hope we can squeeze in somewhere in Trafalgar Square maybe, and get a good view of the procession.'

'You'll write it all up for posterity, I presume? Cup of coffee?'

'You bet I will! Please.'

'Let's go in the kitchen then. I'm supposed to be keeping an eye on the simmering soup and making spam sandwiches. Also, I'm dying to know all the details of your romantic life since last we met.'

'Nothing to tell, really.'

'Tess, you're twenty-five!'

'I also lead a busy life: not many candidates for romance among my patients. What about you? Married bliss, I take it?'

'Of course! I know how to keep my man happy.'

'You always did.'

'I won't rise to that, Tess. I was sorry to hear about Nick, I thought he was a really nice guy.' Roma took a gulp of coffee. She said, rather too casually, 'Seen anything of Moray?'

'Not for three years.' And three months, Tess added silently.

'So long? Is he married?'

'Not that I've heard of.'

'Living in the Surrey house?'

'I don't know. Roma, what are you leading up to exactly?'

'There's something I should have told you, a long time ago.'

'I *know*, Roma.'

'How?' she demanded.

'Moray told me.'

'Moray? I don't understand.'

'He told me you . . . slept together once.'

'Is that all?'

'Yes.' She was being truthful. The rest was only supposition on her part.

'I'm sorry if that spoiled things for you. It wasn't something I intended to happen. Swindon knows – it's behind us. I never think of Moray now.'

'Then why did you ask me about him?'

The door opened and in came the children. The little girls were not shy today.

187

'You're Tess!' Frankie cried. 'Why are you wearing that funny hat?'
'Oh, have I still got it on? I'm a nurse, Frankie.'
'You've got the same colour hair as Pop,' Frankie observed.
'And you've got. . . .' She paused, looking at her niece. Relief washed over her. Frankie's dark hair was bobbed, with a blunt-cut fringe, the quiff not visible. There was a distinct resemblance to Millie Mae, despite differences in colouring; the wide blue eyes were certainly the same. 'You've got nice hair, and so have you, Evie – yours is just like your Mum's.'

'Mine's nat'ral, Mommy gets hers done,' Evie said innocently, then wondered why Roma and Tess were laughing.

'All girls is soppy,' was Paul's opinion, which set them off again.

Penny snatched at the soup pan. 'Just about to burn! Where are the sandwiches Roma? We've worked up an appetite.'

'Sorry,' Roma said, wiping her eyes. She glanced at Tess. 'I really *am* sorry,' she repeated softly.

Barney was *en route* to the Midlands by train on 20 November. He and his companions were transferring to their first real camp. He felt the return of apprehension: what would life there be like? To them this Thursday hardly seemed the day for a wedding, let alone a royal wedding, though the weather forecast for the south was bright intervals and very mild for the time of year. All along their route the bells sang out joyously from every church. Despite the cold air, the young airmen kept the train windows open, and the sound transcended all.

It was supposed to be a simple occasion, in line with the times, but Barney, ever-hungry, could picture the wedding breakfast. All *they* had to look forward to later, if they were lucky, because surely there would be a celebration of sorts, was what the lads referred to as yellow railway cake, randomly fruited, and squares of cheese. He knew from experience that when these luxuries were placed on the table for Sunday tea, on big metal trays, that the general rush would end inevitably in cake being senselessly ground underfoot. They were bound to be more restrained with cutting the royal wedding cake, and they wouldn't be making tea in a galvanized bucket.

Tess and Roma had chattered and chuckled so much in bed last night

188

that Pop had called out eventually, 'Be quiet, you girls! Some of us need our sleep!'

They pinned their patriotic favours to their lapels and edged forward as far as they could. The early morning light was slowly illuminating Whitehall, where the crowd stood six-deep. The Mall, they said was being freshly sanded.

'Where is all the bunting, surely they could have done better than that?' Roma asked. 'And the guardsmen in khaki?'

However, the happy faces of the massed crowd, the good-natured bantering, the excitement, the cheers that greeted even anonymous ministerial motors, made them feel thrilled to be part of it all. Then came the sounds of music from a loudspeaker, while tea was poured from flasks and children sat on the kerb, munching on their breakfast rolls.

Only once did Roma mention her own children. 'Hope they're behaving and allow the grown-ups to listen to the radio!'

'I'm sure they are – look! I'm glad I'm not on duty today, and wearing my uniform, that's the third stretcher I've seen today – it's certainly not the heat.'

'The front rows have been camping there all night, remember.'

Then the bands began to play: first the Royal Marines who marched on, followed by the RAF, who stayed. They struck up with the National Anthem for the Princess's grandmother, Queen Mary, who was followed by the foreign royals.

'*Philip!*' the crowd roared as the bridegroom's car appeared, and his smiling face was their reward. The bridal procession could not now be far behind. The bells were ringing in the Abbey.

More cheering, from those in the street, and from opened windows above, in the Admiralty building, where staff had a grandstand view, when the glass coach carrying the Queen and Princess Margaret at last appeared, proudly escorted by the Household Cavalry on their prancing, perfectly groomed black horses. Eleven o'clock was fast approaching.

Four wonderful state coaches, drawn by Windsor greys: here was the pomp, the pageantry, the colour. Princess Elizabeth looked tiny beside her father, the dress they longed to see concealed by the fur coat draped round her shoulders to keep her warm. A girl on her way to her wedding, radiant and slightly bemused.

189

Tess and Roma were crying, caught up by the emotion of it all. No one was budging an inch until the Abbey service was over and the cavalcade returned, with Elizabeth and Philip, relaxed and waving now, in the glass coach.

'Come on, Tess,' Roma said dreamily, when they finally got to bed that night after all the telling was done. '*We* could do with a wedding in the family: a proper do, not like mine, when none of the family could be there. I want to see you in a white dress, and Frankie and Evie as bridesmaids, and Paul as your page, and Pop giving you away. Oh, do see what you can do before we go back to Canada!'

'You seem to have overlooked the fact there's no groom in sight, and unlikely to be,' Tess yawned.

'Unless-'

'What d'you mean?'

'*Unless – you know* . . .'

CHAPTER TWENTY-SIX

The incidence of polio continued to rise alarmingly, particularly in overcrowded areas and Tess knew of many cases in what she now thought of as her community. One plague being replaced by another as Dolly Day said, although the coughing disease, once known as consumption, now TB was, of course, still with them.

Parents were all too well aware of the range of frightening symptoms: delirium, blinding headaches, stiff neck, desperate fighting for breath and, most dreaded of all, paralysis. The doctor would be called, followed by the ambulance, an emergency dash to the hospital and in the worst cases, the patient, often a child but not always, was placed within the coffin-like but life-saving iron-lung. A few would remain dependent on the respirators for the rest of their lives, but many stricken patients would rely on these for many months. It was to be some years yet before the first vaccine was developed safely and would become available.

Those children who survived and came home after a prolonged stay in hospital were invariably left with a permanent reminder of their illness. It caught Tess's heart to see wasted limbs, leg braces, as those able to struggle along without a wheelchair, made their way determinedly to school. Parents kept their children away from the swimming baths, rumoured to be a source of infection.

Roma wouldn't allow her children to visit crowded places; the promised visit to the little railway never materialized. By March, the family had moved on to the outskirts of a quiet town in Kent, from where Swindon was able to commute to work. Roma drove her girls to a small private day school, where the classes were small, and like

Penny with Paul, kept a vigilant eye on their health.

Tess regretted leaving the hospital, for nurses were badly needed as the wards filled up, but as Dolly reminded her, 'You're needed *here*, Tess, more than ever.'

Summer, and Tess was well overdue for a break, when the letter from Jean in Scotland arrived, readdressed to her by Pop.

Dear Tess

I am prompted to write to you after all this time because I was sorting through some old letters and came across one from you, written when you were first back home in Kent. In it, you promised to keep in touch.

I do understand why your letters ceased, but the fact is I became very fond of you when we saw so much of you in Scotland, and when I feel lonely, which I have to admit is often, with Leo gone almost seven years now and the children long left home, (Sally married an American and lives in the US) I wish I could enjoy your quiet companionship as before.

Of course, I don't know exactly what direction your life has taken since I last communicated with Pop; he did let me know of his marriage, and I was glad about that, and later, I learned that he and his wife had a little son, and that Roma and Swindon were living in Canada.

I also know, because Moray told me, that you suffered yet another sad loss in 1944. It seems that he has heard nothing from you since. You were then embarking on a career in nursing. That did not surprise me, as you are a such a caring young woman, but I do hope you are still writing – Millie Mae would have been so proud of you! Remember what the local newspaper called you? Miss Tess Rainbow of Silver Strand. Please tell Barney that his aeroplane still awaits collection! Moray checks it over from time to time, but he doesn't come here much, being committed to his work these days. Leo would have been both pleased and surprised at this outcome.

And now to come to the real point of this letter, dear Tess. When you can take time off work, would you come to stay with me, for old time's sake? That would make me very, very happy.

Please write soon, and say you will. Much love from Jean at Strand House.

Tess could take a week off, possibly two. Another part-time nurse had joined their team – she was willing to cover for her. She sent a telegram.

Invitation accepted! Coming Friday. Will phone from station.

There were only three days to go. Rail ticket to book; she couldn't afford a sleeper. Uniform to clean, ready for her return. She rang Penny to ask her to send some suitable items from her wardrobe at home, and could Pop please deliver, the day after tomorrow at the latest?

He could. They spent a nice evening together. Later, when she looked in the case he had brought, she discovered that Penny had thoughtfully pressed and packed most of her limited summer wear. Placed right on top was a brown paper parcel. She put it one side to examine later. Probably something Penny had run up for her, she thought. An envelope tucked discreetly among the clothes contained a five pound note 'with our blessing' to spend as she wished on her holiday. They knew, of course, how little she earned despite her onerous duties.

When she unwrapped the parcel she discovered the tangerine dress, folded in tissue. Another note, from Penny: 'Hope an opportunity arises to wear this.'

'I don't know about that,' Tess mused ruefully.

Jean kissed her, then held her at arms' length to look at her properly. 'Wonderful to see you – I never dreamed you'd come so soon – I'm so happy you have!'

'Go on, say it, Jean, I've changed beyond recognition.'

'I'm not going to say anything of the sort! Didn't I hail you immediately, when you stepped down from the train? Your hair is different – I approve, mind – and somehow, when you came hurrying towards me, with such a spring in your step, I thought, good gracious, I can see Millie Mae in her now!'

'I'm glad,' Tess said. She glanced down rather ruefully at her new-length dirndl skirt, printed with four-leaf clovers on white; at her cambric blouse, a cheap outfit from the store for the masses, good old C&A; at her bare legs and Bata sandals. She wished she'd painted her toenails. Roma always did. Then she added, 'Millie

193

Mae, of course, would have looked much smarter when travelling than I do!'

'Our generation is still wedded to our hats and gloves, I suppose, but you look so much cooler and, I'm sure, were comfortable despite a stuffy, long train journey. Here we are, my little Morris: I drive myself nowadays, Tess, don't look so surprised. The old retainers, as Pop used to call them, are no longer retained, but retired. My only help is a young mother from the village for a couple of hours twice a week, but she only cleans, not cooks. Her teenage son mows the grass but doesn't know a weed from a flower. Moray bought me a washing machine for Christmas and I'm still struggling to understand how it works.'

'You look very well on it all,' Tess approved. She settled in her seat, and hoped she wouldn't need to hold on round the corners, as Jean cranked the gears.

'We'll drive by the harbour, for old time's sake, shall we? Not that you and I ever walked along the strand together, did we? Perhaps you and Moray—'

'Moray was mostly incapacitated at that time,' Tess reminded her. 'I went with Barney, occasionally with Pop, and – with Gregor Munro.'

Jean stopped the car. They looked out over the swell of water slapping the quay. The gulls shrieked and the sun made them shade their eyes. The boats were still out, and the harbour was almost deserted this afternoon, apart from a few young mothers in summery dresses, clutching toddlers' hands, waiting for older children to emerge from school. Times had changed here too, in the eight years since Tess arrived early in the war.

'There were others who didn't return,' Jean said quietly. 'The fishing industry is in decline, they say. I heard that Mrs Munro's brother died; that she sold up and moved away to be with a teacher friend of her son's in Edinburgh.'

That would be Moira, Tess guessed. She had intended to see Gregor's mother, of course, but now she felt a sense of relief that this was not to be. Too many years had passed, and Mrs Munro hadn't written of her change of address.

'I am still lacking in culinary skills,' Jean apologized, 'but I remembered your fondness for corned beef hash and decided that would be quick and easy, only I hadn't any baked beans. Tomorrow I promise a real treat though, fresh salmon.'

'I look forward to that,' Tess smiled. They ate in the sitting-room, from trays, an easy option which Jean had taken to, living on her own. The french windows were open to a garden with a mixture of cultivated plants amid wild grasses. She felt the pressures of her daily life receding; pleasure at being with an old friend.

'You like your stepmother?' Jean asked after a while.

'Oh we all do, but we don't think of her as that, just Penny. She and Pop are so right for each other and little Paul, well, that makes it perfect.' Tess paused. 'If it had been you and Pop, you know, earlier, I would've been glad.'

'I know you would. But it wasn't to be. It was a mutual decision. At the time I couldn't see him ever putting someone in Millie Mae's place; and I admitted that despite his infidelity, I went on loving Leo to the end. She sounds so nice, your Penny. I'm really happy for Pop.'

'Pop marrying again gave me the push I needed, I suppose, to leave home.' He was overprotective of me, and Barney to a certain extent, you see, though Roma, of course, wouldn't stand for that.'

'That was only natural, Tess, after losing Millie Mae; sons tend to do what they want to, as they grow up; fathers find it harder to let daughters go. Pop has granddaughters to fuss over now. What wouldn't I give to be a grandma, eh? But Sally tells me she has no intention of making me one for the foreseeable future: she's enjoying life in the US with no ties, apart from Hank, of course.'

'What about Moray?' Tess heard herself say.

Jean glanced at her keenly. 'He's a sober chap these days. More devoted to pursuing a golf-ball than a pretty girl. He sold the Surrey house and rents a bachelor flat in a block not too far from the works.'

'You said he doesn't visit very often?'

'More than I ever believed he would. The house will be Sally's eventually, but I rather imagine she'll do a deal with her brother after I go.'

'Which won't be for years and years yet!'

'Thank you for that! You look tired, my dear; you go on up, if you want to. Lie in as long as you like in the morning, won't you?'

'I'm sorry, you're right, I could close my eyes right now.'

'Then, goodnight, Tess, and God bless.'

*

Jean turned off the main light, then went to switch off the desk lamp. She hesitated for a moment, then picked up the telephone receiver, dialled the operator, then asked for a long distance call.

'Moray? Ma.'

'Is it important, Ma? I was just leaving for the club. I realize it's round about your bedtime these days, almost nine-thirty, but—'

'Moray, listen! You can get here by tomorrow, can't you, if you fly up?'

'I could, that's true. But it would have to be for a good reason – I'm playing golf in the afternoon.'

'Tess is here, Moray.'

There was silence for a moment, then he said, 'Expect me when you see me, Ma, and don't say a thing to her or the defences will be well and truly up.'

It didn't take long to pack a bag. Moray lay fully dressed on top of his bed, waiting for the dawn. He'd spent an hour on the telephone following his mother's call. There was a lot of red tape involved before the clearance was confirmed to fly one of the corporation's private planes to Scotland.

He wondered wryly why he was doing this. If he had any sense he would leave well alone. It was entirely his fault; Tess knew too much about his cavalier attitude to women in the past, including her own sister, to trust him. He remembered the last time they had met. Tess in shock after that deadly rocket fell; cradling her slight body close while she shivered and wept; how protective he felt as she succumbed to sleep. Their joint family history hardly helped, but she wasn't a young, vulnerable girl any more. It was worth one last try.

CHAPTER TWENTY-SEVEN

O n the way to her room she passed Moray's door. It was still adorned by a plywood plane, which he'd told her nonchalantly he'd fashioned with a fretsaw at the age of seven, then knocked in place with hammer and nail. 'Dad gave me a taste of the slipper for that; all the doors here are oak.'

Feeling guilty, but unable to resist the impulse, she turned the door knob, looked in. The room appeared unused; no jumble of books and papers, no clothes lying about. It wasn't as she remembered it at all, from her cheering-up visits when Moray was immobile. Jean's help obviously didn't venture in here often.

She closed the door quietly and went on to the guest room, the other side of the bathroom. There was a towel hanging on the bedrail, but she must eschew the pleasure of a long, hot soak tonight, she decided. A perfunctory wash, then she tumbled into bed and slept the night dreamlessly away.

She had forgotten to pull the curtains; the sun was warm on her face as she opened her eyes next morning. She stretched, looked at her wrist watch. Almost ten o'clock! She snatched at yesterday's clothes and made for the bathroom.

The wafting of sizzling bacon as she hurried downstairs was quite a relief: Jean must have slept in, too. She entered the kitchen ready to apologize, finding Jean at the stove dribbling fat over the sunny-side of the eggs in the pan, obviously more confident in cooking these days than she claimed to be.

'Tess, hello.' She whirled round in surprise, saw Moray sitting at the table, newspaper spread out before him. He obviously hadn't eaten yet, either. He was casually dressed in buff slacks and Aertex shirt, with a paisley cravat. Weekend wear. He didn't look much older, just thinner in the face.

'We'll have what Sally calls brunch, shall we? You don't mind if we eat in here, do you?' Jean was saying, a trifle breathlessly. 'A good fry-up now, and we should be all right until dinner. Slept well?' she asked unnecessarily. She turned back to her basting with a little smile. Tess patently hadn't heard a word.

Moray pulled out a chair. 'Sit down: good to see you. How are you, Tess?'

'What are you staring at?' she demanded in her confusion.

'You've got a white blob − toothpaste? − in your hair − here.' He handed her his napkin. 'By your left ear; oh, let me do it.' He leant forward and rubbed at her hair. 'It's all sticky now, I'm afraid, you might need to wash it.'

'Thank you,' she said primly, feeling that he was joking at her expense. Then, 'What are you doing here?'

'Visiting Ma, like you. Why, isn't that allowed?'

She recovered her composure. 'I'm sorry, of course it is. I just wasn't expecting to see you.'

'And I didn't know, when you and I said goodnight: he only arrived fifteen minutes or so ago,' Jean said, bringing their plates to the table. 'I hope you like the griddle cakes, Tess − not really griddled, I fried 'em, but they're Moray's favourites. Well, do begin, and I'll join you.'

'You've got egg on your front now, Tess,' he observed later, amused, as Tess looked down at her blouse in dismay.

'Moray, don't be so personal,' Jean reproved her son.

Tess recovered herself quickly. 'I haven't quite come to yet! Excuse me, Jean, I must sponge it off quickly before it stains. Thank you, it was a real treat.'

'You've frightened her away,' Jean reproved her son, after Tess left.

'I'm trying the brotherly approach, Ma. I think she likes it.'

'Oh, do you? You can wash up, Moray.'

'But I've only just got here.'

'It's a small price to pay, isn't it, for a phone call?'

He kissed the top of her head. 'I was only trying to disarm her, Ma.'

'Well, you're certainly well-practised at *that*. If you're good, I'll plead a headache this afternoon, and you can walk her along the shore, eh?'

198

'If she'll come.' He poured himself another cup of coffee. 'I'll see to that.'

Tess draped the damp blouse over the bedroom chair. She needed time to regain her composure. Whatever would Jean think of her, running off like that? Why had he got so close, dabbing her hair? As he held her head steady, she was all too aware of the familiar half-mocking smile and the clear blue of his eyes.

She put on a yellow T-shirt bequeathed to her by Roma. It was clean, but she could still discern her sister's scent: Roma always pumped the spray too enthusiastically, from those elegant cut-glass bottles.

'Your hair's all tendrils in the spray. I didn't think I'd like you shorn, but surprisingly I do. I suppose you used to hide your blushes behind those flowing tresses in the old days, eh?' he said, as they walked along. His limp was pronounced today, probably because of the recent rushing around, she surmised. The pallor, tightness around his lips, that was pain, her training told her. It wasn't weather for hurrying, anyway, being overcast and sultry. The beach was deserted, as it had been long ago, when the two of them traversed the crunching shingle at Dungeness, talking so earnestly about life and Millie Mae.

'Take a rest. Here's a rock to lean on.' They'd turn back before the blowhole, she decided. It was Gregor's special place, not his.

'Yes, Nurse, I think I will.' He lowered himself heavily to the ground, and on an impulse, she rolled her cardigan and put it behind his head.

'Sit down yourself.' He patted the sand beside him. 'It's dry here. The tide doesn't come up this far.'

'We need to talk,' she told him.

'Isn't that what we've been doing?'

'Be serious. You knew I was here, didn't you?'

'Yes. Aren't you flattered I literally took off and followed you here?'

'No – I—'

'Can't you admit it, even to yourself?'

'Moray, you know it would never do.'

'What wouldn't?'

'You and me.'

'A few years ago, I'd have agreed. That's why I didn't reply to your last letter, I read between the lines. I'm *different* now, Tess, can't you see that?'

'You look the same, except your hair's shorter, too, and you don't seem to have a chip on your shoulder any more, but—'

'You're still frightened I'll try to seduce you if I get half a chance, is that it?'

'Wouldn't you?'

'No. Only if you invited me to. All this would be resolved, if you'd only agree to marry me – we're wasting so much time, Tess. I'm ready for it now; I'd even be delighted to have a couple of kids like Roma.'

'*Roma!*' she almost shouted. 'Why does *she* have to come into it?'

'You can't come to terms with what happened? It didn't mean anything—'

'How can you say that! It's an insult to my sister.'

'Allow me to modify that: it was something neither of us could help; part of the fever and urgency of wartime.'

'I gathered that.'

'Please forget it, Tess; Roma obviously has.'

The next moment she was screaming, her hands flailing. 'Oh! *Help*! Horrible things all over me—' Her shirt was smothered in a mass of black flying insects.

He hauled himself up, tugged the shirt smartly from her skirt waistband, and flapped it vigorously to dislodge the unwanted visitors. 'Thunder flies; I don't think they sting. They're attracted to the colour of your top, or your scent – here, whip it off, cover-up with your cardigan and hopefully they'll leave you alone.'

She allowed him to help, to button the woolly. His touch was deliberately light, not intrusive, but her heart was pounding. She knew he must have realized she was wearing very little beneath. 'Thank you,' she managed. 'I'm sorry I was so silly.' *Scent*, she thought: the elusive essence of Roma . . .

He moved away, reached for his stick. 'No point in going further; better get back to the harbour and the car, before the skies open up.'

'Take my arm,' she offered, supporting him unobtrusively.

'Don't you think we make a good team, looking after one another?' he asked, as they reached the car. 'I'm told I could become more disabled in time, so a nurse would be the perfect wife for me,' he added wryly.

She gave him an impulsive hug. 'Maybe. You were a very undisciplined patient, as I recall. She'd have to love you to put up with you.'

200

'I think she does, despite all the reasons why she shouldn't. Here comes the summer downpour.' He slid in beside her, tossed his stick on the back seat.

'Can we watch it for a few minutes, I do love to see the sea all stirred up.'

'So do I.' Moray was watching her, not the sea. The rain drummed furiously on the roof of the car and trickled through the windows where the seal had perished. They had to shift closer together to avoid the wet. The rain stopped as abruptly as it had begun. There was even a hint of the sun returning.

'I won't put any pressure on you,' he said, as they drove away. 'I've got four days, and I'd like us to make the most of it, enjoy ourselves.'

'I came to see Jean,' she reminded him.

'And what d'you think would make Ma really happy? Seeing us starting over again as friends. We won't rush it, Tess. Let's take each day as it comes.'

'I'd like that,' she said.

'I haven't got around to the salmon yet,' Jean said, too innocently. 'I think I'll rest up; it's the only way to banish a headache. Why don't you take Tess out tonight, Moray? Don't say you've nothing to wear, look in your wardrobe. Tess, I must confess, I couldn't help seeing you'd hung a beautiful dress on your door.'

'Penny packed it, I haven't tried it on for five years.'

'I can verify that your figure is exactly it was then,' he remarked audaciously.

'Oh,' Tess said faintly. Whatever must Jean be thinking?

'I'll have to ring around to make a booking. Will Elgin do?'

'Rationing; seems no end to it,' he said, looking at the limited menu.

'It doesn't matter. Beans on toast, when I'm working.'

'That's not good,' he reproved. 'Finish tonight with treacle pud and custard.'

They sat in a curtained alcove, with a lamp which cast a rosy glow.

'No dancing, I'm afraid, but I don't think I could manage it after the walk. Mind you, walking's good for me, that's why I took up golf. I can do that at my own pace.' He looked at her reflectively. 'You still look lovely in that dress. I was jealous, that time, because you were escorted by someone else.'

'You were with Sylvia,' she reminded him, not wanting to think of Nick tonight. 'What happened to her? I hope you didn't break her heart.'

'She said not; she invited me to her wedding a couple of years ago.'

'So you remain friendly with all your old girlfriends?'

'Even with Roma, I hope. Though, as I said before, I don't expect she gives me a single thought nowadays, does she? Did *you*, either, these past four years?'

'I did, *I do*,' she said softly, 'but let's follow the pattern you suggested.'

He gave a little whistle. 'No chance you'll let me kiss you goodnight, then?'

'I didn't say that . . .' she whispered, as the Windsor soup arrived.

CHAPTER TWENTY-EIGHT

'See, she's still here.' Moray unfastened the tarpaulin revealing the legend of *Spirit of Millie Mae*. 'Does Barney mention her much these days?'

'Not much,' Tess admitted. 'Like you with Leo, he clashed with Pop. He did well in matric. so he stayed on for the Higher School Certificate; that's why he's a few months older than most for National Service. Pop wanted him to apply for further deferment, go to college first. However, there was no chance of Cranwell, becoming a pilot, as his sight is not twenty-twenty. He told Pop he'd made his mind up: all his schoolmates were being called up, and so was he.'

'He sounds quite different from the young lad I remember.'

'He's more headstrong than I was at nineteen, like Roma in that respect.'

'You had too many responsibilities at that age, but you hadn't even dipped a toe in the sea of experience, then.' He let the heavy cover drop, retied it.

She wondered if he realized how inexperienced she still was, in some ways. 'It's a good day for a swim, Jean says. She's hunting for Sally's school costume, and if it doesn't swamp me, why don't we venture into the water this afternoon?'

'I don't swim these days,' he answered shortly, ushering her from the barn.

'Why? It's ideal exercise for—'

'Those with disabilities like mine,' he finished.

'Yes,' she stated honestly. 'Don't look so grim, Moray.'

He grinned then, relaxed, slung an arm casually around her shoulders as they walked back towards the house. 'I suppose the sight of you in what I recall with a shudder, as thick navy wool, with built-in bloomers is not to be missed. Any other bathers will be ogling you, not me.'

'Well, I don't care, if that means you'll come,' she said, allowing him to know she was pleased by slipping her arm, in turn, round his waist.

They splashed in the shallows. 'I haven't swum since 1939,' she admitted.

'Dungeness?'

'Could be. Or maybe Winchelsea; we occasionally went there.'

'Didn't you swim when you were here?'

'No. Perhaps it wasn't allowed? I know that certain parts of the beach were mined. We were lucky with our stretch of the Strand.'

'You're keeping one foot on the bottom,' he accused, as she launched herself off a bit further out. 'Who taught you to swim – Pop?'

'It was Millie Mae, of course. She was fearless in the water. We used to cling to her back when we were tiny, and we didn't feel scared, even when we got wet in the waves, because she made it all such fun.'

'I do wish I'd known her.'

'You did, until you were two,' she reminded him. She ducked down, came up gasping. 'Despite the heatwave, the water's still c-cold, just as it is in Kent.'

'You'd better go under again, pull everything up, and make yourself decent.'

He was laughing aloud. 'That ancient costume's water-logged from the mothholes, and definitely sagging, I'm afraid. Fortunately those people swimming further along are too far away to see what I can see—'

'Beast!' she cried. 'Go away, until I've recovered my dignity.'

Tess sat under the overhang of rock, as she wanted to avoid getting sunburnt. She removed, with difficulty, the sodden, baggy bathing costume under cover of her towel and re-emerged respectable once more in her sleeveless cotton frock.

Moray, being dark, had no qualms about exposing his limbs to the warmth of the sun, and he pulled on shorts over his damp trunks.

She hadn't seen the scarring on his leg before, but she could deal with such sights now, she thought. She felt compassion for what he must

204

have suffered, both physically and mentally; she hadn't understood the extent of his depression when she was young, she thought, how could she?

The other swimmers left the water, packed up, and were going home for tea. They were alone, but together, in a shimmering place of endless soft silver sand with only the rushing and receding of the sea to remind them where they were.

Moray's eyes were closed; his arms half-folded limply across his chest. Aware that he was breathing rhythmically, on an impulse, she leaned forward and idly stroked the fine hair on his forearms. She was about to move back, when he caught at her hands. She could guess what he was thinking.

'Let me go, please,' she said faintly.

He rolled on to his side, pulling her, unresisting, towards him.

'You promised—'

'I know I did,' he murmured, before their lips met.

It wasn't like the last time they had been so close; it was like the other time he had come to see her at the Last Stop Garage, when she was looking after Frankie as a baby. That was when he told her about himself and Roma, and she had rejected him, because it seemed to confirm her agonized suspicions.

'Now, tell me you don't love me,' he said, triumphantly. He released her.

'I can't say that, because you're right.'

'I'm not altogether like my father. I'll be faithful, if you'll agree to marry me. I've dedicated myself to work these past four years; I haven't looked at another woman and that's the truth. I've sown all my wild oats. I shouldn't have confessed about Roma; it salved my conscience, but it blighted things with you.'

'I believe you,' she said. 'Don't talk about her now.'

'Can we tell Ma what she's longing to hear, then?'

'I can't get married just yet.'

'Why not? You're almost twenty-six, and I've already turned thirty.'

'I'm committed myself to my job for another year, I can't let them down, Moray. Really, I don't want to, you see, I trained really hard for this.'

'I don't mind you working after we're married. Many women do, having got a taste for it, during the war.'

'But I couldn't stay where I am, I have to live in the district, be on call.'

'So you want to settle for an lengthy engagement?' he sighed.

'I suppose so. Oh, Moray, these last three days, seeing you again so unexpectedly, has turned my little world upside-down. When I get married, I – I'd hope to fall for a baby almost straight away, like Princess Elizabeth has. I'd want to be at home, looking after you, and – it – and taking up my writing again.'

'Do you expect me to exercise restraint until then?' he asked bluntly.

She remembered Connie and Nick. That hadn't seemed wrong, because they were so in love. It was as if they knew time was precious, and short. The answer was surely to marry Moray right away, but as she'd told him, she couldn't just abandon her patients now, they relied upon her.

'Don't ask me that – I do love you, *I do!*' Her voice echoed off the rocks.

'That's right, tell the world!' The tenderness of his expression, said the rest.

Jean was thrilled. 'Oh, you must take Tess out and buy her a ring, tomorrow!'

'Come with us, help us choose,' Tess offered.

'Oh, no, my dear.'

'Well, we'll take you out for lunch anyway, to celebrate,' Moray insisted.

'That would be very nice. I accept! I'm glad you're not flying back with him, Tess, you and I have got so much to talk about, haven't we? Where will you get married? From home, I suppose—'

'Slow down, Ma, she's making me wait a whole year.'

'Oh, Tess!'

'Don't sound so reproachful,' Tess told her with a smile. 'We'll see each other whenever we can, we're not too far apart, after all. And then—'

'You'll tie the knot, and make a grandmother of me as soon as you can?'

'Tess says so, and look, I've still got the knack of making her blush.'

She couldn't get off to sleep, after their last evening together. She went to the bathroom to replenish her glass of water. It was a very warm night and she was wearing a brief nightie.

A light beamed under Moray's door. She paused, glass in hand. The door opened, and he stood there looking at her, tousle haired. 'Still wearing the ring?'

She held out her hand. 'I can't bear to take it off. It's beautiful, Moray. I always dreamed of a sapphire ring like Millie Mae's.'

'Coming in for a bit?' he asked softly.

She didn't hesitate. 'Yes.'

'D'you think we've woken Ma up?'

'I hope not. Anyway, I don't think Jean will grumble at us if we have.'

He drew her inside, took the glass from her. 'I'll clear a chair for you.'

'No need to do that, let's make the most of tonight . . . Remember' – her voice was muffled against his bare, slightly damp chest as he drew her close – 'it's the first time for me.'

'I wish I could say that; but it's the first time for me with you – isn't that what really matters? Let's take things slowly, eh?'

Fleetingly, she wondered if she was doing the right thing. What would Millie Mae have advised? Would she have been shocked? Millie Mae fell in love with Pop when she was around the same age as I was, when I fell for Moray in Scotland, Tess thought. She wasn't much older when she married and Roma was born. I believe – I know – Millie Mae would say be wholehearted about it if you're really in love – and I am, and it's wonderful, he's wonderful, and, it's meant to be.

'Don't go, we've only got another three hours together,' he said, first thing. His arms tightened possessively around her. 'No regrets, darling Tess?'

'None,' she said truthfully. She ought to go back to her room of course, what if Jean arrived with a cup of tea for Moray? His flight was scheduled for 9.30 this morning. Her mouth curved at the corners.

'Why are you smiling?' He was curling a lock of her hair round his finger.

'Ah, wouldn't you like to know!' She recalled how she'd discovered Pop and Pen together, just before they announced that they were to be married, and how she'd managed to contain her surprise, and yes, a little consternation, even though she'd believed Penny when she said nothing had occurred. What did it matter if it had? Look how committed they were, one to the other; just as she was now committed to

207

Moray, and he to her. She was finally fulfilled, utterly content.

'Ma won't say anything, Tess. She can be a bit old-fashioned at times, but there's nothing wrong with that, is there? And she'd certainly disapprove if we didn't intend to make it legal eventually, but she adores you Tess, you know that. You'll be the daughter to her, which Sally, somehow never quite could be.'

'I feel the same way about her, of course. I think Millie Mae would have been pleased at that. I wish she was here, so I could tell her about us.'

'And I wish Dad was too, because I'm sure he'd approve.'

She stood with Jean watching the plane take off. 'Don't cry, Tess, or you'll start me off. He promised to ring directly he gets back, after all.' She turned the key in the ignition. 'Forgive me asking, did Moray try to take, um, liberties last night?'

'Jean, will it shock you if I say yes – and that I wanted him to? Very much.'

'If you put it like that, it's all right, except I hope he wasn't, er, irresponsible about it,' Jean said in a matter-of-fact sort of way. 'Town – for coffee, I think.'

'I think you can say he was very responsible indeed, responsible for me feeling happier than I've ever felt in my life. And thank you, Jean, for making it all possible and bringing us together again, when it seemed we never would.'

CHAPTER TWENTY-NINE

She went home before she returned to work. She'd wait and see if Pop and Penny noticed the ring, she thought, before she said a thing.

She caught a taxi there, because she hadn't warned them she was coming. Paul was playing in the garden. He called to Penny. 'Mummy, Tess is here!'

Penny, all paint-smeared as usual, flung her arms round her.

'Hey! Anyone would think I was the prodigal daughter!'

'We don't see nearly enough of you — what a lovely surprise! Peg's down at the shops, but she'll be back soon — I'll summon Pop from his workshop.' There was a ship's brass bell fixed to the outside wall. Penny gave it a vigorous tug.

The clanging brought Pop running too, to see what was up.

'Tess, why didn't you ring me to collect you at the station? We thought you were going to be another few days in Scotland.'

'I couldn't wait to see you — I don't spend nearly enough time with you.'

'Kettle boiling, Pen? Did something happen in Scotland?' Pop looked at her keenly. 'You got on all right with Jean, surely?'

'Of course I did. It's a long old journey.' She took a cautious sip of tea.

Penny's shriek caused her to almost spill it and scald herself. 'Look, Pop! Tess is wearing a ring!'

Tess set the cup back on the saucer. 'That was a near thing, Pen — I didn't quite expect that reaction!'

'An engagement ring?' Pop queried.

'That's just what it is, Pop.'

'Who?'

'Moray, it must be, eh, Tess?' Penny guessed.

'You don't mind, d'you, Pop?' Tess appealed to him.

'Mind? I guess he's older and wiser, and − I always liked him, you know. If you're happy, I'm happy − we're happy, aren't we, Pen?'

'I'm not happy,' came a sad little voice. 'I've been trying to tell Tess I want her to come and see my guinea pig.'

'Let me drink my tea, and I'll be with you, Paul − a guinea pig, how exciting!' She looked down at her ring. 'Just one thing, *I'll* tell Roma.'

There was always a crowd in the NAAFI canteen on pay-day, once a fortnight: it wasn't always worth the bother of being stuck in the queue. If Barney hadn't wangled a weekend pass, he was stuck on the camp, for it was quite a walk to town and those who invited him to join them on a night out had a different view as to what constituted fun. Probably the bragging had very little substance, but Barney didn't want to find out. The propaganda films shown at the beginning of their National Service certainly had the desired effect on Barney and his mates.

Sometimes Barney, Johnnie Scott and others, spent their time off peeling spuds in the cookhouse; chucking them with a satisfying splash into cauldrons of water. The cooks thus relieved of this boring chore rewarded their slaves not with money, but with an illicit fry-up. The spud-bashers often felt queasy afterwards and a boy called Parkin was invariably sick, but always affirmed it was worth it.

Then it was heads under the covers awaiting the return of those who had gone to town, imbibed too much and inclined to raucous song and rude repartee.

One Saturday evening the word went round the stay-in-campers that the hut recently erected on the smallholding directly opposite the camp gates, had actually opened as a café with a view to taking the overflow from the NAAFI.

Barney, Parkin and Johnnie Scott decided to give it the once-over. Someone had painted a big sign: CAFÉ − WELCOME! HOME-COOKING. Under these words was sketched a rather wobbly cup and saucer and the price of tea, 3d.

They trooped in sheepishly. The only customers, they sat down at a wonky fold-up table on a mismatch of chairs and waited for service.

'Come and fetch it, lads.' A middle-aged man appeared through a rear door, in a whoosh of steam and appetizing aromas from what was obviously the kitchen. He fixed a long counter. 'What d'you fancy?' he asked affably, pointing to the blackboard menu. 'Sav'ry ninepence, or with sweet, together a bob.'

Sav'ry was something on toast: baked beans and sausage, poached egg and tomato, grilled bacon, or scrambled eggs. They decided on the latter. The owner's daughter eventually brought out a loaded tray. Two thick cut pieces of perfectly browned toast spread with what tasted like butter, heaped with softly scrambled egg, and really tasty. This treat really didn't need the brown sauce which Johnnie Scott shook all over his plate.

They queued for apple crumble and custard. 'Our own apples; there's egg in the custard, and fresh milk . . . fancy a glass of that instead of a cup o' tea, lads?'

Chrissie delivered the milk to Barney. 'Extra 3d for the drinks, please,' she requested in a low voice. Barney had glimpsed her several times before, when she walked to town, basket on arm. Once, he had seen her climbing a ladder, in the orchard beside the house. She was wearing shorts, revealing tanned, shapely legs. She reminded him a little of Tess, being small but with smooth brown hair, kept in place with hair slides decorated with gilt butterflies. Her eyes were the same colour as her hair. Her dimpled pink cheeks bestowed prettiness on one with a healthy outdoor tan. She worked on the smallholding with her parents.

'Everything all right?' she asked, wiping the crumbs and spills from the table.

'It was really good, thanks.' Barney, for once, spoke before Johnnie or Parkin could get a look-in. He put tuppence under his plate. When she discovered this, Chrissie smiled her appreciation, and slipped the coins in her pinny pocket.

'You'll come again, I hope? Tell your mates?'

'You bet.' Barney had coined this expression from Old Swindon.

'Good. See ya then,' Chrissie said, looking at Barney. Her vocabulary had been influenced by weekly trips to the pictures, and Hollywood films.

Roma had been up West to get her hair done. There was a local hairdresser where the girls had their six-weekly trims, but the word 'ladies' summed up the service for their mother. She didn't want rigid waves and setting lotion dripping down her neck, and pre-war copies of *Home Chat* to read under the old-fashioned dryer, with cotton wool stuffed over her ears because there was a risk of burning.

She had done her window-shopping; even though her purse was full thanks to her generous husband, it wasn't much use when the shops still hadn't a great deal to offer. It really was disgraceful, rationing still in place three years after the end of the war, she thought. She had two hours to fill before she caught the train back to Kent. Swindon had the weekend off and was amusing the girls. He had regarded her keenly this morning, when he brought her breakfast in bed, and told her, 'You need a day to yourself, darling – seize your chance!'

On an impulse, she took out her diary from her bag and checked the map of the underground inside the front cover. She had plenty of time to visit Tess, to impart some important news, but she'd best give her a quick ring first.

Dolly answered: Tess was on a routine visit to a mother who had just given birth, but she expected she would be home at any minute. 'Come anyway, I'll let you in if she isn't. I'm sure she won't want to miss seeing you.'

Half an hour later, she was knocking on Tess's door. Not too bad an area, she thought, relieved, for this was the first time she'd been here: shabbily respectable in fact. Most of the terraced houses looked as if they were occupied by several tenants. She knew that Tess and her colleague shared the top floor of this one.

'I was on the q.v.; Roma, isn't it?' Dolly said, opening the door. 'Mrs doo-dah downstairs has a rest in the afternoons. Follow me up; you can wait in Tess's room. Make yourself a cup of tea; bathroom's on the landing if you feel the need. Excuse me, I've a visitor too, my niece. Make yourself at home.'

Roma wished she hadn't come. The room was dark, plain and functional. The chairs were uncomfortable, it was stifling hot and the window refused to open. She sat down with yesterday's paper, retrieved from the waste-paper basket. The newspapers were thin compared with the ones in Canada, with pages of funnies for the children, she thought, flicking over the crumpled pages.

She heard footsteps on the stairs. Dolly looked in again. 'Someone else to see Tess – this gentleman says he's her fiancé, well, she hasn't said yet, but I certainly noticed the ring – wonder where's she's got to?

All right if he joins you? I'm sure you know each other.' She ushered the second visitor in.

'Hello, Roma,' Moray said, to satisfy Dolly that they really were acquainted.

'I'll leave you to it, then,' she said cheerfully.

Roma jumped to her feet, thinking fleetingly that she was glad she'd had her hair done. It would have been dampening if he hadn't recognized her, but, after all, it was seven years since last they met. She could be exact about that. 'Hello Moray, well, this is a surprise! What did she mean, fiancé?'

'Haven't you spoken to Tess since she returned from Scotland a few days ago? She went home first—'

'I didn't even know she'd been Scotland, or to Kent! I'm always asking her to stay with us, but she never does.' Roma felt distinctly disgruntled.

'I don't think Ma gave her time to say no, on this occasion.'

'Nor did you, apparently. Are you really engaged?'

'We are, I'm delighted to say. Any objections?'

'None at all! I've been pointing her in your direction and hinting for absolute ages. Well, aren't you going to say you're pleased to see me?'

'Of course I am. You're always a sight for sore eyes,' he smiled.

'That's better.' Roma was recovering her good temper. 'Know where Tess keeps the matches? Then I'll put the kettle on.'

'Actually, no. It's the first time I've been here, too, you see. Here, use my lighter,' he handed it to her. 'We were due to meet tomorrow; I decided I couldn't wait that long, and took the chance she'd finish work earlier than she expected.'

As Roma flicked the light to the gas, Moray, glancing idly at the mantelpiece, asked, 'Are these your daughters?' He picked up the silver frame.

'Yes. The little boy in the middle is Paul, Pop and Penny's son.'

'I can see that. The younger girl—'

'That's Evelyn. We call her Evie.' She rinsed the teapot with hot water.

'She's like you, I think.'

'Most people think she looks more like her dad,' she said perversely.

'You know, it's rather uncanny, but, Frankie, isn't it? looks very like Sally when she was about that age – six?'

'Almost six and a half.' Instantly she wished she hadn't said that. She

213

added defensively, 'We call her our honeymoon baby.'

'I always assumed—'

'Assumed what?' she flashed back, turning to face him, full teapot in hand.

'Hey, put that down! It doesn't matter of course, but it did seem to be—'

'A shot-gun wedding? Nothing of the sort! You just didn't hang around in wartime, did you? You snatched at happiness while you could.' She couldn't help thinking of the one night they had spent together.

'Yes, you did, didn't you?' he said deliberately. 'And it's lasted for you, hasn't it?' He was still holding the photograph. 'I'm glad for you both.'

'Thank you. Sugar?' She felt the moment of danger had passed.

'Yes please.' He put the photograph back in place. 'You're very lucky.'

'I hope you and Tess will be, too. She'll be a wonderful mother.'

'I'm counting on her being a wonderful wife, first.'

'I intend to be,' Tess said clearly, coming into the room, looking hot and tired in her uniform, thick stockings and heavy shoes. 'Is there a cup for me?'

Neither of them had been aware of the door opening, of her presence until then. Guiltily, Roma wondered how much she had heard. She blurted out, 'I dropped in to tell you some good news, and now I learn you've got something to impart as well – congratulations, Tess! Both of you.'

Tess sat down next to Moray. He reached for her hand, gave it a little reassuring squeeze. 'Thank you,' she said to her sister.

'You won't forget your promise, will you?' Roma asked.

'What was that?'

'Oh, you have! I said, if you thought of getting married, please do it soon, because the girls, you know, are longing to be bridesmaids before they're much older, and we're moving back to Canada before Christmas.'

'Is that your news?'

'Well, yes, but, haven't you guessed, Nurse?' Roma patted her rounded stomach ruefully. 'It must be the air over here, Swindon says, as we're expecting another baby next spring, so he's not renewing his contract because we want the baby to be born in Canada, like

Evie; the hospital there was so good.'

'Congratulations to you and Swindon, too. I'm not sure I can oblige on the bridesmaid front, because we can't fix a date yet.' There was something she wanted to discuss with Moray, but not now, in front of Roma.

'I'd better go,' Roma consulted her watch. 'Train to catch.'

'I'll run you to the Tube in the car,' Moray offered, 'While Tess gets changed. We're going out tonight,' he said to her. 'You need a break, and so do I. Throw a few things in an overnight bag, eh?' he added deliberately.

They both observed Roma flinch, but she recovered her composure instantly to advise Tess, 'Seize the moment, as they say, little sister!'

They didn't go out on the town after all. Moray drove Tess back to his flat and made a meal for them there. Cold cuts and salami from the nearby delicatessen; watercress, tomatoes and lettuce from the Saturday market; boiled new potatoes; hunks of seedy bread spread with what she suspected was his weekly ration of butter; and a bottle of chilled white wine, opened with a flourish.

They hadn't talked much during dinner. Now, as he served coffee, Moray asked. 'Tess, what's wrong?'

'I'm – tired.'

'No, it's more than that, isn't it? Roma?'

She said softly, 'I suppose so. Can I tell you my news before we talk about that? I called in at the office, on the off-chance there was some-one there and I spoke to the nursing co-ordinator. She said a couple of months' notice would do, that the part-time nurse would be happy to be permanent; they'd always welcome me back with open arms if I decided to come back later.'

'That's great news: it means we can get married sooner, doesn't it? How d'you feel about that?'

'Earlier this afternoon I felt elated, relieved, because, I can't help it, Moray, I feel guilty without—'

'That necessary piece of paper,' he finished sharply. 'Does that mean you want me to take you home tonight?'

'I-I didn't say that, the last thing I want is to upset you – please, Moray.'

'Then stay,' he insisted.

'I brought my things, didn't I? We've wasted so much time, and all—'

'Because of Roma. Darling Tess, I must have been blind. Seeing that picture of Frankie, *I knew*. Did Roma tell you?'

'No, she's never said; only what you told me, too – like you, she said it was best forgotten. But, seeing Frankie again, I thought I'd been mistaken.'

'Maybe because you wanted to believe you had. She's not so much like me, but the image of my sister as a little girl. Ma would realize instantly, if she saw her. Best to avoid that.'

'What are you going to do?'

'Nothing. Roma would deny it, possibly Swindon doesn't know, and would be dreadfully hurt; they are obviously a happy little family – I can't do anything to damage that security, can I? We'll have a family of our own, soon enough.'

'I'm glad they're going back to Canada.'

'What about a Christmas wedding? No embarrassing meetings then.'

'Oh, Moray, yes: I do love you so much.'

'Then allow me to show you just how I feel about you . . .'

216

CHAPTER THIRTY

'**I** know you're awake, Roma; what's up?' She had gone to bed early, left Swindon to tidy up the chaos in the living-room left behind by their energetic daughters.

Roma wiped away her tears with the sheet, keeping it up over her face so that he couldn't see she was distressed. She mumbled something, hoping he would feel contrite instead for disturbing her sleep.

He switched off the lamp, settled down gratefully in bed beside her. 'Flying a planeload of passengers is nothing compared with coping with two small girls all day,' he observed. 'Come on, cuddle up and confide, as they say.'

'You always know when I'm bluffing.' She allowed him to lower the sheet, to kiss her damp cheeks, hug her to him. His hands caressed her silk-clad shoulders, soothing her. 'I went to see Tess, I said I might, if I had time, remember?'

'And?' he prompted gently.

'Moray was there.'

'Moray?' He was tense now, too.

'Yes. We waited for Tess, together, in her digs; she was seeing a patient.'

'How long is it since you saw him last?'

'Not since we, you and I saw him – that time in Surrey, with Sally – well, you know how long that must be, as well as I do,' she whispered.

'A month before we were married.'

'I think he's guessed, about Frankie: Tess had framed that photo we sent her of the three children together, you took this spring. He said' –

217

the tears were gushing again – 'he said, Frankie looked just like Sally at that age . . .'

'Did he question you?'

'No, because fortunately Tess arrived then, and I told her about the new baby and perhaps he thought it best—'

'Perhaps he thought it best to say nothing more. To let it go. That must be it.' Sometimes he was too ready to assume a problem was solved.

'It might be because Tess and Moray met up again in Scotland a couple of weeks ago after not seeing one another for years. They decided they were in love, had been all along, and, would you believe it, they actually got engaged!'

'Then I don't think you need to worry: this is not something he'll want Tess to know, any more than we do.'

'Swindon, I've got a confession, please don't be angry with me, will you? I told Tess a while ago, when I guessed she was keen on him, that we, Moray and I, had been . . . foolish once, but we didn't even contemplate marriage because we knew very well that we weren't right for each other. Then she said he'd already been frank with her about it.

'He seems to have changed for the better. I saw the way he looked at her – I felt I was intruding – he never, ever looked at me like that.'

'Do I?' he demanded.

'Of course you do! I still go weak at the knees when I realize how lucky, and loved I am.'

He kissed her fiercely, almost taking her breath away. 'You're so beautiful, so precious to me, Roma. I can't imagine really what you see in me.'

'Can't you? It's like Millie Mae always said: "I married Mr Right!" When I was little I'd ask, "Who's he?" and she'd laugh and say, "The most wonderful man in the world". Then, one day when I was a bit older I realized she meant Pop.'

'He tells me you grow more and more like your mother.'

'And like her, I'd like two girls and a boy, then call it a day, my darling!'

Barney was walking back to his hut, still in a bit of a happy daze because he'd actually dared to kiss Chrissie goodnight for the first time, even if it could be classed as a brief encounter, when he cannoned into another airman.

'Sorry, I wasn't looking where I was going,' he apologized.

The other chap paused, stared hard at him. 'Barney?'

'Dougie? It can't be!'

'Well, it is – who'd have thought we'd meet up again here?'

'You came with the new intake two days ago?'

'Certainly did. Coming to the NAAFI for a chat? That's where I was off to, hoping to find more congenial company than some of the lads in my hut.'

'Well, I've just come from the café over the road, the grub's great there, but I can always manage another cup of tea. Have we got time?'

'Half an hour before they close.'

Dougie was still lanky, thin and ever-hungry; scoffing two large sticky buns in quick succession. 'They'll be stale by tomorrow.'

'Half-price then! Thought you were going to university,' Barney observed.

'I am. Going to read medicine, I hope. Thought I'd get my service over and done with first. Can't believe my luck, seeing you again.'

'Sorry I didn't keep the letters up, but after the first year—'

'I know. Me, too. But I often thought of you, over the years. What's the news of your family? Tess and Pop – oh, and Roma?'

'Pop's married again, we all approve of his choice, and guess what? I've got a little brother, Paul! Pop's aspirations are pinned on him, now. Roma married Old Swindon, the Canadian, you met him, I know, and they've got two daughters and, I've just been informed, there's another on the way. They're going back to live in Canada in November. They were there for a long while before.'

'And Tess? Did she become a famous writer?'

'No, but we still have hopes! She's a nurse.'

'I had a crush on her, you know.'

'You didn't! She's nearly six years older than you and me, we were just kids. I wasn't the least bit interested in girls, then, I thought you were the same – don't tell me that's why you never minded tagging along when Tess made me go for walks with her, eh? I thought you were mad on aeroplanes like me!'

'I was, I still am, to a lesser extent. I've still got that super Gladiator you gave me, and it's not come unglued or broken or anything. Perhaps I'll become a flying doctor out in Australia, eh? Remember when you fell out of that tree, and Tess sent me shooting off for help, only Gregor turned up just as I was all set to impress her, and they walked home, starry-eyed? Nice chap though, I liked him. Shame about what happened, eh? Did Tess marry someone else eventually?'

'Not yet. A month ago I'd have said, "not likely", but she's just surprised us all by getting engaged to someone else from your part of the world.'

'Scotland?'

'That's right. She's going to marry Moray Tann. Remember him?'

'Of course, he was our hero, wasn't he? Battle of Britain pilot and all that. The reason, I suppose, we both chose the RAF when we got our call-up. Did you ever take possession of the light plane his father gave you?'

Barney shook his head. 'Hardly given it a thought the last year or two,' he admitted. 'My dreams of flying – well, that's all they were, just dreams. I'll tell you all about it another day. Now, what about you? Got a girlfriend?'

'Looking for an intellectual redhead like Tess, maybe. You?'

'Going in the right direction, I hope . . .'

They were in the lift, to Moray's flat, when he asked her, 'D'you mind starting married life here, Tess? You haven't said where you'd like to live, you know.'

'Well, we obviously can't settle on the marsh, or in Scotland, because of your work, so, I really don't mind.'

The lift doors glided open, and they stepped out on to his landing.

'Ready to set a date yet?' he asked, as he inserted his key in the lock.

She shook her head. 'Fortunately, Roma hasn't said any more about us getting married before they return to Canada, and now their departure is almost here, ten days away, in fact. I thought we'd agreed on Christmas?'

'Cutting it fine for then, banns to be read and all that. Have you actually given your notice in yet?' he pressed. He helped her out of her coat. 'Your hands are really cold,' he told her. 'You must wrap up in this damp, foggy weather.'

'Oh, I'm not a poor specimen like I used to be! The nursing profession is going through a period of upheaval, remember, with the National Health Service taking us over. It must be for the best, of course, because now the people who really need medical care and who can't afford it, are able to have it, for free. Though I suspect it's just as well I'm about to leave, because I don't feel I'm nearly as dedicated as I was, with you to distract me. And to answer your question, now I've finally made it official. The end of this month. Then I'll pack up and go home to Pop and Pen, and allow them to make all the arrangements!'

Tess was spending the day helping Roma with her packing. 'Leave that heavy bag,' she counselled. 'I'll carry it downstairs. Are you feeling all right?'

'Don't fuss,' Roma retorted, just as she had when she was expecting Frankie. It was the girls' last day at their school; tomorrow they would be, as Roma put it, "under foot" and she wouldn't get much done, although Swindon would be here to see to the last-minute things. Roma was expecting him home tonight.

'You must take care: you're almost six months pregnant after all.'

'At least the journey home will be much quicker, going by plane.'

'Put your feet up for five minutes, rest on the bed, there's a good girl.'

Tess sat down beside her, taking hold of her sister's wrist, feeling her pulse.

'It's a bit erratic, you know. Stay put!'

'At least I needn't worry if I go into premature labour, you being a nurse.'

'Don't make jokes like that! Stop fidgeting, Roma, please.'

'Tess, have you delayed your wedding on purpose – 'til we've departed for Canada, I mean?'

'Well. . . .'

'I'm right, aren't I?'

'Roma, the last thing I want to do is to hurt your feelings.'

'You haven't, because I believe I know why. You're trying to avoid any awkwardness, aren't you? I tried to tell myself you hadn't realized the truth about Frankie's birth, but, of course, Moray will have confided his suspicions to you.'

'I'd already guessed; from when she was a tiny baby. Moray has no intention of spoiling things. When he realized the truth, he accepted that you were happily married and that Frankie had a good father already, that he must never come into the picture again. There, feel better now?'

'Tess, thank you! Yes, I do. And when you and Moray have a family, as I hope you will—'

'Oh, we will! Right away, I've warned him. And if the first one's a girl, can we lay claim to the name of Millie Mae?'

' 'Course you can! You're the best sister I've got!'

'I'm your *only* sister, and now you can direct operations from the bed. We'll finish the packing and then have lunch!'

It was time to fetch Frankie and Evie from school. Roma and Tess went along quarter of an hour early because Roma had presents to give, and goodbyes to make to the teachers who had looked after her children for the past year.

'I didn't tell the girls you were coming today,' Roma said, as they walked along the corridor to the staff room, their first port of call. 'They would have tried hard to find a good reason for staying at home, and missed seeing all their friends on their last day here. They'll be so pleased you've decided to stay overnight.'

'Well, I suddenly remembered that it may be quite a while before we all meet up again, and, of course, I wanted to see dear old Swindon, too.'

'We'll make it a special evening, eh? All the luggage neatly lined up in the hall, awaiting collection; we'll send Swindon out for fish and chips.'

'You'll get heartburn,' Tess teased.

'It'll be worth it,' Roma said.

Then a little whirlwind came bursting out of her classroom. 'My teacher said I could! Tess, what're you doing here?'

'I came specially for the party tonight, Frankie.' Tess hugged her niece. Frankie had a special place in her affections.

'What party?' Frankie demanded.

'It's the first I've heard of a *party*, too – ask your auntie.'

'Tess?'

'Hellos and goodbyes – impromptu parties are often the best.'

'What's impromp-tu,' Evie asked, joining them.

'You don't know nothing,' Frankie said, as her mother winced at her grammar. 'It means we don't have to wait, it starts the minute we get home!'

CHAPTER THIRTY-ONE

'**O**ne more call,' Tess told Dolly Day, at five o'clock, 'the very last one, before I hand in my uniform tomorrow at the office.'

'It could wait for me to see to in the morning, couldn't it? It's only Mrs Fredericks's neighbour wanting you to look at a rash.'

'Could be the start of a bed-sore, Dolly, I can't let her down.' This patient was a bedridden, dignified old lady who had known better days. She was a particular favourite of Tess's because she had a rich fund of stories of an eventful life spent mostly overseas. 'There – you can spin a tale about that, can't you, my dear. I don't mind, as long as you call it fiction!'

'The fog's coming down, and you've got a nasty cough already,' Dolly worried, echoing Moray, with, 'Wrap up well.'

'*Smog*, the papers have dubbed it now,' Tess said, as she pulled her hat down over her ears. 'Factory chimneys, coal fires – there's that awful smell and yellowness of sulphur; it seems to go straight down to your lungs: pea-soupers they called 'em in the nineties, didn't they? The kind of fog you could almost cut with a knife. Back in an hour; if not, mount a search party,' she joked.

She began choking and coughing the minute she set foot outside the front door. She wouldn't ride her bike, too hazardous.

This swirling, thick stuff was evil, she thought; she could barely see a yard ahead. It affected her eyes and she had to concentrate to keep them open. When she got back, she thought, she would have to bathe them, unglue them, to remove the horrible sooty deposit. Most people who couldn't avoid going out in this weather suffered from sore, red-rimmed eyes.

Many of the shops and offices had obviously closed early, and staff sent home. The occasional bus was creeping along, guided by men carrying flaming torches. It was a surreal sight. The trams still clanked along, spitting sparks; close behind them, cars cruised cautiously in their tracks.

Sometimes Tess stumbled inadvertently off the kerb into the gutter. Once, where the smog was densest, where the gas lights failed to penetrate, she fell against a lamppost, saved by her bag which took the impact, but winded her in the process. She clung on to the cold metal, struggling for breath.

'All right, miss?' The local bobby peered down at her, shining a powerful battery torch. 'Nurse Rainbow, isn't it? What are you doing out in this?'

'Patient – to see . . .' Tess managed. 'Butlers Buildings.'

'I'll walk you there,' he decided. 'Will you be long?'

'Don't think so – thank you.'

'I'll wait, then. See you back. Take my arm, eh?'

He helped her up the steps to the flat, carrying her bag. 'All right?' he asked her again. She nodded, coughing as she opened the door, left on the catch.

She had to sit down, while the bobby explained about the smog to old Mrs Fredericks, lying in bed in that fusty room; wrapped like a mummy, as she remarked wryly, because the gas fire was only kept going by precious sixpences.

Tess applied soothing cream, padded the patient's hip.

'Sorry, her-next-door called you out, dear, just a rash, as I told her. She'll be in later to settle me down. You go now, there's a good girl, and inhale some good old Friar's Balsam . . . oh, and thank you for all you've done for me these past months.' She rummaged under her pillow. 'I'm sorry this is goodbye, but I hope you'll be very happy when you wed your young man. This is for you, not much, I know, but I carried it at my wedding, and I hope it brings you luck, like it did me.'

The silver paper horseshoe, with its crumpled spray of artificial white heather, was ancient, like Mrs Fredericks, but Tess accepted it in the spirit it was given.

'Thank you – I shall treasure this.'

Out in the foul air once more Tess was racked by more coughing. The gripping pain in her chest – she knew what it meant. She was about to be really ill, as she had been when she was younger and suffered from bronchitis every winter. The bobby caught her as she collapsed. His voice seemed to come from a distance. 'Hospital, my dear.' He blew his whistle.

There was something over her face and she put up a shaky hand. An oxygen mask. She was propped up in a hospital bed. She couldn't recall being brought here in the ambulance, the last thing she remembered was that piercing whistle. Her gaze flickered to the locker beside her – a carafe of water, a jug of velvet-petalled red roses – in November? A paper horseshoe? She frowned in perplexity.

One nurse greeted another. 'She's awake now.'

'Good. Breathing easier?'

'Slightly. Tell her father he can come in now for a few minutes.'

Then Pop was there at her side, patting her hand, and talking in a husky voice as if he, too, had a bad cold, she thought, and he was saying that he'd been here for two days and this was the first time he'd been allowed to see her.

Her brow puckered again. She gestured: take away the mask, let me say something, he interpreted. He shook his head. 'No, I mustn't. Here.' He closed her fingers round a pencil; held a notepad for her. 'Can you write something?'

The shaky capitals asked: G. FEVER?

'No, no. Your old trouble, I'm afraid.' Bronchial pneumonia, actually, but he mustn't alarm her. A few years ago, she would have been unlikely to survive, but now, thanks to the wonder drug M&B, as it was known, she had a good chance.

The pencil wavered again. MORAY.

'Yes. He's here with me, has been all along.'

'Time's up,' the nurse said briskly. 'Tests to do.'

Pop stroked her forehead. 'The family send their best love. Moray will see you soon; we're both staying. They let me in first, next-of-kin, you see.'

The screens were trundled into place round the bed. The mask was lifted, briefly. 'Cough, there's a good girl – spit!' Words she'd often said to a patient herself, holding the sputum bag steady.

Time seemed to have no meaning. She drifted in and out of consciousness. Injections, drips, doctors applying the chill stethoscope to her chest, drumming fingers on her back. Lifted from a pool of sweat, gently bathed and changed into a clean hospital gown, subsiding gratefully once more on cool, smooth, dry linen. . .

Dark days before Christmas: the blinds were down in her little room off the main ward and, as the nurse switched on the light, Tess opened her eyes wide and seemed to see clearly again for the first time in many days. The mask had been removed and she could speak. She cleared her throat, and the nurse turned at the door. 'Want anything, Tess?'

'Is – is Moray here?'

'I'll see. Doctor said he should return to work, visit you in the evenings, now you're getting better. Ah, here he is, that's good – go straight in, Mr Tann. You'll find her wide awake at last!'

He was laden with hothouse blooms, a carrier bag of fruit. Nurse relieved him of the flowers. 'I'll see to these. Ring if you need me, but stay as long as you like, only don't let on I said so!'

'Hello, Tess,' he said softly. He looked gaunt, eyes heavily shadowed. She wondered, as she had earlier with Pop, has he been ill, too?

'Where have you been?' she asked uncertainly.

'Here, most of the time. They kicked me out now and then.'

'How – long?'

'Nearly three weeks.'

'Then . . . it's almost . . . Christmas?'

'Almost. They'll be moving you into the ward soon, they tell me. That's a positive sign: means you're out of danger, at last.'

'Can't I go home?'

'Not just yet, I'm afraid. Tess, darling, it's been touch and go – but you're making good progress.'

'We were getting married.' She held out her arms weakly. 'You haven't kissed me yet,' she reproached him.

'Sorry; you look so fragile, Tess: I'm afraid of hurting you.'

'Please . . .'

He embraced her gently, but she could sense the holding back. 'I love you, Tess,' he whispered. 'We took so long to find each other again – I've been so afraid I was going to lose you.'

'Have I been as ill as all that?'

'Yes, you have.'

'The wedding. . . .'

'Don't worry about that; spring might be a better time, anyway.'

'Spring, yes.' Her eyes were closing. 'I need to sleep . . . but don't go . . .'

'I won't,' he promised.

The year had turned, it was January 1949, before she was finally allowed home. She was sitting out in a chair, screened from the other patients in the ward, resting after a morning of tests, when the doctor came to see her.

'You're looking much better,' he said encouragingly.

She gave a wry smile in return. Her pallid face reflected in the bathroom mirror first thing, had not been a pretty sight, she thought.

'Your fiancé is collecting you, I understand, after lunch?'

'Yes. He is driving me home to Kent.'

'You have someone to look after you there?'

'My parents. My stepmother was a nurse,' she added, just in case he thought of changing his mind and keeping her here.

'Good. You still need plenty of rest.'

'Why . . . why is my recovery so slow?' she asked.

'What did the specialist say?'

'He said my lungs were healing nicely.'

The doctor cleared his throat. 'He also told you, I'm sure, that your heart was weakened; bearing in mind that from childhood, you have—'

She interrupted. 'He said I could live a normal life, but that I wouldn't be able to go back to nursing. I said it didn't matter, because I am getting married—'

'And Mr Pickles reassured you that there was no reason why, ah, you should not have, ah, an intimate relationship with your husband?'

'Yes.' She looked at him. 'You want to be sure that I understand the rest of it? That it would be advisable not to have children . . . How do I tell Moray that?'

'You don't have to, Tess. He knows.'

The doctor carefully turned her clenched hand, wrist upwards. 'Relax . . . What have you got in your hand? I'll just take your blood pressure one last time, eh?' She let the little paper horseshoe fall on to the coverlet. I shouldn't marry Moray now, she thought, I must give him the chance to break things off gracefully if he wants to. I promised him a family; he has a daughter he can't acknowledge, and now there won't be a new little Millie Mae, *ever*.

They didn't talk much on the journey home. Moray swathed her in blankets, placed a covered hot water bottle on her lap, a cushion behind her head. She covertly watched the miles slip by, hoping he would think she was napping.

The house was ablaze with lights, warm and welcoming. Pop came rushing out to help her indoors, while Moray collected up her things.

'For you,' Penny said proudly, showing off the new reclining chair. 'A late Christmas present, from all us 'Ps', including Peg.'

'I cross-stitched the arm covers and the chair back,' Peg beamed. 'Took my mind off worrying about you, Tess.'

'I'm not going to lie about all day,' Tess knew she must sound ungrateful.

Penny smiled. 'This evening you are: doctor's orders after the journey. Sit down: hog the fire for once, while you've got the opportunity, eh?'

'Good to have you home,' Pop said softly, covering her knees with a rug. He gave her a kiss to let her know he forgave her lack of grace.

'Make the most of her, before I marry the girl and whisk her away again, to hog the fire with *me*,' Moray reminded them with a smile.

'I don't want to talk about weddings today . . .' Tess was suddenly weeping, and Moray was on his knees beside the chair. She tried to push him away. 'Leave me alone, don't you understand? I don't want to be fussed over!'

Pop looked helplessly at Penny. They'd anticipated a joyful homecoming.

'Come and give me a hand with the meal, Pop.' Penny plucked at his sleeve. 'Leave them to it,' she added in a whisper.

'I didn't mean it,' Tess sobbed.

'You're tired.' Moray straightened up, moved a chair close beside her, reached out and took her hand firmly in his.

'I'm not!'

Perhaps it was unwise of him to say, 'You sound like Roma now.'

'*Roma*! You see, you do still think about her.'

'Only in a sisterly sense. What's really up, Tess darling?'

'The doctor told me,' she stated baldly, 'that we can't have children.'

'Not exactly that, eh? It might not be advisable now after you being so ill, but later on, when you regain your strength.'

'I'm twenty-six now.'

'That's not very old – look at Penny.'

'I don't want to wait until I'm in my forties!'

'We could adopt a baby.'

'It wouldn't be the same.'

'How do you know? It would be giving a child a chance to have loving parents, wouldn't it? Hurry up and get well, that's all I want right now.'

'Are you sure, Moray?'

'Of course I am. Didn't I once say anyway that I didn't envisage being a father? The most important thing is that we love each other, and there's nothing to prevent us showing each other just how much.'

'So long as you don't try to rush me into church,' she said. 'I want to look radiant on my wedding day, not all drooping and dismal.'

'A lot of loving will work wonders, you'll see,' he said.

CHAPTER THIRTY-TWO

Tess was sitting on a stool at the sink, peeling and rinsing potatoes for their main meal. She counted them out. 'One for me, one for Peg, a small one for Paul, two medium for Pen, three big ones for Pop, and – this giant one cut in four for Moray?' She smiled, and Penny smiled back at her. It had been a long two weeks since his last weekend visit. Penny understood.

The rain rolled relentlessly down the windows. 'February fill-dyke,' Penny observed. 'I'm not looking forward to turning out to meet Paul from school.'

'Second post,' Peg came in, waving an air letter at them.

'Roma's baby – it must be!'

'Addressed to Pop and you, Penny.'

'Oh, inside it'll say, "Dear all", it always does.' Fortunately, Pop came through the door at that very moment, kicking off his muddy boots.

'What's all the excitement?' he asked mildly. 'And where's the tea and scones? Some of us have been working, you know.'

'Shall I open this? It must be the news we've been waiting for.'

'Go on, then.'

It was mostly good news. The best bit, of course, was that Roma and Swindon had a baby boy, 'Quite a bouncer,' as Roma wrote, and they could detect the wincing in the words. 'Over ten pounds – I ended up having a caesar. I'm still hobbling about. Tess will know how I feel.'

Tess was wincing, too, inwardly, because she didn't know, how could she?

'Name?' Pop queried impatiently.

Peg was reading over Penny's shoulder. 'Steven, she says.'

'Stevie, I reckon,' Pop said. 'You know what Barney's reaction will

231

be? Poor kid, two bossy older sisters, just like me!'

'About time we saw *him* again, isn't it?' Peg asked.

'In a couple of weeks we hope. He's asked if he can bring a friend.'

'More great boots lined up to fall over,' Penny remarked. 'And you can just put yours on again Pop, and get the car out to meet Paul from school. Hurry up, and I might have that tea on the table by the time you get back!'

Strange, Tess thought, Pen's beginning to sound exactly like Millie Mae, and I don't mind, because it means we're a real family again. 'Does Roma say if the baby's got red hair?' she wondered aloud.

'Haven't managed to get that far with all the interruptions – ah, here we are – black hair, like Frankie when she was born.'

Roma would be pleased at that, Tess guessed. It meant that Frankie would not look the odd one out. But I suppose, she thought painfully, it's me who will fill that role in the family, in the years to come.

They had the sitting-room to themselves at last. Time for talking about their future. Sitting in the firelight, very close. 'You're looking so much better, darling,' Moray told her.

'I feel it.'

'Then, can we set a date?'

'Not yet, it's not wedding weather, is it?'

'I'll soon warm you up,' he teased.

'You've been very patient.'

'*Steady, Barker!*' The catch phrase of Eric Barker, a favourite of wireless comedy. 'That's not the only thing on my mind, you know.'

'Isn't it?'

'Your fault if it is. You shouldn't be so delectable.'

'You make me sound like a cream cake!'

'Give me a taste, then . . .'

She couldn't tell him that she was afraid to succumb to her feelings; it wasn't just what the doctors had said, though that was a good part of it; maybe she wasn't ready yet. Could the magic generated at Silver Strand ever be repeated?

'We ought to try . . .' he murmured, softly, as if he could read her thoughts. He stroked her hair back behind her ears. '*Please*, Tess.'

She twisted her engagement ring on her finger; it was very loose. 'When this fits more snugly, Moray, I'll know I'm putting on weight, really recovering. I know how unfair it is, but will you wait?'

'*Can* I wait, d'you mean? Haven't I *proved* that to you?'

'Moray, we *will* be married, I promise. There's nothing I want more. I'll try not to keep you too long in suspense.'

Barney and Chrissie were at the pictures. Not in the back row because Chrissie didn't approve of the goings-on there. As she told Barney: 'I'm not that sort of girl.' But they sat as close together as the seats permitted, and he sneaked an arm round her waist. Now and then, because she worked so hard and she was tired, her head would droop on to his shoulder, and Barney would feel protective and did not complain about the discomfort this engendered.

'Sorry!' she exclaimed contritely, coming to just as Al Jolson sang the thrilling 'You made me love you'.

'Shush!' came the loud whisper from the row behind.

'I know Larry Parks wasn't really singing, but he makes you believe he's Al Jolson, doesn't he?' she said, as they walked home from town. No privacy on the last bus, more embarrassing couples in clinches.

'He got the Best Actor award,' Barney said. That rich, deep, voice, he thought, expressing what he didn't yet know how to say to Chrissie himself.

They paused at her gate. Other young servicemen had followed them on their way back to camp. '*Aye, aye!*' came the raucous chorus, then a wolf whistle.

'Ignore them,' Barney said. He waited until the followers passed, then bent to kiss her goodnight. He was experienced at that now. So was she.

'Don't laugh, will you, Chrissie, but I'm going to marry you one of these days – sooner than you think, too.'

'I'm not laughing, Barney. Does that mean—?'

'Yes, it means I'm in love with you, and I can tell you feel the same, but I know everyone will say we're too young, too – green.'

'You're over twenty, and I'm twenty-one – that makes us old enough!'

'I'll be demobbed this summer, I'll have to leave you, Chrissie.'

'No you won't. I'll follow you, get a job.'

'I'll get one, too. I'm going home this weekend, Dougie's coming with me.'

'I wish it was me.'

233

'So do I. Anyway, I'll ask Pop if he'll take me on in the business.'

'Barney, I do love you, I really do. I don't know what Mum and Dad will say, but they like you, and they know you treat me with the proper respect. I never had a boyfriend before,'

'And you're my first girlfriend. My parents were married very young, and that worked out – I'm sure it will, for us. I'd better go, before I get locked out, eh, and posted AWOL.'

'Hello Tess,' Dougie said bashfully, fiddling with his forage cap as she greeted him. Barney had instantly gone in search of Pop, and Penny and Peggy were hastily tidying themselves, as the young men had arrived earlier than expected.

'Dougie! How nice to see you again, after all this time. And you don't have to say I look just the same, because I know I don't, and nor do you!'

'You seem even smaller than I remember,' he said.

'That's because you've grown so tall, like Barney! How nice it must be for you both, catching up on your friendship.'

'Yes, it is. I heard you were engaged; congratulations, Tess.'

'Thanks, Dougie. Do they still call you that, or is it Douglas, now?'

Barney used the old nickname; the blokes on the camp called him Doug. Only his parents kept to Douglas. 'Dougie suggests short trousers and buck teeth, me as I was, when we first met,' he said. 'I prefer Douglas.'

'Good, then Douglas it is. Barney tells us you intend to be a doctor; it's a name that suits that profession, I think.'

'I brought you a bar of chocolate; Barney said you needed fattening up.'

'Oi, don't give all my secrets away,' Barney said, appearing unexpectedly. 'You're sharing a room with me apparently, so follow me!'

'Boy's thinking of getting married,' Pop told Penny later, as they prepared for bed. 'Only left school a short time ago, no job in view when he's demobbed—'

'Hasn't he?'

'What d'you mean? D'you know something I don't.'

'No, of course not. Haven't you been taking in all those heavy hints?'

'No. Enlighten me.'

'He wants to work with you, Pop. You get on well now, after the

234

hiccups of his growing up, eh, and you could do with help; you keep saying how the business has grown beyond all you hoped for, and who better than your son? Peg would be pleased to think you'd got another family concern off the ground with her help. She's very fond of Barney, you know – and Tess, of course.'

'We'll see. The other thing's more pressing right now.'

'What, Chrissie?'

'How come you know her name and I don't?'

'Because you don't listen properly when I read out his letters at breakfast.'

'Letters? He's only written a couple since he went in the forces.'

'Maybe. But I can read between the lines!'

'He's too young.'

'He'll be twenty-one later this year. He knows his own mind, that's obvious.'

'We haven't met her yet.'

'Suggest he brings her with him next time, eh? Then you can say yea or nay.'

'Where would they live? I couldn't pay him much, Pen, you know that.'

'Plenty of room here, for a start, when Tess goes, marries Moray.'

'What's the hold-up there, d'you reckon?'

'Tess told me and I don't think she'll mind if I confide in you.'

'What then? I know she can't go back to nursing, but—'

'She's been advised, no children, Pop.'

'Oh, I see.'

'It won't affect their married life, and you come to accept it, I know I did – before you – and Paul. Maybe the doctors will change their minds, after all.'

'*That's* why she was upset – oh, she tried to cover up, but I know my Tess too well – when Roma produced yet another bonny baby.'

'Just as well Roma doesn't live on our doorstep,' Penny said wisely.

'Pop didn't say a thing against it,' a jubilant Barney told Chrissie, after a double helping of scrambled eggs in the café.

'Haven't told my mum and dad yet,' she whispered back. 'We might have to elope – I could bring a sack full of apples,' she joked, wiping the table top.

'Wait until I've handed in my kit bag then! They really want to meet you.'

'And I want to meet them, I really do. Another cup of tea?'

'Go on, then,' he said.

CHAPTER THIRTY-THREE

'**H**eard the clackety-clack and the carriage whizzing back – knew it must be you.' Pop looked at his watch, tapped it as he did the barometer as if he thought it must have stopped at 4.30 this morning, plus a minute or two.

'Sorry, I didn't mean to wake you,' Tess said contritely.

She was seated at the desk in the sitting-room, having shifted Pop's accounts and ledgers to one side, to make room for her typewriter, which had been relegated to her bedroom since her return.

'You shouldn't carry that heavy machine yourself; you only have to ask, you know,' Pop reproved her.

'I know, Pop. I was awake for ages, ideas buzzing in my head, then I got out and grabbed my dressing-gown and slippers, because I felt compelled to write the beginning of a new story, though I haven't any idea where it's leading to.'

'Well, I'll make a cup for you and us, take ours back to bed. You've got that look you had on the train that day we steamed off to Scotland.'

'A brand new chapter in my life, then, Pop. Now I believe I'm ready for another challenge.'

'That's good news, but don't use this as an excuse, Tess dear, will you?'

'What d'you mean?'

'To put off your marriage to Moray. That would be so unfair, after he proved how devoted he was, while you were in hospital. You *love* the feller, don't you?'

'Pop, of course I do.'

'Then don't keep him hanging on any longer. He'll be delighted you're writing again, he'll give you his blessing to do so, and you might produce your best work yet, eh? I'll make that tea, now.' Had he said too much?

'Thanks, Pop,' she said quietly.

'What for? Telling you off?'

'For putting me right,' she said. She fitted a sheet of paper round the roller; she knew she'd made a good start to the new story. The rest would follow. There was something else she must do first. *Dear Moray*, she typed decisively.

A week went by. No reply to her letter. No joyful phone call. Nothing. Tess felt uneasy. Should she ring him? It was difficult to know the best time to do this; he was rarely back in his flat until late in the evening and he wouldn't like it, she thought, if she called him at work.

Pop finally put her out of her misery. 'I've got a query one of the older chaps at the works might help with. I'll ask casually if Moray's around, and if the telephonist will put me through. Perhaps he didn't get your letter, eh? Am I right in thinking you were sending good news?'

Tess nodded. 'When you came upon me typing at dawn, you talked sense into me, Pop. I – I said, I'd marry him as soon as it could be arranged.'

'Stop fretting,' Pop said. 'Get on with that writing, I should, before you get wedding fever – for which there's a very good cure, incidently.'

'Pop!'

'Don't stand over me, and I'll make that phone call right now,' he said.

Chapter Eight, Tess typed, and she sat and stared unseeingly at the blank page, and wondered why Pop was so long on the phone.

'Sorry,' he said, 'Todd kept yarning and it was some time before I could mention Moray. Then, I'm told he's away, and they're not sure when he'll be back – business in Scotland, the switchboard girl thought. Maybe you should try ringing Jean, he might be there.'

'They didn't say, when he left?'

'About ten days ago.'

'Must have been after he came here, for the weekend. D'you think I gave him the impression that I was putting the wedding off indefinitely, and—'

'My dear Tess, how would I know? But if you did—'

'If I did, maybe he's gone away to think things over, and because he hasn't read my letter yet, he might . . .' she paused fearfully.

'Millie Mae always said you let your imagination run away with you. Ring Jean now, blow it being long distance, and tell her what you've told me, eh?'

'Moray?' Jean sounded rather evasive. 'Yes, he's here, Tess, but not here right at this moment, if you get my meaning. How are you? I meant to write again, but I've been . . . busy . . . with Moray around.'

'It was my turn to write to you! I'm much better, thank you, Jean. Please, will you get him to ring me later?'

'If I see him. He went off to Edinburgh and he could be gone a day or two. Look, don't worry, Tess. There's nothing wrong, I'm sure of it. Just some project he's absorbed in. Take care of yourself! Kind regards to all the family.'

Tess replaced the receiver. Jean had sounded almost flippant; that hurt.

'Was he there?' Pop asked, reappearing, after tactfully leaving her to it.

'It's a mystery, Pop – he is, and he isn't.'

Another four days: it would be March shortly. She'd written: 'How about April? Just time to make all the arrangements!' No phone call from Scotland, still no letter. Her pride wouldn't let her telephone Jean again.

'I'm making a special supper,' Penny said. 'You need cheering up, and oh, the good news is, Barney rang earlier to say he'll be home this evening. Forty-eight-hour pass, that's all, but it's always good to see him. Suppose he'll be full of talk about Chrissie: he hasn't been able to afford an engagement ring yet, but tells us to expect a wedding not too long after he's demobbed this summer . . .'

How could she? Tess thought. Penny's usually so tactful, and here she is going on about two – *babes* – getting married, and here I am, having been foolish enough to let Moray go.

Whatever Penny was cooking, it certainly wasn't yet bubbling away on the stove. Tess thought. 'Where's Paul?' she asked. Amusing her little brother might take her mind off her troubles.

'Helping Peg tidy up his room to make room for Barney.'

'Pop?'

'Still in the workshop. Feeling at a loose end?'

'You could say that. Can I help you?'

'Everything going to plan, you could say, but thanks for the offer.'

The telephone rang. Penny glanced at Tess, saw the apprehension on her face, and went to answer it.

'Barney,' she reported back. 'At the station. Will you tell Pop to go and meet him, please? Put your coat on,' she added, 'there's a cold wind blowing.'

'Maybe I'll go with Pop to the station.'

Pop left the powerful outside light beaming across the forecourt.

'I still miss the call to the pumps,' Tess said, settling down next to Pop.

'So do I. Even though it's obvious we aren't going to revive that side of the business, they remind us this was once the Last Stop Garage, I suppose.'

'Future plans, Pop?'

'Making a real go of the light aircraft side; looking forward to Barney's involvement after demob. Pen expanding the pottery – she's talking about a shop and tea-rooms to attract the summer visitors.'

'Barney says Chrissie is a jolly good cook.'

'There you are, then – she can run that side of it!'

And me, Tess thought, I'm detached from all these developments. Now that Moray has obviously given up thoughts of marrying me, and I can't blame him, I have to work out what to do next. I can't stay at home for ever, I do know that.

'Here we are, and here he is, laden down as usual.' Pop wound down his window. 'Barney!' he called, and he came hurrying towards them.

While Barney humped his stuff inside, Pop caught at Tess's arm. 'Come and have a quick-see what I've been making in between-times in the workshop.'

She gazed at the model of the *Spirit of Millie Mae*. 'It's lovely, Pop.'

'To scale,' he said proudly. 'See the little figure in the cockpit?'

'Moray . . . is this for Barney?'

'No, it's for *you*, Tess, with my best love.'

'To remind me, I suppose?' she said sadly.

'You don't need reminding; he's always in your thoughts, isn't he?'

'Like Millie Mae was for you?'

'*Is*, Tess, even though Pen's made me so happy. She understands, bless her. Leave the plane here with me for the moment, I've a bit more to do on it.' He paused. 'Can you hear something?'

'What?'

'Shush. Listen . . .' He beckoned her to follow him outside.

They scanned the darkening sky. A small plane was circling the area, preparing to land, guided by their light, like a wasp to the jam pot.

'He'll make a smooth landing this time, don't worry,' Pop said. He gave her a little push forward. 'Go and meet him, Tess. I'll wait indoors with the family. Take your time. I'll leave the workshop open, go in there, if you want to.'

She waited in the shadows until he emerged from the *Spirit of Millie Mae*, climbed down, looked around him, blinking in the bright beam. 'Tess?'

She rushed at him then, nearly bowled him over. 'Moray, oh Moray, you came back!' She felt the chill dampness of his flying jacket as she embraced him, though she knew the sheepskin lining would have kept him warm on the inside.

'Hey, steady – my bad leg's hardly come to yet. Of course I've come back! I thought this little jaunt might prove something to you. Bringing *Millie Mae* to Barney as promised.'

'Come in the barn for a minute,' she said, still clutching him determinedly. 'We don't want to be in the spotlight, do we, while I prove something to you . . .'

In the house, Barney held the speared bread to the glowing coals of the living-room fire. His look of concentration was the same as when he was a small boy. It made Pop clear his throat noisily.

'Unearthed the old tin plates,' Pop said, as Penny cut slices of cheese.

'The smell'll draw 'em back,' Barney observed confidently. He wanted to rush out to examine the plane, his excitement thoroughly rekindled.

'When are we going to eat? I'm hungry,' Paul said. 'Is that all there is, one round each?'

Peg sneaked him one of her extra strong mints.

'You'll spoil your appetite,' his mother said.

'No, I won't! Can I go and call them?'

'Here they are,' Pop said, with a broad grin.

'You knew, didn't you? *All of you!*' Tess cried, but they could see she didn't mind one bit.

'Everything all right now?' Barney asked, layering toast with cheddar and sliding the plate under the grate, with, 'Hope I haven't lost my touch.'

'Well, we can't let you and Chrissie beat us up the aisle,' Tess replied, 'now can we?' This time, she didn't care who saw them, as she and Moray embraced and kissed as if they had all the time in the world.

'You don't have to keep the plane, you know,' Moray said, trying to have a mouthful of toasted cheese, with Tess curled up beside him on the settee drawn up to the fire, intent on distracting him.

'What d'you mean?' Barney asked, startled.

'You could sell her. It'd be a good start for your married life; security. I expect Pop could tell you a few names of those who'd be interested.'

'What d'you think, Pop?' Barney turned to his father.

'Well . . .' Pop hesitated.

Tess interrupted. 'You said you'd brought *Millie Mae* home, Moray!'

'Yes, but even if Barney did let her go, well, the memory of her would endure, the *Spirit* part of her – does that sound sentimental?'

'Practical,' she admitted.

'She'd take up quite a bit of space, need maintenance – that wouldn't matter of course,' Pop said, 'if you were going to fly her, Barney.'

Barney smiled sheepishly. 'Chrissie wants me to keep my feet firmly on the ground – I promised her, I would!'

Peg levered off the lid of the pre-war Quality Street tin. 'Who'd like a piece of Penny's flapjack? Hands off, young Paul, you can pass it round!'

'Made up the bed in the studio for you, Moray,' Penny yawned much later. 'All this excitement, we should sleep well. Off you go, Paul, Pop – leave the washing-up, Peg, do; we'll tackle it in the morning.'

'Goodnight you two,' Barney said gruffly, the last one to go. 'And thanks, Moray, it was a great idea.'

'Flying *Millie Mae* here? I had an ulterior motive, of course.'

'I know that. Tess, I couldn't help thinking it must be fifteen years since Moray landed here first – this time, don't let him get away!'

'I won't,' Tess promised. 'Goodnight, Barney dear.'

'Coming?' Moray asked, rising with difficulty.

Tess nodded. She slipped an arm around his waist, steadying him. 'I'm going to look after you from now on,' she said firmly.

'Who says?'

'I do!'

'Funny, I was just about to say the same thing to you.'

'Well, we'll look after one another then.'

'Starting tonight?' he teased.

She didn't hesitate. 'Oh yes, I'll be looking after you, tonight . . .'

CHAPTER THIRTY-FOUR

There was no looking back. Tess was determined to be really fit by her wedding day, to look good for Moray. Roma couldn't be there, of course, because of the new baby, or Sally, but Jean was travelling down from Scotland, to stay with her son, and Barney was determined to get leave and to bring Chrissie with him.

'A simple wedding, like yours and Pop's,' Tess insisted to Penny.

'Ah, but that was wartime. Please don't stop us from giving you a special send-off, even if the wretched rationing hasn't ended yet. Fancy! the war's been over four years already! We've all waited long enough for this day, as it is! Will you let me make your dress? Peg'll help, I know.'

'Depends what you have in mind! No to white satin – and, before you say it, to tangerine!'

'New look, thanks to the inspired Mr Dior; new length, of course. Oyster-coloured silk, how does that sound? Moray passed on a message from his mother: she has a precious length of material which was orig-inally intended for her own wedding dress, only because she married during the Great War, she wore a costume instead.'

'A sleeveless dress, with a little jacket, nipped in at the waist? You won't need one of those torturous waspie corsets. An outfit that'd be useful for social occasions later.'

'What social occasions?'

'Have you forgotten Moray's position in the Tann Corporation?'

'I'm marrying him, not the Corporation!'

'Of course you are,' Penny said soothingly. 'Before you know it, you'll be flying up to Scotland for the honeymoon, and you'll have the house to yourselves, as Jean's staying on in London, until your return . . .'

*

Millie Mae's church again, but with the bells pealing and flowers in every nook and cranny. An April day, with more sun than showers, and happy smiles all round.

Tess with her hair longer and loose, adorned with a stiffened band of the same material as her dress, sewn with clusters of artificial orange blossom – she had refused to countenance wearing a veil. Likewise court shoes in favour of ballet-style satin pumps. Worn only once; second-hand – not quite the 'something old', Penny had in mind. 'Well, now you can say "only worn twice". Just be thankful she isn't wearing her district nurse clodhoppers,' Pop said cheerfully.

The shoes ensured her smooth progress down the aisle on Pop's arm, to where Moray waited, with his best man, Barney. Behind, walked Chrissie, the last minute bridesmaid, because Frankie and Evie couldn't do the honours; in a borrowed outfit. The traditional music seemed to lift them, carry them along. *And I'm wearing shoes for dancing*, Tess thought.

Tess handed her bouquet, the colours and flowers of spring, yellow, white and green, to Chrissie, as Moray stepped beside her. His expression told her everything: he was marrying her because he loved her. The past was gone, and the prospect of the future, together, was thrilling.

There were toasts, and telegrams, at the hotel reception. Congratulatory cables, from Ottawa and New York. 'When do we get to be alone?' Moray whispered in Tess's ear. 'All this fuss . . .'

'Is wonderful, you know it is!' she reproved him, softly.

After the cutting of the two-tiered cake, a joint effort by Penny and Peg, they mingled with the guests, until it was time for Tess to slip away, with Chrissie on hand to help, to change for the journey ahead.

'It's such a lovely dress,' Chrissie sighed, folding it carefully.

'Would you like to borrow it, for your wedding?' Tess offered impulsively. 'We're about the same size, aren't we? I'm sure it would fit you – it *ought* to be on show again. Try it on, when you get back to Pop and Pen's and, don't worry if you decide no – you won't hurt my feelings, I promise!'

'D'you think Penny would mind? She made it for you.'

'Of course she wouldn't! When you know Penny as well as I do, you'll understand why!'

'She's just like a mother to you, isn't she? Barney's really fond of her, too.'

'Yes, she is. But there's someone missing today, that's óur real mother, Millie Mae. I'm not sure if Barney remembers her, he was so young, but I do.'

'She's with you in spirit,' Chrissie observed awkwardly. She paused a moment, then, 'Are you a bit . . . nervous . . . you know, about tonight?'

Tess knew exactly what she meant. She wouldn't disillusion this sweet girl, who was much as she had been at that age – not yet *stirred* she thought. 'When you love someone and they love you, you'll know when it's the right time; well, there's no need to worry at all, is there?' She hoped fervently she'd said what Chrissie hoped to hear; passion, fulfilment, they weren't the words to use.

'Then I won't!' Chrissie said, relieved.

'Better get back for the send-off,' Tess said. 'I hope they won't be too disappointed in my going-away outfit, but I had to think of my mode of transport.' She looked down ruefully at her slacks and jersey. 'Wait till they see the duffel coat and boots! But they're just the clothes for Scotland, and wild walks along the cliff-top.' She gave Chrissie an unexpected hug. 'I'm so happy, and I know you will be, too – July will be much warmer for a wedding, with any luck, and it'll be here before you know it.'

'You'll be my matron-of-honour, won't you?'

'I thought you'd never ask! I just hope I can perform my duties as competently as you have for me.'

She was crying, she couldn't help it, kissing the family in turn and saying how much she'd miss them, and Pop said, 'Go on with you!' and ruffled her hair, just as he had done when she was young. Then he whispered, 'Betcha don't know how much we love you . . .'

'Yes I do, Pop, I do!'

Jean said, 'Such a shame Roma and Sally couldn't be here – it's been a wonderful day, Tess, a day I've been hoping for ever since you came to our house that first time.'

'Thank you for letting us stay there, Jean. I can't think of a better place for a holiday – honeymoon,' she amended shyly.

246

'Make the most of it,' Penny put in. 'Did I say you're a beautiful bride?'

'You did, Pen, but I don't mind how many times you repeat it!'

Barney gave her one of his bear hugs. 'Thanks for putting up with me, Tess, all those years. I know I didn't always appreciate your ideas on bringing me up at the time, but Chrissie seems to think you made a jolly good job of it.'

'That's good. I'm glad you'll be with Pop and Pen, Peg and Paul, when you get married,' she said, ''til you manage to get somewhere of your own – that's important, Barney.'

'I know it is. You approve of Chrissie?'

'Oh, I do!'

'You don't think we're too young to know our own minds?'

'No, when you find the right person – grab 'em!' she joked. 'Don't wait around until you're ancient like me.'

'And even more ancient, like me,' Moray said, listening in.

'You said it, Moray! Oh, by the way, Dougie sent his best.'

'Please thank him for that! Pity he couldn't come, wasn't it?'

'Someone had to guard the camp, eh?'

'You did a good job, today, thank you,' Moray observed.

Tess caught up with Peg reproving Paul for asking for a second slice of wedding cake.

'Go on, let him have it, Peg – he's just like Barney at that age – bottomless pit for a stomach.'

'No I'm not, I'm like me!'

'And Pop, too, of course,' Peg remembered. 'Just wait until you have a boy like that around the house. We'll keep the top tier for the christening!'

Tess wouldn't flinch, not today. Anyway, who knows? she thought. Moray and I are together, at last: this is the most wonderful day of my life.

Flying, not in the *Spirit of Millie Mae*, but in a private company plane: an uneventful journey, and a perfect landing in Scotland.

The heating was on in the house, a meal prepared by unseen hands.

'I couldn't eat a thing,' Tess confessed. 'Will it keep for breakfast?'

'I reckon so. Let's put the perishables away in the fridge; spread the cover back over the rest . . .'

'Oh, you should have something, Moray.'

'A piece of pork pie, and a glass or two of champagne, so we can tell Ma how good it was, when we speak to her. We'll have a picnic upstairs. Go and warm the bed up, eh?'

'You can still make me blush,' she told him.

'Good! Tess . . . .'

'Yes?'

'Why on earth didn't we do this years and years ago?'

'We weren't ready then; we are now. Don't be long.'

'I won't, that's a promise.'

They walked along the cliff path, resting regularly when Moray indicated that his leg was seizing up. The air was so good.

The old cottage was deteriorating further. Tess was moved to tell Moray the story behind it, and just a little about the young man who had been in her life such a brief time. Tears came in her eyes, when she remembered the blowhole, and the poignant message, *back on the tide!*

'*You* came back, Moray didn't you? Just when I thought I'd lost you for ever. We must never be parted again, oh, promise me that.'

'Didn't I make the most solemn promise of my life, on our wedding day?'

'You did – so did I!'

'Well, if you think about it, we will be apart from time to time, for business reasons, but we'll always be together.'

'In spirit – of course!' she exclaimed.

Like Millie Mae and Pop, she thought. Oh, darling Millie Mae I just know you would have been so happy for Moray and me. I wasn't aware of it until this moment, but it's turning out to be about people like us, the book I'm writing now. The next chapter in my life, well, that's another story, and I can't wait for it all to unfold.

EPILOGUE

1969

There really was no need for the tall girl with long, straight black hair, beaded, tasselled waistcoat and the briefest of denim skirts to hold up a placard with her name written boldly on it. Tess, hurrying from the station car-park, guessed immediately that this was Frankie.

'Knew it was you, by your hair,' Frankie told her, as they loaded her luggage. 'You're lucky; Mom says she doesn't wish to know, thank you, how grey she is, she'll stay baby-blonde for ever. Dad, of course, doesn't have that problem: you have to look hard to find hair on his head.'

'Don't be so disrespectful about your parents, or I'll put you on the next train back to London.' Frankie's lightheartedness was definitely catching, she thought.

Frankie smiled at her, as they drove off. 'Good to see you again, Tess. How many years is it?'

'Too many. You were seven, and Roma was expecting your brother.'

'He's twenty-one now!'

'I know. I did send a card.'

'We didn't come back I guess, because Mom decided to launch herself back into the working world. Dad retired, didn't fly after 1954 when they bought the farm. She said she wasn't ready to be put out to grass, even if he was, and he could look after us children, being home all day, and it was her turn to fly high.'

'She still drives that tourist bus? I can just picture her at the wheel, talking away to the microphone, describing all that wonderful scenery.'

'Not now, she's all glam. in pants suits and boss of the whole outfit!'

'Of course; she would be!'

'We've seen most of the family from time to time. I know Mom and Dad invited you too, Tess, but you didn't come.'

'Well, since Moray had to use a wheelchair . . . We came to Scotland a few months ago, to be with his mother, so that I could care for them both, together.'

'You were a nurse, weren't you? I do know you cared for me as a baby. I know you write – Dad built a special shelf to hold the books you sent Mom!'

'Did she read them?'

'You want me to be honest? Mom's very proud of your success, but reading the end first is her motto. You inspired *me*, though, Tess. Not to write books; like Mom, I can't sit still for long, but to be a journalist. I had the good fortune to be posted to Great Britain; hence my looking you up. I haven't got as far as "Letter from Scotland" yet; there's lots of Scots in Nova Scotia.'

'Here we are, Strand House,' Tess said, as they swept up the drive.

'Gee, quite a stately home!'

'Not exactly, but I'm glad you like it!'

'Chat to Moray, Frankie, while I fetch Jean,' Tess suggested. She wondered if Moray was aware of Frankie's constant flicking back of the lock of hair which couldn't decide which side of the centre parting to go. It was a habit of his, only now at fifty-two, twenty years after their marriage, he was already grey-haired.

He made light of the arthritis which had literally crippled him. He clung stubbornly to independence, an electric wheelchair. 'I'm not going to be pushed around,' he insisted. There wasn't much he couldn't do for himself.

Jean, who had developed Parkinson's, relied on Tess much more. She was always appreciative of her help, but lately, the doctor insisted Tess be backed up by the village nurse. Money wasn't a problem, so she also had help in the house.

If, when something happened to Jean, and Tess didn't like to think about that, they would leave the house, of course, because it would go to Sally, even though she seemed unlikely to live there. They rented out their home in Rye.

'The last time I actually saw you, apart from photographs, you were rattling the bars in your playpen and Tess was rushing to attend to you,' Moray observed.

Frankie stretched out her long legs, tossed her hair back. 'Pop's place?'

'Yes, it was.'

'What were you doing there?'

'Trying to persuade Tess to trust me enough to marry me.'

'You had a bit of a reputation? Well, Mom said you did, but I guess she was the same: took Dad to tame her, but he reckons he doesn't always manage it; she usually gets her own way. I'm like that too, I must admit.'

'I thought you might be. How old are you now?' he asked.

'Twenty-seven. Don't tell me you hadn't got that worked out.' She looked directly at him, from her chair opposite. 'Want me to be frank? You're still a handsome hunk. I could see you more with Mom, than Tess.'

'Maybe. But Tess was always the girl for me. She kept me waiting long enough, before she agreed to be my wife,' he said evenly.

'Well, in case you're wondering, I'm keeping someone waiting, too, back home. He's been married before, got a couple of kids. I'm not sure I can cope with an instant family.'

'So you've put the ocean between you, to think about it?'

'That's right. I guess you can understand that.'

'D'you love the guy?'

'What's love – can you define it?' she challenged.

'Love is – what Tess and I have, she's my life, my rock. You'll know, if you feel that way some day about someone.'

'You never had children, was that a disappointment?'

'A sadness to Tess, maybe, earlier, but we accepted our lot, a good one.' He smiled at her. 'Questions, questions – you're in the right profession, Frankie!'

Jean was unwell. Tess kept her in bed to be safe and called the doctor.

'Rest should do it,' he said reassuringly. 'She's had a bit too much excitement, perhaps, with your lively young visitor – she's not used to the emancipated generation, not having grandchildren.'

'News travels fast! Come and meet her, Douglas. Stay for lunch!'

'Thank you, my afternoon off, actually; I'd like to,' he said. 'Moray about?'

'He's supposed to be entertaining our guest, but it's probably the other way around – she's Roma all over again!'

'Oh, I thought you'd be an *ancient* family doctor, in a kilt – with sandy hair.'

'Got that, the sandy crop. And a dagger in my sock, for lancing boils!'

'*Ouch!*'

'Douglas and Barney met as boys during the war: he's not forty yet.'

'Forty-one actually; I'm forced to admit it.'

'Married?' Frankie asked.

'Not yet.'

'Oh, you've still got hopes.'

'I wouldn't say that, but . . .' Douglas was laughing now.

'Douglas sounds so sober – so *fortyish!* Mind if I call you Doug?'

'Yes, I do: it reminds me of my late, unlamented national service. Dougie's what Barney still calls me.'

'That'll do!'

'I could hardly believe it,' Tess said to Moray later. 'Douglas – Dougie, suggesting they go for a spin and see some of the sights.'

'Maybe it's time, Tess, he gave up carrying a torch for you.'

'Me? Oh, Barney did hint, but he's nearly six years younger than me, after all. But Frankie – I can't imagine—'

'We couldn't imagine Roma and Swindon together, originally,' he reminded her. He was sitting on the sofa, watching her, as she tidied up the scattered newspapers. He stretched out his arms. 'Come here, Tess; sit down and relax for a few moments, before Ma thumps the floor with her stick.'

He can still stir me, she thought. Frankie'll think we're a couple of old fools.

'Frankie,' he said softly, 'is a lovely girl. She's just what I hoped she'd be.'

'You thought about her, over the years, then? I suppose I guessed you would. Her mom and dad, as she calls them, have done their job well, haven't they?'

'Better than Roma and I would have.'

'No regrets darling?'

'None,' he said. 'None at all.'

*

Frankie bunched her hair before she climbed into bed. She'd enjoyed exploring the harbour, the beach with Dougie. 'I guess I take after Mom,' she said to herself, 'I kinda feel comfortable with older guys.'

She lay awake for some time thinking. Mom doesn't know I made the connection, after Sally came and made peace with her. But, Dad's my dad, and I couldn't do without him; he's my ally against Mom when she gets in a spin and cross with me when I do what I want to do, not what she thinks I ought to do. I never showed her the letter Sally sent me, I didn't want to hurt her, or Dad. It's strange to think that one day this house could be mine. I kinda feel at home here, already. As for Moray, he belongs to Tess, and I'm glad, really glad . . .